Credits:

Edited by Linda Ingmanson

Cover Design by Deranged Doctor Design

# ENEMY CHASE

TRIDENT RESCUE

A.L. LIDELL

OTHER BOOKS BY THIS AUTHOR:

**TRIDENT RESCUE (Writing as A.L. Lidell)**

**Contemporary Enemies-to-Lovers Romance**

ENEMY ZONE (Audiobook available)

ENEMY CONTACT (Audiobook available)

ENEMY LINES (Audiobook available)

ENEMY HOLD (Audiobook available)

ENEMY CHASE

ENEMY STAND

**IMMORTALS OF TALONSWOOD (4 books)**

**Reverse Harem Paranormal Romance**

LAST CHANCE ACADEMY (Audiobook available)

LAST CHANCE REFORM (Audiobook available)

LAST CHANCE WITCH (Audiobook available)

LAST CHANCE WORLD (Audiobook available)

**POWER OF FIVE (7 books)**

**Reverse Harem Fantasy Romance**

POWER OF FIVE (Audiobook available)

MISTAKE OF MAGIC (Audiobook available)

TRIAL OF THREE (Audiobook available)

LERA OF LUNOS (Audiobook available)

GREAT FALLS CADET (Audiobook available)

GREAT FALLS ROGUE

GREAT FALLS PROTECTOR

~

SIGN UP FOR NEW RELEASE NOTIFICATIONS at https://links.alexlidell.com/News

# 1

## Aiden

Aiden accelerated his Harley out of the curve, the bike gaining speed down the freeway. Cars streamed and lagged in his wake, the wind rushing against his face and slicking back his hair. The scent of the forest that lined the highway of Denton Valley, Colorado filled Aiden's lungs.

It felt good. The speed, the road, the bike's power beneath him. Aiden eyed the next turn and took it without slowing, just tilting that heavy machine beneath him as he flew and drank the adrenaline. He righted the bike and wove between two cars that bumbled along at barely a few miles an hour over the speed limit, then caressed the throttle again and—

Blue lights flashed in Aiden's side mirror.

*Bollocks.* Aiden pulled the bike over to the side of the road, hiding a wince. If he wasn't careful, he'd lose his license…again. And that would be a problem on all sorts of levels. Settling his bike, Aiden kept his hands visible on the handlebars while the officer parked the cruiser behind him and walked up.

"License and registration." The man in uniform look unimpressed by the Harley.

Aiden dismounted his bike and reached into the inside pocket of his leather jacket to hand over the documents.

"Do you know how fast you were going, Mr.…McDane?"

Aiden scratched the back of his head. The question never fully made sense to him. Was it preferable, in police eyes, to be speeding in ignorance or to be fully aware of your law breaking? Aiden tilted his head at the officer. "Is there one answer that's more likely to get me out of trouble than another?"

The officer glared at him over his sunglasses.

Aiden's gaze, however, was suddenly shooting over the man's shoulder toward the curved road he'd just been conquering. He didn't know what exactly had made him look, be it the sound or just the sixth sense of awareness the special forces had drilled into him—but whatever it was, it was now bringing his whole attention to bear on a Corvette that was taking the same turn he just had. At the same speed. And headed right for the officer interrogating Aiden.

Lunging forward, Aiden grabbed the officer in a bear hug.

Predictably, the man went for his weapon. Shifting in midmotion, Aiden clapped his hand over the cop's, ensuring the gun stayed where it was as Aiden dragged them both off the roadway a breath before the Corvette left track marks in the spot the officer had been standing in.

With a soft curse, Aiden released his captive and stepped back, his hands in the air. He could see the man's pale face, his pulse pounding at the side of his temple. That was dangerous. Aiden knew better than most what impulse a terror surge could spur. "You all right, mate?"

The officer looked in the direction of the speeding-away Corvette, his chest heaving as he recovered his wits and radioed the Corvette's details to someone on the force. "That guy is going to kill somebody."

"Can't say you're wrong," Aiden agreed. "But at least it's not going to be you just now."

The officer blinked and refocused on Aiden. "Who the hell are you?"

Aiden motioned to the license and registration still in the cop's hand. "Aiden McDane. Also known as the idiot who was driving fast enough to be noticed and slow enough to be caught."

"You know what I mean," said the cop.

Aiden did. But this wasn't the time to rattle off a résumé of his time in the Scottish special forces or explain what brought him to the States. So he settled for the most expeditious answer that would tell anyone in Denton Valley, Colorado all they needed to know. "I work for Trident Security."

AIDEN PARKED his bike just outside Café Italia, a gelato and pastry shop that even somebody as discerning about her food as Dani Mason would appreciate. It was their unspoken arrangement: so long as Aiden kept finding new coffee shops, Dani would keep meeting him there—and Aiden could keep pretending he wasn't *really* seeing a psychologist. It helped that Dani was married to one of his best friends and was thus, by extension, family.

Choosing a table in the back, Aiden placed a gelato order for them both along with a latte for himself and "whatever drink that's green in color and is considered healthy" for Dani. The food was delivered just as Dani walked inside.

Aiden rose, holding out her chair. "I got you…something green and blended. It smells like kale, so you'll probably love it."

"Delicious." Dani sat and took a sip and grinned. "So how did you find this place? Putting insomnia to good use?"

"I sleep like a baby."

"In other words, waking up every few hours in inconsolable tears?" Dani and Eli had two little ones at home. Her smile faded. "I'm serious, Aiden. You have a month-long gap in your memory, and while one can argue that *not* remembering the details of hostile interrogation is a good thing, we aren't dealing with a surgical type of amnesia. Your subconscious is well aware of what happened.

Hence the night terrors. The daytime attacks. We have to be able to confront things slowly to move past them."

Aiden didn't disagree, though he wanted to remember for a different reason. His captors had never been apprehended. Once he figured out who they were, he would hunt down the bastards and kill them. "Too bad there isn't some kind of electric shock that could shake everything loose," he muttered, then held up his hands because Dani got *that* look. "Yes, yes. A couple of Tylenol helps, a bottle at the same time fries the liver. I know the analogy."

"Oldie but goodie." She took another sip of her green concoction. "So. Back to our slow and steady ways. Talk."

"I remember the details of the deployment. My unit didn't usually operate in the Afghan theater, but we'd been deployed for training. I was out on recon."

"Alone?"

"Yes." Aiden's hand curled around his coffee. They'd been over this before, approaching the memory from various angles. It was a little easier to say the words each time. "It was more a mapping operation than anything. There were no known hostiles in that sector. No indigenous groups at all. At least that's how it was supposed to be. I was ambushed. The next thing I remember, a team was coming in to get me."

"Do you remember anything about the rescue? Try to hear the team talking. Do they have an American accent? Scottish? Your unit?"

Aiden closed his eyes, but saw only darkness. Heard only silence. "I don't know," he said. "I know it wasn't my unit because they'd have told me, classified or not. But it's all hazy again until I'm at the hospital. The docs said my wounds were consistent with interrogation." They also said he should have been dead several times over, except for the antibiotics coursing through his system. "The bastards had injected me with drugs to ensure I stayed alive longer." Anger heated Aiden's skin, his fingers turning bone white against the cup.

Dani glanced down at the grip. "You get angrier talking about your captors' doctor than their interrogator. Why do you think that is?"

"If there was someone whose job it was to push your body beyond its endurance, wouldn't you be upset at them?"

Dani pointed at him with her spoon. "Don't try spinning the tables on me. You aren't my first or last special forces friend. If someone made me run a few miles by way of good morning, I'd be pretty upset at them too, but you lot take a certain amount of pain with your morning coffee. So. Answer the question."

Aiden shifted in his seat, the café suddenly feeling too small. Too hot. "I don't know. It just does. I don't know why. I don't remember why. I don't even remember—" He cut off, his jaw tight.

Dani touched his hand. "Tell me."

Aiden blew out an irritated breath. "You asked me about accents before. Occasionally, in my dreams, there are voices. But they all speak perfect English. American English."

"Why is that important to you?"

"Because it means my mind is playing fucking games. The SEALs sure as hell didn't kidnap and torture me, Dani. It means all these attempts to jog my memory, everything we're doing, is bloody useless." He put his hands flat on the table, gasping for breath as he checked his voice and his attitude. Talking with Dani wasn't useless. It was just damn difficult. "I'm sorry. I didn't mean to snap at you."

"Yes, you did. But anger and doubt, that's all part of the process." She scooped up her gelato and savored the taste. It was a trick she used often when she thought Aiden needed a few moments of breathing room. Then she came up with a flank assault. "Speaking of processes, how is it going with your cousins? I hear Cassey is going to run the North Vault for Liam."

Aiden leaned back in his chair and groaned. "He is. The bugger didn't have much of an uphill battle talking Liam into it. Between Jaz being pregnant and the wedding coming up, Liam's up-to-his-neck busy. Briar is still deciding what he's going to do—but he won't have much trouble finding employment."

The twins, Cassey and Briar, had just gotten out of the Delta Force. With word about Trident Security spreading like wildfire through the special ops community and with Aiden being here, the pair had decided to give Denton Valley a shot.

"How was the reunion?"

"Awkward. They know what happened to me, so it's an elephant in the room. It's only a matter of time until they try to corner me about it." He rubbed his face. He'd left Scotland to get away from his family's probing questions, and here was his family nipping at his heels again.

"Maybe we should give them some credit before condemning them as busybodies? They might have some depression after Delta."

"Possible," Aiden agreed. "And it's also possible you'll let Eli get Ella a set of drums. It's just bloody unlikely."

"I HAVE A NEW ASSIGNMENT FOR YOU," Liam said, coming into Aiden's office at Trident Security and Rescue. "And no, the fact that you kicked my ass in training today has nothing to do with it."

Despite the preamble, Aiden perked up. Trident Security was top-notch, its business centering around providing protection for individuals in high-risk situations. In the last six months, Aiden had negotiated the release of a hostage in Mexico, deployed with a client to Central America to ensure the man didn't get kidnapped, and taught a class on weapons and tactics to a police department in Colorado. It kept him busy. And he liked to be busy.

"Tara Northpoint." Liam handed Aiden a file with a headshot of an attractive redhead in her midtwenties clipped to the front. "She needs to be found."

Aiden turned the page to find another printed shot. This one looked like surveillance footage and had Tara wearing some sort of tactical gear, though no insignia showed on the uniform. His hand stilled on the photo, which had caught the young woman looking off to her left with intense focus. Though he'd never seen her before, the potency of her gaze had an electric quality to it, the kind that drew the eye.

"Does Tara know she's lost?" Aiden asked. Trident took on cases of missing adults, since the police seemed to have a policy of ignoring them. Still, sometimes the person in question had left of their own free will, not because of peril. In those situations, Trident didn't force a return.

"Oh, she knows," Liam said grimly. "Given that she has a warrant out for her arrest. Murder."

Aiden's attention jerked away from the file. "Why are we bounty hunting?"

"Because Tara Northpoint is an Obsidian Ops operative. Or was."

Obsidian Ops wasn't just Trident Security's evil twin of an organization, they had nearly gotten Liam's fiancée killed. This was personal.

"Last month, Tara was part of a two-man on a job in Denver. Something went south, and they blew up the security checkpoint at Denver Research Group—together with the guards who were inside."

"Fuck." The focused look on the photograph took on new meaning. "What happened to her partner?"

"Died in the explosion. Talk about karma. Tara, however, is in the wind. Actually, per the intel guys, she's in Las Vegas."

Aiden looked back at the file. "She's a liability to Obsidian now. She'll be in their crosshairs."

Liam nodded. "Which is why you're going to find her first and bring her back here. Tara Northpoint is going to prison—and she's going to take Obsidian down with her. She just doesn't know it yet."

# 2

Tara

Tara Northpoint slid her oil-slicked fingers along the beefy, hairy back of Big Nose Rolex Wrist, whose actual name was Harvey—or possibly Pauly—and focused on the music she'd put on to drown out the pleasured groans the man emitted while she massaged him. Harvey—or Pauly—was dumb, rich, and more than a little hammered on the free booze the casino downstairs had slid in front of him. Exactly the kind of man Tara had spent the day hunting for.

"You do this a lot?" Harvey's words were muffled by his pillow. Even this runt of a Las Vegas hotel had no problem delivering massage tables to rooms. "You have very good hands. Dex… Dexterous. What was your name?"

"Bunny."

"That's not your name." He sounded proud of himself for putting that much together.

"In Las Vegas, it is." Tara slid her hands over his shoulders. "I like it. I think it suits me. Don't you think Bunny suits me?" Given that she was currently running like a hare from a pack of wolves, the name suited better than Big Nose could imagine.

Tara wasn't quite sure when her life had turned into its current iteration of hell. Though it was a matter of philosophical debate whether the situation could be traced to a single catalyst. There was the most obvious: when Obsidian Ops had picked her up off the streets and offered food and shelter. At eight, she didn't understand indentured servitude or what she was getting into. Then there was the great eye-opener six years ago, when Obsidian sent her to support an interrogation team in Afghanistan. And of course, there was the *final disaster*, when Ray Brushings had decided to play God at the Denver Research plant, ignoring her calculations about explosive materials. Innocent people had died. There was no coming back from that. Not even back to Obsidian Ops. Not for her.

Ray had been of a different opinion, rushing back to Obsidian to pledge his lifelong loyalty in exchange for their cover. So far as the authorities were concerned, Ray Brushings had been killed in the explosion, his remains identified only by DNA records. Obsidian, who usually ensured none of their operatives' DNA was on file with the national registry, had even carefully injected an old record into the system to ensure the detectives could make a match.

Tara, who wasn't willing to go back to Obsidian after that final straw, was a fugitive wanted for murder by the state of Colorado.

On the massage table, Big Nose muttered something lewd. Tara picked up the thread of conversation and steered it firmly away from his insinuations of what else she might do with her hands. The three hundred and twenty dollars Harvey had had in his wallet when they'd first come up to his room was already in her pocket, but that made up only a drop in the thirty thousand she needed to secure her relocation package out of the country. If she lasted that long.

Speaking of time… Tara stepped away from the table. "That's our time, big boy."

"Already? But you haven't gotten to the *good part* yet." Harvey turned over onto his back, the tenting sheet covering his waist leaving little doubt as to the part doing his thinking just now. "I didn't pay you fifty just to tickle my back."

True. He'd actually paid three hundred twenty; he just didn't know it yet. Tara tsked. "We agreed to a hundred, hot stuff."

Harvey grinned, showing a pair of gold teeth that nearly matched the rest of his mouth with their yellow color. "I was just testing you." Dropping the sheet to the ground, he waddled bare-assed to where he'd left his clothes and reached for his wallet. Fat fingers parted the fine leather and withdrew a bill.

Tara stepped forward with a smile, which faded into consternation. "What's that?"

"The other hund—" Harvey frowned at the one-dollar bill he was holding. That was a trick Tara learned early on. If someone finds their wallet empty, they look for a thief. If they find the bills being incorrect, they blame themselves. True to pattern, Harvey pulled back the note and rummaged through his remaining cash. A couple more ones and a dingy five, if Tara recalled correctly.

"What the fuck?" the man muttered.

"No problem, it happens," Tara called over the top of Harvey's head, then disappeared into the bathroom. "But there is an ATM in the lobby. I'll wait here and wash up a bit while you get this squared away."

At this point, the marks did one of two things—got the hell out of Dodge, or went and got more cash. Both options required them to put on their pants and leave the room, so Tara didn't care which one was currently in Harvey's mind. She had a bad feeling about this one, so the moment he was out of the room, so was she.

Having stashed all her clothes and things in the bathroom, Tara now slipped from a slutty dress into a pair of stretched bootcut pants and crop top. Hanging her backpack on her shoulder, she listened at the door as Harvey stumbled around trying to get his pants over his ass.

But then the sounds abruptly shifted from their pattern. Where there should have been the usual hopping about, slide of zipper, and curses as the man tried and failed to get his feet into shoes, now there were heavy footsteps. Instead of receding toward the entry door, Harvey was ambling toward the bathroom. A moment later, he shoved against the closed door.

It creaked, and every muscle in Tara's body went taut.

"So this is how it's gonna be? You like to be chased a little bit?" A disgusting chuckle sounded on the other side of the door. "All right. I know the game." He pounded with his fist, his voice low and menacing. "Open up, bitch. Don't make me come in there after you."

"I'm not playing a game, Harvey," Tara said. "Not 'hard to get' or 'chase' or any other kind. Our session is over. If you could kindly go get the rest of the payment—"

*Booosh.*

Harvey slammed his shoulder into the door hard enough for the hinges to shake. Once. Twice. On the third bang, the flimsy lock surrendered to the abuse.

Tara jumped away from the swinging door, which had opened to reveal Harvey in all his bare-assed glory. Having apparently abandoned the battle with his pants, the man now stood in shoes and nothing else, the reek of booze, body odor, and lavender massage oil filling the chipped-tile bathroom.

"Now, where were we?" Reaching out, Harvey seized Tara's bicep and yanked her toward him, his free hand grabbing her left breast and squeezing painfully. Though he had no weapon, at two hundred and fifty pounds, the man's sheer mass was dangerous.

With a practiced jerk, Tara freed herself from the asshole's tight grip, then repositioned both her hands against his. Her heart pounded. The stench, which seemed to magnify as time slowed to a crawl, choked her nose. Holding her breath, Tara shifted her weight to fold Harvey's wrist over, throwing her whole weight behind it.

The sound of snapping bone bounced off the porcelain tile. Harvey bent over double and howled. Grabbing a towel off the rack, Tara clamped it over his mouth, then knocked him backward onto the floor with a sweep of her foot.

"Now listen up." Her voice was steady despite her heart's pounding as she kept the towel gag stuffed into his mouth. "You're either a john who got his ass handed to him by a little masseuse you tried to rape, or you slipped on the hotel's unsafe tile and hurt your hand. The former gets you arrested, the latter probably gets you a comped room. Are you following me?"

Harvey nodded, his eyes wide and a pungent odor trickling along his thick thigh.

Tara gagged, though she'd been trained to be used to a lot worse that a weak bladder. Trained by people who now wanted her dead.

"Good," she told Harvey. "So you fell, didn't you?"

He nodded again.

She got up, grabbed her backpack, and backed toward the door. "Now, once you hear the door close behind me, give a count of one hundred and then you can get up."

It took all Tara's willpower to keep from bolting as she slipped out into the hallway and out the back door. She was done here. Tomorrow, she'd need to find a new place to scope. Maybe she'd take a break from casinos and lie lower still. Less money, but safer. The thought of it made her tired, but she didn't have a choice. Wouldn't have a choice until she could get the money she needed. As Tara passed by a dumpster, she allowed herself one moment of weakness and was neatly sick over the side of it before continuing on to the used car that she called home nowadays.

This was karma. She was getting what she deserved. But damn it, she wasn't ready to give up yet. Somehow, someway, Tara would find a way to survive.

# 3

## Tara

Tara pulled her legs up against herself and stared at the burner phone she'd purchased for cash in Walmart. Her fingers hovered over the keypad. Outside, the relentless Nevada heat was beating down on the car roof, and sweat now soaked Tara's undershirt. Everything inside her screamed against making the call, but the one stubborn bit of hope made her pick the phone up again. Swallowing, she dialed a memorized number.

"Ralf's Pizza," a familiar deep voice said on the other end. Lucius. The Obsidian Ops commander who'd been the only thing in Tara's life that ever resembled a father figure. She hadn't spoken to anyone from Obsidian since disappearing after the explosion in Denver, and it was entirely possible that this call was suicide. But she was so very alone that even that failed to stop her. On the other end of the phone, Lucius cleared his throat in annoyance and repeated the demand for a pass code. "Hello? Can I have your order?"

"Three large with stray rat," Tara said into the line. *This is Tara Northpoint. I'm in trouble.*

"Fuckin-a," Lucius swore. "Have you lost whatever goddamn mind you have?"

"I…I need help. I don't have anyone else to call."

"And you decided to call *me*? That is stupid even for you. Listen to me, because I will say this only once. Get out of the country. Throw out that fucking phone and I'll destroy mine. I'm not in charge of the cleanup for Denver, but the next time I even catch your scent, I'll personally trace the damn call and put a bullet in your head. You copy that?"

Tara's eyes stung, but she didn't let the tears fall as she disconnected the line. Of course Lucius wasn't going to help her. Other Obsidian Ops operatives were recruited from highly trained military specialties, usually following dishonorable discharges. Lucius had picked her up on the street as a stray. A charity case. She'd always been second-class. A servant to the fighter and professionals. To think that Lucius would go out of his way now that she was a liability to boot had been stupid.

Pulling herself together, she stepped out of the car and crouched to give a slice of bacon from her sandwich to the stray cat who lived in the abandoned lot. She could survive without it, and for him, it would be nearly a whole meal.

The orange tabby—who Tara named Overload, despite knowing better than to name strays—peeked out from behind a scraggly bush long enough to snatch the meat and scamper off. He was a smart cat and knew better than to trust a human over a piece of bacon. She should take lessons from him.

Two hours later, having cleaned herself up at a McDonald's bathroom, Tara clocked in for her shift at Rural Minnesota—an off-strip diner where she'd gotten herself hired on as a temp. After last week's incident with Harvey, she decided to stay clear of casinos for a while. Rural didn't have the best pay, but its owner asked few questions and allowed her to take the guests' unfinished meals for herself. That the owner offered the half-eaten meals as an employment perk was telling.

Plastering a bland smile onto her face, Tara set down a plate of mashed potatoes and chicken tenders in front of a harried-looking mother and her preschool-age boy, who dug into it hungrily. The mother watched the child chew each bite, but took none of the food for herself. Tara knew that look on the woman's face, just as she knew what kind of thing left the fingerprint-like bruises she saw on the woman's wrist.

To avoid looking so long at the mother and child, Tara went to deliver the next meal, a large burger, to a man at an opposite table who was keeping company with his beer. Grabbing the order slip from beneath the plate, she quickly added a few pen strokes to it and waved the paper to get the cook's attention.

"Hey, Henry, table four was a burger *special.*" The difference was only a couple of dollars, and given the amounts of alcohol the guy was consuming, she was certain he wouldn't notice. "Do you have that side salad, fries, and drink for table four?"

The cook frowned. "Shit. Didn't see that."

"No problem, I can put the plate together." Grabbing the food —along with an extra helping of bread and butter—Tara returned to the mother and little boy. "It comes with your meal," Tara told the woman, who'd opened her mouth in protest. "No extra charge. You might as well keep it."

Turning away before she had to watch emotions play over the mother's face, Tara headed for the back table where a man with a broad back had seated himself. "Welcome to Rural Minnesota. My name is Delaney," Tara said with the hint of the Southern drawl she'd been perfecting and grabbed her pen and pad from her pocket. "Can I get you started with a cup of coffee today?"

The man turned toward her.

He wasn't just handsome, he was damn gorgeous. The black motorcycle jacket he wore over a white T-shirt was well broken in and did nothing to cover the honed lethality of his body as he studied the laminated menu. His face was equally gripping. Short-cropped red hair, a bit of stubble that outlined his square jaw, and a smattering of freckles that would look goofy on someone else but somehow managed to make him seem masculine. Piercing blue eyes. The kind that seemed to sparkle despite the grim room.

Tara's stomach turned at the familiarity. Those eyes. That body.

The damn freckles. It was impossible that she'd met this man before, of course. Quartz—she'd never learned the real name of the red-haired, blue-eyed prisoner Obsidian Ops had captured in Afghanistan—unlikely to have survived what they'd done to him. Plus, that man had been from Scotland. More to the point, this restaurant guest wasn't trying to cut Tara's throat, which Quartz would certainly do if he ever saw her again.

Tara's mind was playing games on her, as it sometimes did.

"A cup of coffee would be welcome, lass." The man's Scottish burr sent a chill through her. "What do you recommend for lunch?"

"The, um, burger is good." She leaned into her Southern drawl. Her pulse quickened.

The customer looked up, studying her, his large muscular body seeming out of place on the rickety chair. "Verra good. I'll have that, then."

Tara flashed him a quick smile and started to step away.

"Wait." He reached out a hand, his finger brushing her wrist.

Every nerve ending in Tara's body wakened, her heart pounding from the brush of his touch. *It's not him. It can't be him.*

She pulled her hand away from his, stepping back farther and bumping the mismatched table behind her. The ketchup bottle tipped over. Fortunately, there was no one sitting there, and Tara could quickly walk to the other side of the table to right the bottle—and put an extra obstacle between the man and herself.

"Do you have any taramisu?" the man asked.

Bile rose up her throat. Had he said tiramisu? Or *Tara*misu?

"Sorry, we don't serve anything like that. But I do recommend the chocolate cake." Actually, she didn't recommend it at all. The thing was five days old.

The man tucked his hand into his jacket pocket. "That's unfortunate. I'll think about the cake."

"Of course." She walked away as quickly as she could without drawing more attention. The blue eyes and the freckles. The ghost from another continent.

"Everything all right, Delaney?" the short order cook asked from the other side of the serving window, where heat and the stench of oil hung heavy in the air.

Tara realized she'd stopped with her order pad still in her hands and was now staring at nothing but her memories. "Sorry, Hank. I've a bit of headache."

"The omelet for twelve is ready."

Tara shook herself back to reality. "Can you ask Mary-Ann to bring it over? I'm going to wash my face. Also, table fifteen wants a burger."

"Sure thing."

Sidestepping into the corridor on the far side of the kitchen window, Tara headed to the bathroom. She liked this bathroom. It had a window into the back alley.

*Tara*misu. Maybe—likely—most certainly—it was a trick of his accent. Her own imagination. Ghosts didn't exist any more than coincidences did. But there was still a chance. And the one thing Tara had learned in Obsidian Ops was that chances weren't to be taken lightly. Not if she wanted to survive.

Tara clicked the bathroom lock closed. Since the thing wouldn't stop a determined toddler, she also stuck a wedge under the door before she climbed on top of the toilet. Pulling out the multitool she always carried, Tara selected a screwdriver and made short work of the window lock.

Even if that man was Quartz, Tara wasn't the same scared, useless eighteen-year-old she'd been six years ago. She'd learned to use her hands and body since then. For lockpicking. For fighting. For other things.

The window came loose with a soft pop. After laying down the frame, Tara hoisted herself through it, hung on her hands, then dropped lightly into the back alley. Sending a mental farewell to Rural Minnesota and the paycheck she wouldn't get now, Tara jogged along the shadows toward the end of the alley. Dumpsters and tall back walls of stone buildings streamed by on her right and left. But there were no people. The stench alone kept the place clear.

She had just reached the corner when something large and metal rolled into her path. Jerking to a halt, Tara realized the something was a Harley motorcycle. With the man from the restaurant sitting on it.

*Fuck.*

# 4

## Aiden

Aiden was glad that he had a good liver for alcohol and a better eye for billiards, because after nearly a week of hitting three places a day, he'd stressed both skills. Frankly, he was getting tired of Liam's cat-and-mouse bounty game. The combination of well-placed payoffs, PD reports, and casino security network contacts Trident Security had cultivated all came back with the same information: a woman matching the description of Tara Northpoint was somewhere around Las Vegas. On the move. The best intelligence placed her wreaking havoc at Hooligan Hotel and Casino a wee bit ago and not returning since. Less reliable informants put her at a dozen other locations, at least one of those in Alaska.

Aiden had initially profiled Hooligan's clientele and made the rounds of similar establishments. A drink, some billiards, a chat with bartenders. Nothing. Two days ago, he'd finally gotten a tip on her car, though—which was what brought him to a run-down diner by the absurd name of Rural Minnesota. Sitting in the back booth, Aiden used a small mirror to watch two young women in waitress uniform scurry around. Mary-Ann and Delaney, according to the name tags.

*Delaney's* short-cut black hair didn't match Tara's profile, and neither did the Southern drawl, but both of those things could be faked. The way she finagled a meal to a hungry mother, though—that was an odd move for a cold-blooded murderer. If it was her.

Seeing the waitress set course for his table, Aiden put the mirror away. Time to get a live look.

"Welcome to Rural Minnesota. My name is Delaney." As the woman slid her order pad from her pocket, Aiden could see a bit of stained skin near the hairline. Dye. The hair color was fake. "Can I get you started with a cup of coffee today?"

He raised his face to get a better look and felt his stomach tighten despite itself. Though he'd only ever seen Tara in photographs, the sight of her penetrating eyes sent a shot of primal familiarity through him. Maybe it was the week he'd spend chasing the little cat down, or that she had the kind of beautiful, alert face that lit a fire in a man's soul, but the woman's sheer presence was washing over him like a tidal wave of adrenaline. Of electricity.

Delaney's—Tara's—eyes widened, her hand turning white on the notepad. As if she'd somehow sensed that he was the hunter tracking her.

"A cup of coffee would be welcome, lass," Aiden said. "What do you recommend for lunch?"

Tara deepened that Southern accent. "The, um, burger is good."

"Verra good. I'll have that, then." *Along with you in handcuffs.*

She started to step back, and Aiden knew that the smart thing to do was to let her go now and pick her up without a scene when she left the restaurant. But he couldn't help himself. "Wait." Aiden touched her wrist, her hot skin sending a new, inexplicable rush through his blood. "Do you have any *Tara*misu?"

She froze. Covered it up with some stammering about cake. Yes, with that one little clue, she'd made him. And if she were smart, she would be getting the hell out of here now.

Tara did not disappoint.

Aiden sat long enough to see her disappear into the bathroom, then strode outside to pick up his bike and headed to block off the most likely route the lass would take back to her car. In the back of his mind, a small voice berated him for his lack of patience, but he told it to shut up and listened for footsteps. Five. Four. Three.

Aiden rolled his bike to block the alley's mouth just as Tara stepped into it. Their gazes met, and that primal pounding came over Aiden again. As if his body knew something he didn't. Not that it mattered. Whatever reason something inside him reacted the way it did to the woman, Aiden was here for one thing only.

"Tara Northpoint," he announced as he took out the set of handcuffs tucked into his belt. "You're under arrest pursuant to a warrant in the state of Colorado. Turn around and place your hands behind your back."

Tara crouched, the white apron of her waitress uniform shifting in the wind. Her eyes darted about, but this part of the alley was long, and with no escape to the right or left. "I'm Delaney," she insisted. "I don't know who Tara is. Please leave me alone."

Aiden took a step toward her.

"Come any closer and I'll scream."

"Somehow, I don't think you will," said Aiden.

Twisting on her heels, Tara sprinted away from him, her boots pounding the pavement. Aiden ran after her. She was fast, but Aiden expected no less from an Obsidian operator. In a marathon, she might have been able to outrun him, but in a sprint, Tara had no chance.

Aiden was on her in seconds. He reached for her.

Tara twisted, the blade in her hand catching the light as she slashed Aiden across the chest. With the leather motorcycle jacket taking the brunt of the slice, Aiden grabbed Tara's knife hand. It was a damn multitool that she'd managed to pull out while moving. Aiden folded the woman's wrist onto itself until the blade dropped to the ground with a resounding ring.

She grunted.

Aiden pressed the wrist farther, dropping Tara to her knees.

Instead of resisting, Tara rolled over her shoulder, relieving the pressure. Then she was up again, in a fighting stance, her eyes flashing with murder. Aiden's chest tightened as he recognized the one advantage Tara had on him. She was willing to kill him to get away.

Now weaponless, Tara kicked his knee. Aiden turned in time to take the shot on his thigh instead of letting the heel of her boot shatter his kneecap. Undeterred, she closed the distance, going for his groin. His fingers. His eyes.

Ducking beneath her swing, Aiden managed to grab hold of her upper arm and dragged her wrestler style across his body. Stepping behind her, he snaked his hand under her armpit and cupped the back of her neck in a half nelson. Blood rushed through Aiden's veins, pounding his chest though the fight itself hadn't been long enough to take his wind. Yet he felt as if it had been. As if Tara Northpoint was his kryptonite.

Before the scuffle could start up again, Aiden kicked the back of Tara's knees and dropped her hard to the ground. Snatching his cuffs once more, he secured the woman's arms behind her back with a few practiced clicks.

Then, Tara still on her knees, he leaned down to whisper into her ear, her fresh apple scent stirring a memory he couldn't put a finger on. Not that it mattered. The time for games was over. "So, here's how it goes, lass. My name's Aiden McDane, I work for Trident Security, and my job is to deliver you back to Denver. Which I'll be doing. You have two choices just now. Either you stand up nicely and go with me under the power of your own two feet, or I knock you out and carry you. Well, there's also the option of you screaming your head off until someone calls the cops—but if you think the Vegas boys in blue will protect you from Obsidian Ops, you're delusional."

"How do I know you aren't going to kill me?"

Aiden snorted and pressed the side of his hip into Tara's back, letting her feel the metal of his holstered weapon. "If I wanted to kill you, I would have by now."

# 5

Tara

In a run-down hotel room, Tara sat in a chair, her hands shackled to the armrests and her feet secured to the wooden legs. The number of restraints Aiden thought were needed to hold Tara was a backhanded compliment. Aiden. Tara swallowed. Six years ago in Afghanistan, the man hadn't given up his name despite a month of questioning—yet today, he'd just volunteered it. As if it were nothing of consequence.

*If I wanted to kill you, I would have by now.*

Yes, but why the hell didn't he want to? It made no sense. None at all. Just like the giving up of his name made no sense, and the care he'd taken in the alley not to hurt her more than he had to.

At first, Tara thought that her memory was playing tricks. That Aiden's blue-gray eyes and intense face were not those of the man her team had held captive in Afghan caves. But now that he'd removed his leather jacket, all doubts were gone. Despite a tattoo that now encircled his left biceps, Tara could see the star-shaped scar of the burn she'd never forget giving him. Yet… Yet he seemed to have forgotten her. Or, more likely, failed to recognize her. Yet.

In Aiden's defense, between the drugs and the torture, he'd been in bad shape back then. And Tara had been different too. Not just surface differences like the makeup and dyed hair, or even the natural change of body that happened between eighteen and twenty-four, but truly *different.* The girl Aiden had met—had saved, really—was an eighteen-year-old snot-nose kid, crying and begging her betters for mercy. The woman she was now didn't care for others' opinions. She was a chemist. A professional. Most importantly, she knew better than to show vulnerability to anyone. Most especially men.

Now Tara surveyed her captivity and captor with sober eyes. Aiden had brought her to the corner unit of a motel about an hour's motorcycle ride from the Rural Minnesota. The ride itself had been a terrifying experience, sitting with her hands cuffed, in front of Aiden, with only her balance and the iron cage of his body keeping her in place.

The motel was the kind of place that had cracks in the walls, bugs in the corners, and staff who were likely used to tuning out groans and screams of various types. Newspaper clippings from the Denver bombing, which Aiden had been reading until recently, were scattered around the writing desk while the man himself stared out the window.

Tara couldn't tell the direction of the man's thoughts, but for now, she had the advantage of knowing more than he did. Unfortunately, knowledge didn't always make things simpler. She'd learned that lesson six years ago too.

*The day after her eighteenth birthday, Tara Northpoint found herself sitting in the back war room of the Obsidian Ops' New Jersey compound, excitement coursing through her veins like alcohol. She tried to appear cool and collected as she looked around the room at the real Obsidian operatives who'd gathered there—most former special forces men. The back war room was the place where* real *operations were discussed, not the piddly things she'd been helping with by running social media searches and posting multi-account Twitter comments. Real operations that, until now, Tara was given no access to.*

*"Our client requires information about the operation of the Scottish Black Watch units." Standing at the head of a conference table, Colonel Lucius clicked*

*a PowerPoint slide, bringing up the elite unit's emblem. The men around the table nodded their understanding, and Tara copied them. Lucius clicked over to the next slide. "We ran several operational models and concluded that extracting the intelligence from an operative directly carries the best risk-to-reward ratio."*

*Extracting intelligence from an operative? Tara frowned. That sounded like a fancy way of saying—*

*"So a basic snatch and chat." Gio Welch grinned, showing a set of yellowing teeth as he stretched out the words with his Texas drawl. The Stetson he wore whenever he was out of combat gear slid up his forehead. "My specialty. I thought we weren't allowed to go wet in Europe and North America? That finally lifted?"*

*Tara bit her lip, bile slowly rising up her throat. After years of wondering what they discussed in this closed-off conference room, the thought of social media searches and Twitter suddenly had great appeal.*

*"Negative." Lucius paused, catching Tara's glance at the door. He scowled and waited until her eyes returned to the PowerPoint before continuing. "But a unit of the Black Watch is scheduled to train with the Americans in Afghanistan next month. You'll run the op there."*

*Welch grinned. "Yes, sir."*

*Tara snuck another glance at the door.*

*This time, Lucius ignored her, his attention on Welch. "The op was only green lighted because of the camouflage opportunity the Afghan venue offers. None of this comes back to us or the client. Clear on that?"*

*"Yes, sir." Welch dipped his Stetson, then pointed his chin at Tara. "Are we popping the stray's cherry there too?"*

*"Language, Welch," Lucius snapped. "But yes, Ms. Northpoint has turned eighteen and will be accompanying your team to fulfill her wet work requirement. Get her through it."*

*"Wait!" Tara raised her hand. She knew better than to interrupt, she truly did, but they couldn't seriously be suggesting that. "What does wet work mean exactly?"*

*Lucius gave her a no-nonsense glare. "Exactly what you think it means."*

*"But… I don't want to hurt anyone. I wouldn't be good at it." That was an understatement. The last time Tara saw blood, she fainted outright.*

*Welch and the others at the table chuckled.*

*Lucius didn't. "I don't expect you to like it, Northpoint. I expect you to do it.*

*Getting your hands dirty is a security measure. You're too old and too involved with us to put this off any longer." He nodded to himself as if this settled the matter. "Be grateful I'm sending you for information extraction and not termination."*

*Tara's jaw tightened. "Grateful? I'm supposed to be grateful that—"*

*The cocking of a gun cut her words short. Turning her head slowly, Tara found herself looking down the barrel of Randy's Beretta, its muzzle aimed at her forehead.*

*She froze.*

*Welch grunted, then, slowly, moved the muzzle to point at Tara's kneecap instead. "You heard your orders and I heard mine. You're coming for the ride, stray. Your only choice is whether to ride in the saddle or be dragged behind by a rope. The destination will be the same, I promise you that."*

"Am I interrupting important thoughts?" Aiden's words jerked Tara back to the present. Without waiting for her to reply, the man picked up a chair with one hand, brought it over, and straddled the seat backward. "Since we'll be spending some time together, I figure we should get properly acquainted." He crossed his forearms over the top of the backrest, his confident blue-gray eyes oblivious to his words' irony. "You're Tara Northpoint, an Obsidian Ops operator wanted by the Colorado State court for setting off a three-victim explosion at the Denver Research facility. I'm Aiden, the man from Trident Security who pulled the unlucky lot to ensure you get to said court."

Right. She was just a bounty prize for him. Tara lifted her chin, meeting her captor's eyes without flinching. "It wasn't *my* explosion. My explosion wouldn't have killed anyone."

He shrugged one shoulder. "Glad to hear that. Point is, my job is to get you to court, not punish you for whatever crimes you did or did not commit. Work with me, and this trip will be easy on us both."

"Otherwise?"

"Otherwise it will be easy for only one of us."

Tara pulled on her restraints. "A friendly drive with life in prison at the end. An offer too good to resist."

"What's there to worry about? I thought you said you were innocent."

"I thought you said you were intelligent."

"Nay, I'm certain I didn't."

Tara snorted. She hadn't known Aiden had a sense of humor. Not that their last meeting had given him occasion to use it. Leaning forward as much as the restraints allowed, she tried to meet him confidence to confidence. "Look here, Trident Security. If you've done even an inkling of homework, you know that Obsidian will never own up to a disaster on US soil. According to them, there was no job in Denver. I went rogue and somehow forced Ray Brushings into joining me—to his tragic demise. Obsidian is happy with that version of events. So you see how my showing up with an alternative tale would be highly inconvenient. And by inconvenient, I mean they'll kill me."

Aiden shrugged. "Sounds like you picked a hazardous work environment. I wouldn't want to be you."

Tara showed her teeth. "Let me use smaller words. The moment word gets out that I'm headed to Denver, Obsidian will make me disappear. If you're near me, you'll disappear too. So here's my counteroffer: let me walk out that door, and you get to keep living and catching bounties."

"Tempting, but…" Aiden clicked his tongue. "No, I think we'll stick to my version." His voice became serious. "As for Obsidian, I know what I'm dealing with. It isn't our first dance."

*You have no idea how right you are.* Tara doubted Aiden suspected Obsidian's involvement in his capture and interrogation, and wondered who he thought had been responsible. The Taliban? A local insurgent group? Did he remember the accents? They'd kept a bag over his head most days, and with the drugs and pain, Aiden had become delusional by the end. Hell, Gio Welch, who'd led the op, had moved up in the world and was now a public-facing executive for Obsidian Ops' Pacific branch. Working for Trident, Aiden would have seen his picture on the internet. The fact that Aiden hadn't gone for the man's throat meant he didn't remember Welch either.

But there was a world of difference between a picture on the internet and sharing the same breathing space with someone who'd once put you through hell.

"I can keep you safe from Obsidian, Tara," Aiden said seriously. "And right now, you've no one else. Take my offer. It's your best bet to come out of this alive."

Tara studied Aiden's face. Strong and determined. Just as intense as the rest of him. He truly believed what he was saying. Which meant that unless Aiden was playing a hell of a mind game, he'd somehow blocked many of his memories. Sooner or later, though, something about Tara would trigger the lock. A smell, a voice, a movement, and suddenly, Tara's self-declared protector would be the first in line to tear her limb from limb.

She couldn't wait around for that to happen.

"I'd like you to turn me over to the police," she said. "If you insist on playing by the rules, I'd like to be released into police custody and talk to my attorney."

"You think Bumbleville PD will stop Obsidian?" he asked. "Nothing secret about an arrest report."

"I think I want to take my chances with the law." That would give her a chance to get the hell away. "So go ahead and call them."

"I would, except the boss has decided that you're to be our guest until the trial." Aiden opened his arms in mock apology. He'd seen through the whole call-the-police move, and they both knew it. "You're more than welcome to sue Trident Security when this is all over, though."

"Kidnapping and imprisonment are serious felonies. Are you ready to spend some time in a jail cell yourself, Aiden?"

A muscle tightened along his jaw, and Tara snapped her mouth shut, wishing she could snatch the words back. She was three kinds of idiot for bringing up the notion of a cell to him.

Aiden leaned away from her, his gaze narrowing on her face. Getting a better look.

Tara's pulse jumped, her limbs tingling with blood that rushed to her muscles, her heart, her lungs. She'd made a mistake. And she had moments to correct it. Wiggling her thighs, Tara jutted her chin toward the bathroom. "I need to pee," she said quickly. "I really, really need to pee."

Aiden hesitated, his attention shifting to the tap dance her feet now made on the floor.

"Come on." She made her voice effortfully reasonable. "If we're going to be spending any time together, I'll need to pee on a regular basis. And right now is one of those. Do whatever you need to do to make yourself feel safe. Check out the bathroom. Watch me tinkle, if you must. But please do it quickly. Making me pee my pants won't be pleasant for either one of us."

He took a long breath, and a longer look at her, but finally got up and went over to check the bathroom—returning with everything the motel had placed inside that could be turned into a weapon. He even took out the ceramic soap dish that could be broken for shards. Finally, he returned to Tara's chair.

"Sorry." She gave him a wince. "Really need to go."

Lowering himself to one knee, Aiden undid her left foot restraint. Then her right.

Tara held still, playing possum. "Thank you."

He grunted and eased off the left handcuff, tucking the set into his belt.

Almost there. Tara's pulse hammered her ribs, and it was an effort of will to keep herself slumped loosely in the chair. But she had to. Aiden was bigger and stronger, and her only chance of escape depended on having the element of surprise.

He gave her a final warning look and released the handcuff half that was snapped onto the arm of the chair.

Tara lifted her hand slowly, part of the handcuff still attached to her wrist. "I'll be quick," she promised as she stood up and took a step to the bathroom. Twisted around. And attacked.

# 6

### Aiden

The wildcat leapt from her chair, swinging the open handcuff like a bloody nunchuck. The serrated metal from the open cuff sliced against his brow, a high-pitched sting following in its wake. Wiping away the sudden gush of blood that fell into his eye, Aiden lurched after his captive. He had to give Tara credit—the lass had played the complacent damsel so convincingly that he had lowered his guard for a moment. Gotten cocky. And now they were both going to pay for it.

As Aiden got his bearings, Tara was already at the door, ramming her shoulder against the door with enough force to beat the flimsy lock. She would have succeeded if Aiden hadn't prepared the room when he first got to Vegas and temporarily reinforced the motel's awful hardware with his own. He had extra latches on the windows as well. Not that Tara would have known that.

Stepping back, he watched the small woman slam into the door that should have given way and caught her around the waist on the rebound. This was the second time she'd gone after him, and the pattern had to end.

Locking his arms around her, Aiden dragged her bodily into the bathroom. Wrenching her arms slightly harder than he had to, he secured Tara's wrists behind her back—an easy feat considering that one of the cuffs was still around her right wrist—and forced her into the tub on her knees. Despite the rough handling, she made no sound of pain or protest, which didn't sit well with Aiden as he used a spare set of cuffs to clip her shackled hands to a sturdy handicap assistance bar inside the bath stall. He didn't like the thought of her being used to such manhandling.

Stepping out of the tub, Aiden crouched to get on eye level with his captive. On her knees, with hands shackled awkwardly to a bar behind her back, Tara had to be uncomfortable as all hell. If Aiden did this right, they'd only have to have one conversation of this sort.

She kept her eyes straight ahead, not looking at him. Her chest heaved with quick, panting breaths, her heart pounding so fiercely that he could see the soft part of her neck pulsate with each beat. With her arms pulled behind her, Tara's small chest protruded forward, her breasts pressing against her T-shirt. Damn, she was beautiful.

"Tara. Look at me," said Aiden.

She didn't.

Reaching forward, he shifted her chin toward him.

Tara recoiled from the touch, her eyes dilating as she took in his face. With the next heartbeat, her body curled in on itself as much as the restraints allowed, her muscles trembling as if expecting a blow. Bracing for it as terror radiated from every line of her body. Considering that it'd been she who'd done all the hitting between the two of them, Aiden wasn't sure what to make of the sudden change. Except that he didn't like it.

He tasted copper and realized his brow still bled, the thin trickle of blood snaking all the way to his mouth. Right. Whatever the strange reaction of his body to the woman, Aiden needed to remember who he was dealing with. An Obsidian Ops chemist wanted for murder. The one who'd tried to kill him in the alley and manipulated his trust just moments earlier in the hotel room. Fool me once, shame on you. Fool me twice, shame on me.

Aiden realized he still held Tara's chin in his hand and that she was holding her breath as she awaited his next move. More like awaiting a certain execution.

Dropping his hand from her skin, Aiden rose to his feet. "Cool off," he said tightly and turned on the shower's cold water. "We'll talk later."

Back in the room, Aiden pulled out a medical kit from his bag and closed the gash over his forehead with some skin glue and butterfly strips. Any medic would have told him to get stitches, but he wasn't into doctors, and it was hardly the time to be parading around ERs anyway. As the shower in the bathroom continued to run, Aiden pulled out his phone, updated Liam on the status of the bounty, and then dialed a familiar number through FaceTime.

"Aiden!" Dani's face appeared on the screen, her open expression changing to concern a moment later. "What's wrong?"

Aiden closed his eyes as he suddenly realized he didn't know what to say. His bounty was getting to him. He was angry at her for the latest escape attempt. *Angry.* As if it weren't the nature of the beast. As if she didn't have every reason in the world to try to get away. Anger was an unprofessional emotion. But noticing her body as he shackled her was unprofessional as well. Everything about his reaction to her was unprofessional. Down to how much that terror in her eyes stayed with him still.

Aiden reached for the red button. "Sorry, Doc. I actually meant to call someone else—accidental dial."

"Bullshit." Dani held a finger out to the screen. She was sitting at her dining room table, a green smoothie in her hand while cartoons played on a television screen in the living room behind her. "You disconnect this line, Aiden McDane, and you're a coward."

He made a resigned sound in the back of his throat.

Dani and her smoothie relocated to an office, the background cartoons out of sight. "What's wrong?"

Fine. "I'm in the middle of torturing a woman, and it bothers me that she doesn't seem to like me very much for it."

Dani spit out her smoothie. "You what?"

He pinched the bridge of his nose. "It's complicated. I've a woman wanted for blowing up a building in custody. She attacked and tried to escape. I restrained her."

"Is the gash from her?"

Aiden nodded.

Dani pushed away her drink. "You usually take better care than to allow that."

Aiden flinched. True. He should never have let the situation develop as it had, but Tara had his mind and body tangled since the first moment he saw her. "Does it make sense, from a psychological perspective, that a cold-blooded murderer would be finding a way to sneak food to a hungry family? I saw her do that."

"I didn't know you passed the Colorado bar, much less received an appointment to a judicial bench," Dani said. She reclaimed her drink. "That's your usual line, not mine. Why are you so keen on knowing whether your bounty is guilty or not?"

"I'm not." He crossed his arms over his chest. "I just like knowing what I'm dealing with."

"And what are you dealing with?"

"A gorgeous woman." He nodded to no one in particular. Yes, that made sense. Tara was beautiful and he was a man, and his body was doing a million little things to mess with his mind. Hence this havoc. "I think that's just it. Testosterone poisoning. I'll get it in hand and get my head screwed on straight. Thanks, Doc." He reached for the Disconnect button again.

"She isn't, you know," said Dani.

Aiden paused. "Beg your pardon?"

"Tara Northpoint, right?" Dani appeared to be scrolling through a computer screen. "She isn't beautiful by conventional Playboy standards, from what I can see. More of a nerdy kind of girl. And she isn't the tall blonde type you've said you like either."

"What the bloody fuck, Doc?" Aiden cringed, shoving down the wave of indignation shooting through his chest. "Anyone else feel like dragging me through the mud?"

Dani raised a brow at him. "I'm saying, whatever you're feeling, I don't think you can blame it on your cock alone. You see something in this one. Not your reproductive system."

"No, offense, but you're off your game. I told you, I've worked it out. She—"

A choked-off scream cut off Aiden's words. *Tara.* Shutting off the phone, Aiden drew his gun from its shoulder holster, his senses alert as he sprinted toward where the woman screamed again. A glance at the front door and windows assured him they were locked and the bathroom had no other exits. With his hand on the doorknob, Aiden made himself stop. Breathe. *Fooled me once,* he reminded himself.

Now moving with deliberate slowness, he pushed the door open and swept the bathroom with his weapon. Steam rushed at him, clouding the air and fogging the mirror above the vanity. Wet heat wrapped his skin, seeping through his clothes. Why was there heat when he'd left cold water running?

Twisting toward the bathtub, Aiden found the thermostat regulator on the bathtub floor where Tara seemed to have kicked it during her struggle. Apparently, the bar proved a more difficult target, which now left the woman writhing beneath the hot stream of water.

Fury pounded through Aiden, gripping his chest. He tossed his weapon into the empty sink, then dashed into the shower, swearing as the near-scalding liquid poured onto his skin. The bloody motel hadn't put a temperature safety on its boiler, and the water now pouring relentlessly from the shower head was far too hot. As Tara pressed against the wall, away from the water, he tried to turn the damn thing off, but that required first fishing the handle of the contraption from the bathtub floor, then fighting through steam to get it back on. By the time he managed to turn off the water, he was furious enough to snap Tara's neck.

"What the hell did you think you were doing?" Aiden screamed into her face, gripping the woman by the front of her wet shirt. "Do you have a death wish?"

"How was I supposed to know they had no temp ceiling on the boiler?" Tara said through clenched teeth as she raised her face toward him. The water had slicked back her hair, which outlined her hazel eyes and made them look even bigger that they were.

Between them and the curve of her hips, Aiden's cock tightened painfully, further spurring his fury. No one this impossible should be that attractive.

Pulling a cuff key from his back pocket, Aiden made short work of freeing Tara's wrists, then shoved her up against the wall again. "We aren't playing a game," he hollered into her face with the kind of voice that made junior soldiers jump. "In case it escaped your notice, I found you. You go back out there, and the next one to get to you will be Obsidian Ops. And they won't be putting you into a time-out for bad behavior, they'll be putting you underground. Is any of that not clear?"

She stared at him, her chest heaving with breaths as deep as his own. A ball of fierce energy constrained into a soaking wet package. She shoved him in the chest, the motion making up in furious intent what it lacked in power. "Let me go."

She went to shove him again, and Aiden caught her wrists in midmotion, pressing them into the tile wall above her head. "Go where, pray tell?" His breaths came quickly now, too quickly, and the wet clothes plastered against his skin felt too tight.

The tip of Tara's tongue darted out from between her lips. "Go to hell."

"Been there, done that."

She tried to knee him, and he blocked the assault with his thigh, stepping in closer to prevent further attempts. Tara's face lifted to him, her eyes fighting and daring. Blood rushed through Aiden's ears. He wanted to kill her. He wanted to fuck her. He didn't realize he was moving until his mouth covered hers, his tongue plunging inside.

Tara met the kiss with the same wild determination she did everything.

# 7

Tara

The coiled spring of tension and fury inside Tara exploded as her mouth met Aiden's, her self-restraint a distant trembling memory. His taste filled her, his clean masculine musk driving away all remains of conscious thought. Her core burned with the need to…to do something. Fight. Run. Fuck.

Yanking her arm free of Aiden's hold, Tara raked her nails down the side of his shoulder.

Aiden grunted. He was all muscle and power and demand. But so was she. Mouth still on Aiden's, Tara put her arm on his wide chest and shoved, keeping pace with him as he retreated and turned, until it was *his* back against the wall and *her* hips grinding into his.

Her heart raced, her muscles burning with tension. Even now, with their tongues locked in combat and his fingers gripping her ass, it wasn't enough. She wanted vengeance for what he'd done to her. She wanted to run through him. But most of all, she wanted relief for the deep primal need that gripped her sex and sent shots of blinding arousal through her nerves.

Aiden's hands gripped her shirt and ripped it open, the buttons pinging against the tile as they flew from sheared threads. Tangling his fingers in Tara's short hair, he pulled her away from the kiss, his hungry eyes studying every line of her face. Beneath the wet shirt that clung to his sculpted muscles, Aiden's chest heaved.

Tara threw her head back, gulping lungfuls of the steam-filled air. Instead of bringing relief, Aiden's firm grip on her somehow intensified her arousal, which was becoming unbearable to the edge of pain.

He growled softly, his teeth showing. "Get the hell out of here," he whispered, his words escaping from a clenched jaw, his whole body going taut with restraint. A muscle on the side of his neck pulsed in rhythm to the twitching bulge of his cock. "Get. Out. Now."

He shoved her away.

Tara stumbled back into the opposite wall, her hands bracing the cool tile as her hot sex closed around emptiness. Fury rose, hot and pulsing, simmering her blood. "Or what?"

"Or I'll take you." His chin lifted, his chest expanding with desperate gulps. "Hard. Right here and now."

Meeting him glare for glare, Tara closed the two-step distance between them and ripped open his shirt, tearing the fabric with ruthless brutality to expose taut, wet skin. Aiden shuddered, his hands trembling against the tile. "Tara…"

She didn't stop. Didn't slow. She just reached for Aiden's zipper. As it opened, the massive length of him sprang free with enough force to flick bits of moisture through the shower stall.

Aiden sucked in a breath and lunged forward. One moment, he was still against the wall, and the next, he was making short work of what remained of Tara's clothes. Then his hands were on her ass, hoisting her up onto his hips. For a heartbeat, Tara wanted to protest that she was too big for that, but Aiden maneuvered her easily, and her legs gripped his waist on instinct.

Lifting her, Aiden thrust himself inside her, sheathing himself to the hilt in a single powerful stroke. Tara called out at the sudden fullness inside her, the intrusion simultaneously painful and perfect. She slid herself up and down his shaft, desperate for more sensation. For relief from the tsunami of arousal assaulting her sex.

*Thrust. Thrust. Thrust.* Faster. Harder. Deeper. Her channel stretched, accommodating his great girth, and her hands gripped his shoulders with all her might. As she panted, her body screaming with rising arousal, Aiden's strong grip took over the rhythm. His hips pumped against her ruthlessly, driving her higher and higher toward a spinning abyss.

Tara came with a scream, every muscle in her body—from her sex to her toes to her neck—contracted in orgasm. Endorphins flooded her as she arched, Aiden's powerful hold the only thing keeping her upright.

As the final shuddering wave ended, Aiden lifted Tara off his shaft and…and turned her around, bending her in two as he took her a second time, now from the back. Tara gasped, bracing her hands on the edge of the tub as he drove into her again, her body rousing despite having done so already. She'd had sex before, but never like this.

The weeks of pent-up fear and running coalesced together into this moment as she gave herself over to him. Because she had no strength left to fight, only to feel.

*Thrust. Thrust. Thrust.* Aiden held her hips, driving himself into her. Hitting every reawakened nerve. Her breasts swung free, full and aching. His heavy sac slapped wetly against her backside. *Thrust. Thrust. Thrust.*

As Aiden's hand swung around to fondle her clit, Tara's arousal mounted a new roller coaster, soaring to a frightening height before ebbing and climbing again, again, again.

Aiden's thumb flicked over her engorged bud, his teeth nipping into the curve of her neck a split second later. The small sting above coupled with the infusion of sensation below merged like a lit fuse to set off another climax. Explosions of pleasure flared through her body. Her heart raced. Her sex clenched around his hard pulsing shaft. She screamed again, moaning as the orgasm returned for another round.

Her voice still echoed from the walls as Aiden grunted and

pulled himself free, spilling himself over Tara's back instead of inside her channel. A distant part of her brain that still had a semblance of function told her that this was good. The rest of her couldn't hold on to the thought.

They stayed in place for several heartbeats more before Tara straightened and Aiden turned on the shower's cleansing stream. Even then they said nothing as the water washed them both, the evidence of fury and lust, pleasure and shame, disappearing into the drain.

Aiden stepped out of the tub first. By the time she came out, her back stinging and a towel wrapped around herself, he was already dressed in a fresh pair of jeans.

"I found some extra clothes." Aiden motioned to the bed, where he'd laid out a clean T-shirt and a pair of sweats. Both were several sizes too big, but there was nothing else, and the pants had drawstrings to keep them from falling off her completely. As Tara pulled on the clothes, she could smell his scent on them. Clean male musk, with a hint of sea.

"Thank you," she said.

Aiden, who'd turned his back while she changed, continued staring out the window. He was shirtless, his muscles tightly hugging his frame. Heartbeats of silence stretched between them, filling the room with tension.

Shifting his weight, Aiden stuck his hands into his pocket. "You can go."

Tara rubbed her face, fatigue ebbing through her. "Go?"

Without turning around, Aiden waved his hand toward the door. "Go. Leave. Escape. Do whatever it is you half killed yourself multiple times today trying to accomplish."

Tara glanced at the door, then back at him, her brows pulling together. "Why the sudden generosity?"

"Does it matter? You wanted to leave. I'm stepping out of your way."

The man had a point. Why didn't matter. What mattered was getting the hell away. Without waiting for Aiden to reconsider, Tara grabbed her shoes and rushed to the door—this time noticing the extra lock with brand-new hardware. No wonder she'd been unable to break it open before. Aiden had taken care to reinforce the room.

Except now. Now he just stood there, looking out the window, not watching her leave. *The why doesn't matter. None of it matters.*

Pushing open the door, Tara let herself out.

# 8

Cassey

Cassey's fingers caressed the piano keys, the music filling his soul. *Da-da-dee-ta-da. Da-da-dee-to-da.* As the conversation between the notes took on an escalating rhythm, the collective of the North Vault's early evening patronage seemed to hold its collective breath. Cassey could feel it. Just as he felt the music and the ever-present need for vengeance that hadn't left him for six years.

Yes, taking over the club from Liam Rowen, whose commitments to Trident Security and upcoming fatherhood were overtaking his waking hours, was a smart move. The North Vault suited Cassey perfectly. Plus, he and Briar had been angling to get to Denton Valley ever since Aiden appeared to have settled there. Or settled for now.

But the fact that there was a club in the mix, well, that was icing on the cake.

Cassey felt many eyes on him as he coaxed the last climax of sounds from the baby grand, but an instinct born of his time in the Delta Force warned that one person was paying more attention than most. Finishing off the song, Cassey snagged his scotch from the top of the piano and turned to Eli Mason.

A former SEAL, Eli was one of the core members of the makeshift family Aiden seemed to have found here. Which didn't mean Cassey trusted him, but it did mean he noticed him.

"Beautiful instrument." Eli's gaze brushed the piano's polish, his fingers twitching at his side. Another musician. Cassey could smell it.

Cassey ran his fingers along the edge. "Hands off, Brit. She isn't that kind of lady."

"Well, a man can dream." Eli's accent felt out of place in Denton Valley. It reminded Cassey of the way he felt when he went home to Scotland, with his Scottish burr nearly washed away after most of his life spent abroad. Just a bit different from everyone. The way Cassey liked it. Eli stuck his hands into the pockets of his slacks and nodded toward the bar. "Speaking of ladies, I'd give good coin to find out what havoc my Dani is planning."

Dani. Wasn't that the therapist Aiden was speaking to? Taking a slow swig of scotch, Cassey turned to where Jaz, Liam's bride-to-be, huddled conspiratorially with four other women and a tall, pretty young man.

"When that bunch gets together, smart men run for cover," Eli added with a wince.

"I believe their current mission set has something to do with a last-minute bachelorette party," Cassey informed the other man. "But I'm not against a bit of recon for a good cause. Just give me a minute first."

Saluting Eli with his glass, Cassey strode to the back of the club where his twin Briar, nursed a drink in solitude. The North Vault's soft blue lighting and dark natural wood furniture created an intimate décor, while a large dance floor kept the place from feeling claustrophobic. In the weeks since taking over, Cassey had also upgraded the sound system and, of course, brought in the baby grand for himself.

Briar, meanwhile, had gone over every inch of the place's security and finances. For the first time Cassey could remember, his twin had actually been satisfied with both. Liam ran his businesses well.

"I'm glad to see that your natural broodiness has in no way been sullied by the party all around you." Cassey slid into the seat opposite Briar.

Briar shrugged. "This is your scene, not mine."

"Yes, that's because I have taste, and you have that dark broody thing going." Cassey spread his arms open atop the backrest and shook his head. "That we look alike is truly a cruel trick of fate."

"Where's Aiden?" Briar asked.

"Spoilsport." Cassey sighed. "Away on a detail in Las Vegas. He'll be back. He lives here. He won't be able to avoid us forever."

"I think we should leave him alone," said Briar. "If he wants us, he knows where to find us."

Cassey wrinkled his nose. "Spoken like, well, you."

Briar's hand curled around the beer bottle he was holding. "I was right there with you when we pulled Aiden out of that Afghan hellhole, and I want to find and kill the scum that held him as much as you do. But Aiden doesn't remember anything, and the whole op was dark until what, a year ago? So what do you propose we do?"

"For once in my life, I was considering telling the truth."

"Right. Let's see how that conversation would go. *Hello there, little cousin. You know how you don't remember anything about that time you were tortured half to death? Yeah, well, see, we were on the team that pulled you out, except we couldn't tell you that because, you know, dark ops. But now that we aren't in Delta, we'd really like to go hunting, so how about a trip down memory lane? Let's start with all the gory details—might be something we can use there."* Briar took a swig of his beer. "Let sleeping dogs lie. If Aiden wanted to know the details of what happened to him, he would have looked harder. So let him be. We came to keep an eye on the kid, not interrogate him."

Cassey considered. Briar had a point, and Aiden did have a mile-wide defensive wall he'd build around himself. "Maybe it's not Aiden we should be trying to talk to." Leaving his scotch, Cassey made his way over to Jaz's group at the bar and signaled…Delilah, his newly hired bartender, to serve another round of drinks.

Delilah raised a manicured brow at him. Dressed in tight leather pants and a tighter top, she ruled over the liquor with the kind of intensity that set most patrons' cocks twitching. A gathering with a pregnant lady wasn't her kind of crowd, and she knew it wasn't his either. Not usually.

As Delilah set out the order, Cassey snatched Jaz's drink just as the woman reached for it and took a big gulp. That proved to be a mistake. He grimaced as he swallowed and held up the glass. "*What* is this?"

"Shirley Temple," Delilah informed him.

"It has more sugar and less alcohol than those liqueur bonbons."

Jaz, the physically smallest of the bunch if one were judging by height, took the drink from his hand. "It has no alcohol."

"Who plans a bachelorette party without alcohol?" Cassey demanded, taking Jaz's drink back from her and pouring it out into the sink on the other side of the bar. "How about a rum and coke at least?"

"I'm pregnant," said Jaz, pointing to her belly as if he were blind.

"Does that go better with red?" Cassey asked. He was usually much better at establishing rapport, but Jaz was insulting his liquor collection. "We have a decent Cabernet. If I was expecting the end of life as I know it, I'd at least do it with good alcohol."

"That explains so much," said Jaz.

Shaking his head at Jaz, Cassey regarded the rest of the group, trying to match names and descriptions he'd heard to faces. The tall man with the beautiful body had to be Bastian. Cassey spared a quick thought as to whether the young man might be interested in a threesome before reining himself back to his mission. The small shy-seeming one had to be Ivy, the ER doctor, and the blonde with a ponytail and outgoing vibes was likely Sky, the investigative journalist. By process of elimination, Dani and Addie were the two taller women just to his right. Fifty-fifty chance. He turned to the redhead with pale jade eyes.

"Was that your husband over there, drooling on my baby grand?" he asked.

She laughed. "Probably."

Bull's-eye. He'd found Dani. From Cassey's intel, Addie hadn't remarried after losing Bar.

"I take it you're Cassey, Aiden's cousin?" Dani's voice had a nice open sound, not the voice one usually associated with shrinks.

"And the proprietor of a very fine club." Cassey turned his back to the bar, resting his elbows on the lip. "Maybe Aiden will actually set foot inside here one of these days."

Dani smiled at him over her drink. "Let me save you some time and effort. No, the Tridents aren't getting details of our bachelorette plans. Yes, we're talking about you. And no, I'm not telling you anything about my patients."

"I'm wounded," said Cassey. "I asked you nothing of the sort."

"You didn't have to," Dani told him. "That's just how brilliant I am."

To Cassey's dismay, the ladies actually closed rank and turned their backs to him, shutting him out completely. Even Bastian gave Cassey no more than a salute with his glass before choosing his side.

Unbelievable.

Behind the bar, Delilah smirked at him and went back about her business.

# 9

Tara

Halfway down the hallway, Tara stopped herself and cursed. *Stop looking a gift horse in the mouth and keep walking,* the brighter part of her brain instructed. *Or better yet, don't walk—run.*

Yes. That was exactly what she should be doing. And yet, here she was. Standing in the hallway, halfway between freedom and the mess of things that was Aiden McDane. With a curse at herself, she took a deep breath, turned around, and walked back into the room.

Opening the door, she found Aiden still at the window, his bare shoulders hunched slightly. Despite a tattoo, she could make out the star-shaped scar she'd left on his left biceps six years ago, keeping company with so many others.

"What's going to happen to you if I leave?" she demanded.

Aiden turned, surprise playing over his too-beautiful features. "What do you mean?"

"It's your job to bring me back, right? So what's Trident Security going to do to you when you show up empty-handed?"

Aiden raised a brow at her. "Does it matter?"

"No."

"Exactly. So, go."

Exactly. That was exactly what she should be doing. And yet she wasn't.

Aiden slipped his fingers into the back pocket of his jeans, which made his six-pack abdomen stretch and shift. "This isn't Obsidian Ops. I'm not going to lose my life or get thrown into some dungeon cell for punishment."

"But you could lose your job?"

"Will I get sacked once I tell my boss that I took advantage of my bounty while she was helpless in the shower?" He snorted. "I think I forfeited my job when I let my cock do the thinking for me, don't you?"

"I think your cock thinks too highly of itself. There were two of us in that shower." She crossed her arms over her chest. "I was right there with you every idiotic step of the way."

Aiden shook his head. "It's different. I literally had you cuffed in the bathroom. Being held captive… It messes with you." His eyes became haunted for a moment before a mask of stone settled over him. A mask that probably fooled everyone else in his life, but not Tara. Not when she knew exactly what he'd been through. Maybe this was the world's way of righting that fucked-up month.

Stepping farther into the room, she leaned one shoulder against a wall and crossed her arms under her breasts, her mind spinning too quickly to process all her thoughts. "Look, do you think we can eat something first and figure out how to best destroy each other's lives after dinner?"

An hour of tense silence later, a knock at the door announced the delivery of way too many bags to just be dinner. As Aiden pulled out clamshell containers that smelled of seasoned steak and vegetables, Tara opened another large bag that he'd grabbed from the delivery girl and tossed at Tara's chest.

"What's this?" Opening the package slowly, Tara pulled out a pair of blue designer jeans that were several steps higher than anything Tara had been able to afford. Beneath the denim lay a ribbed burnt-orange top that brought out the color in her skin, and beneath that—a set of Victoria's Secret underthings of a soft silk variety. The pieces looked to be a perfect size, though Aiden had barely thrown a glance at her while making the phone call. "You got me clothes? How? Why?"

"Yes." Aiden ticked the answers off on his fingers as he laid out dinner. "Shopper Express. Because I want my stuff back, and I destroyed yours."

"I can't take this." She'd never worn such silken underclothes. Could never afford them.

Aiden shrugged. "I still want my stuff back. You're welcome to walk around naked."

"But..." Tara cut off her protest because the reality of the situation had caught up to her. She couldn't refuse to give Aiden's stuff back, and she couldn't wear the clothes that were destroyed. "I'll pay you back." With what money? She didn't know. But a significant portion of those funds was now earmarked for Aiden McDane.

She went to change while Aiden finished laying out dinner. Despite herself, Tara had to admit that the clothes made her feel like more of a human being than she had in some time. When she came out of the bathroom, Aiden had morphed the hotel suite's coffee table into a makeshift gourmet restaurant—minus the fancy flatware.

Mouthwatering steak, juicy and cooked to perfection. Golden potatoes, still crispy and hot. Green beans tossed with oil and almonds. A bottle of wine. Her stomach growled. Then her gaze slid to the dessert on the writing desk, where crepes with vanilla custard and fresh berries peeked through the clear plastic clamshells.

"That looks delicious," Tara said, drawing Aiden's attention away from setting the table.

He looked up and froze, an appreciative gaze caressing Tara from shoulder to chest to hips. Heat touched her cheeks. Guys like Aiden, the ones who could pose for statues of Greek gods, didn't look at girls like her.

Aiden shifted his feet. "Sorry, what did you say?"

"The food." Tara waved at the spread. "It looks good."

He made a distinctly Scottish sound in the back of his throat and tossed a wrapped set of plastic utensils at her chest.

As agreed, the cease-fire of conversation continued throughout dinner, but as Tara polished off the last of her crepe, the coming judgment loomed over the lifted mood. She was no longer hungry, but with the adrenaline waning, her body was reporting in with every fatigue and ache it had amassed in the course of the day's kidnapping, captivity, and escape.

"First, to set the record straight," she said, venturing back into the war zone. "This whole 'high and mighty hero who took advantage of a schoolgirl' thing is bullshit. Frankly, I enjoyed it." Aiden opened his mouth to say something, but Tara cut him off. "The problem we have is that the moment I'm a threat—and being near Trident Security is most certainly a threat—Obsidian Ops will hunt me down and silence me. And I'm not ready to die yet."

Aiden considered her words, his blue-gray eyes intense. "They would be hard-pressed to get to you in Denton Valley. That's Trident Security's domain, and everyone knows it."

"And then what?" Tara fingered the quality denim that stretched over her knee.

"Then you tell the truth. Provided you didn't actually murder a bunch of innocent people—"

"I didn't." For some reason, it was important that he believed her.

Aiden shrugged noncommittally. "Then you testify to what actually happened. Expose the truth about Obsidian's less than savory operations. I'll talk to Liam, but I'm sure Trident will help support your defense if you tell the truth." He put down his fork, his body shifting toward the dominance that seemed to come to him so naturally. "Obsidian hurts a lot of people, Tara. If you can expose that side of the operation, you'll be saving lives."

"And paying for it with my own," she fired back. "What if I'm not ready to be a martyr?"

"There is witness protection—"

"Hilarious."

"What do you want, then?" Aiden asked.

Tara considered the question. What did she want? She wanted to stay alive. She wanted to *have* a life. Maybe not friends—she'd long ago accepted that no one actually wanted her as a friend—but acquaintances. A normal job. Teaching chemistry, maybe. Or women's self-defense. She wanted… "A plane ticket to a country of my choice, documents to get me there, and seventy-five thousand in starting money, divided between cash and at least two different bank accounts. Cash upfront."

"Twenty-five thousand, cash, once everything is over. You figure out your own documents."

Once everything was over? *If* it was ever over in a way that any of this still mattered. Dead women didn't need money. "Fifty thousand. I need something to live on."

"Fifty thousand on the back end, plus a limited per diem allowance, room and board." Aiden stretched his back. "We all know the public defender's office is useless, but Trident's council can pick up the slack. I'll have to make a call to Liam, but I think I can talk him into it."

Tara's heart jumped. She hadn't expected this to happen when she'd started the conversation, and yet here they were, making a devil's bargain. Though it was debatable which of them was the actual devil in the plan. Seeing Aiden start to pull out his phone, Tara reached forward to stop him. In for a penny, in for a pound. "Wait. I have another requirement."

He raised an unamused eyebrow. "Yes?"

"We drive my car back."

Aiden, who'd taken a sip of orange juice, nearly spit out the liquid. "That piece of junk is going to leave a crumb trail of parts falling off it."

"And Overlord comes with us." Tara tapped her finger on the table. "That's the cat I've kind of tamed. In fact, we should probably go get him now. He's probably hungry."

# 10

## Aiden

Aiden stared at the collection of bolts, scrap metal, and engine that claimed to be a Ford Fusion. The car was once cobalt blue, but now streaks of rust and scratches decorated most of the exterior. By the smell of the interior, rain had gotten inside at least once. He'd seen Tara's car from afar before, but now, up close, it was even more of a disaster than he remembered.

"What is this?" Aiden enunciated each word as if that might make a difference in the answer.

Tara crossed her arms over her chest, her chin rising defiantly. "This is Wilfred."

"Wilfred is a health hazard. We aren't driving this thing down the block, much less to Colorado."

"Then it looks like we're staying in Las Vegas."

Aiden turned his head toward a scraping sound behind the dumpster and cursed as a stray tabby jumped out from behind the metal and landed in the driver's seat as if to say *mine*. "I imagine that's Overlord?"

Tara nodded.

While Aiden prayed that the feline wasn't inclined to mark upholstery, Tara pulled out a little plastic bag with a few bites of leftover steak and offered it to the stray nuisance. The cat snatched it so quickly that he left a small bloody nick on Tara's finger.

"Let me get this straight." Aiden fought for every bit of self-control as he spoke. "You would like us to drive this piece of, errr, antique machinery from Las Vegas to Colorado under Overlord's supervision? I thought staying alive was a rather relevant part of your plan."

"And your plan was to ride a Harley back?"

"It's rented. My plan was to fly back."

"Overlord doesn't have vaccination records. He can't fly."

Aiden sighed and looked inside Wilfred again. The ragged interior was as clean as one could make it and contained a few neat piles of clothes and some toiletries. It wasn't just Tara's car, it was her home. And it was probably the most valuable thing she owned at the moment. He opened the hood to take a look inside to find the maintenance decent. "Who's been taking care of it?"

"Me." Tara pushed past him and closed the hood. "And hands off. When I want you near my engine block, I'll let you know."

As they returned to the hotel for the night, Aiden struggled to wrap his mind about what he'd just gotten himself into. The wildcat managed to surprise him at every turn, and just when he'd thought he'd finally gotten her number, he discovered something new about her. It was disconcerting. And almost addictively intriguing.

"So how long have you been with Obsidian Ops?" Aiden asked as they bedded down for the night. Overlord had taken poorly to his relocation to the hotel room and now hid behind the toilet, threatening death to anyone who considered taking a leak.

Tara, who'd had her back to Aiden as she changed into a set of loose clothing she got from Wilfred's back seat, paused, her muscles tensing. He hadn't meant the question to be a threatening one, but it was difficult to predict anything with this woman. Hell, it was difficult to predict what his own body would do when around her.

"I ran away from a foster home when I was eight. A colonel in Obsidian picked me up. No one was happy, but he had enough clout that I was allowed to stay." She pulled a shirt on, covering skin still pink from the shower escapade, and turned toward him. "If you're waiting for me to call Obsidian Ops some evil organization, keep waiting. We're mercenaries. Judgment isn't in the job description."

"And blowing up civilians is?"

"No." She crossed her arms under her breasts, clearly oblivious to the effect that had on his cock. With a loose shirt and no bra, Tara's nipples tented the fabric so deliciously, Aiden had to think of ice water to keep himself in check. "There are some problem children. Unfortunately, some of the worst offenders have high-up protection."

"You realize you're defending an organization that would like you dead?"

"Yeah." A flicker of pain clouded her face, and Aiden had the oddest feeling of wanting to pull her against him. A feeling that disappeared with her next question. "Where were you held captive? You mentioned it when I was in the hallway."

He had, hadn't he? Aiden considered telling Tara to mind her own business, but given what they'd done to each other in the past day, it seemed petulant. Plus, it wasn't as if she wouldn't find out the basic facts as soon as she got to Denton Valley. There were too many people around there trying to *help*.

"I was in the military. Doing some training in hostile territory. Long story short, the location I was in wasn't nearly as empty as it was supposed to be, and I was captured and held for a while. Woke up in a hospital a month later, my blood full of drugs. I don't remember the details."

Tara swallowed, her hand clutching the hem of her shirt. "Do… Do you know who held you?"

He shook his head. "It was in Afghanistan, so probably someone from the Taliban." The Delta team that had finally pulled him out was operating dark, and Aiden hadn't been able to get any details from the military. Though with Cassey and Briar in Denton Valley, maybe he could lean on them to find something out. "But the more I think about it, the more certain I feel it was someone stateside. A group of insurgents just happened to be in the middle of nowhere, ready for an ambush? It's too clean and neat, unless someone leaked the location."

Tara, who'd just started to relax, tensed again. "So you think someone in America might be responsible?"

"I think someone from America was *involved*. But it's all speculation." Aiden secured his gun under his pillow and got into bed. "I'll figure it out one day. And when I do, I'll kill them."

That night, Aiden slept like hell. More accurately, he tried to sleep in short bursts lest the nightmare crept up on him while Tara snoozed on the nearby bed. He rarely woke up screaming, but the wildcat was an X factor, and he didn't like the thought of thrashing about either. Especially since he didn't trust her to stay asleep and not wander out in the middle of the night to bring another stray along for the ride.

Fortunately, Aiden had been trained to operate with little sleep and was able to keep Wilfred in the lane as they headed toward Denton Valley. Tara was quiet on the ride, which Aiden found strangely disconcerting since silent was the way he always preferred his bounties. Always. Except now. Problem was, he didn't know what to say to her either. So he kept his mouth shut and set course for Staden's place—a waypoint about halfway through that he and the other Trident men often used for layovers.

The wildcat, who'd been dozing in the passenger's seat, became awake and alert the moment they pulled off the highway. Her gaze narrowed suspiciously.

"There's a vetted Airbnb here," Aiden said before she could get too riled up. "Staden, the owner, is a former Ranger. The security is top-notch, he keeps his mouth shut, and there are good amenities."

"Amenities?"

Aiden grinned. "Yep. I'll let you see for yourself. But something tells me you'll like them."

Taking an unmarked exit, Aiden pulled off onto a dirt road and to Staden's guest unit, which opened with a keylock. Standing aside, he let Tara precede him into the apartment that looked like a standard one-bedroom until you figured out that there was a basement to it. A basement that was furnished with a full gym that catered to security types.

Free weights. Punching bags. And a hell of a sparring ring in the corner, with padded walls on two sides and ropes on the others. Blading his body enough to be able to watch Tara's face as she took in the entertainment, Aiden secretly savored the bouquet of emotions running over her beautiful face. Excitement. Suspicion. Weariness.

He'd suspected that she wanted an outlet for the tension building between them as much as he did, and this room was just the thing. "Given that you've been trying to kill me on a regular basis, I thought we could make it official," Aiden said, rocking back on his heels. "Unless, of course, you can't summon the courage unless your life depends on it."

"But why?"

"Field research. I want to know if Obsidian is any good at training its operatives."

"I'm a chemist with a liking for making things go boom."

"Then I'll just enjoy kicking some Obsidian ass on Trident's behalf." Aiden crossed his arms, squaring his shoulders in challenge. Goddamn it, he was acting like a schoolboy with a crush who was determined to pull a classmate's braid. But in his defense, the woman was driving him insane, and something had to give in the tension that had been quietly growing during the long ride. Plus, he needed her to sleep deeply tonight. Deep enough that she wouldn't be disturbed when he woke up in a cold sweat. He didn't want to go another night with no sleep, and the memories were dancing closer to the edge of his mind than usual. Clawing at his subconscious. "And maybe I want to tire you out enough to not have to worry that you'll run off in the middle of the night."

Tara walked slowly around the room, brushing her hands over the fingerless sparring gloves. Aiden knew they were good quality, supple leather. There was a drawer full of training weapons as well, but he didn't feel like digging into that just now.

"Let's do it," Tara said finally, her energy shifting with the decision in a way that sent a bolt of doubt down Aiden's spine.

He'd been inviting her for a bout of friendly sparring. But Tara... Tara was readying for a death match.

# 11

Tara

Tara balanced on the balls of her feet, her hand up loosely as she circled Aiden. The man was twice her size, and the way his muscles coiled beneath his sleeveless shirt promised power. Deadliness. He hit her with a roundhouse that Tara blocked easily, then followed up with a series of punches. All were controlled. Careful. Aiden was playing with her. Testing what she could do.

Blocking the next attack, Tara slid in with a push kick into the crease of Aiden's hip that almost took his balance. He nodded in acknowledgment of the touch. It was still a game to him. But Tara knew that at any moment, he could snap and play for real. Yet even if that never happened, the sparring ring was never a playpen for her. The ring was a battleground for respect. Status. Survival. And the sooner he got that through his head, the better.

She waited for him to throw a kick at her head and lunged inside his space, closing the distance as she blocked to take advantage of her smaller size. In the inner envelope, the distance was too close for Aiden to get a good swing, but just perfect for her.

Tara's heart drummed an even rhythm as she blocked the kick

with one forearm at the same time that she punched him in the solar plexus. Full force.

He grunted, his gaze narrowing.

Tara struck again, keeping her momentum as she kicked at his knees and threw an elbow at his chin. Again, again, as Aiden backed away, his face darkening. His nostrils flared slightly, and his next blow struck her so hard that it took her breath. Good. At least this way, she knew what she was up against.

With Aiden's greater size and strength, the only way this would end in Tara's favor was to attack something vulnerable. His joints. His neck. As he punched next, Tara ducked beneath Aiden's arm and slid behind him, snaking her forearm around his neck.

Aiden ducked his chin before the blade of her forearm could slide into place, shifted his weight, and threw Tara over his shoulder onto the mat. She landed hard, slamming her arms down to dissipate the force. Before she could rise to her feet, Aiden dropped down to the ground, his intent to pin her to the mat clear in his blazing eyes.

Scrambling up to her feet in the nick of time, Tara kicked Aiden in the head—something she could only do because he was low. Blood trickled from Aiden's split lip, a small snarl curling his mouth. A trickle of fear rushed along Tara's spine. But relief too. No more games. If he wanted to punish her, he was entitled to it. She'd take it without complaint. It was better than the disrespect of being toyed with.

Aiden moved in hard and fast. Grabbing the back of Tara's head with both his hands, he wrapped his legs around her waist and took himself backward onto the mat, bringing Tara with him. Although Aiden was now on his back, his grip on her gave him an advantage and jerked her forward each time she attempted to escape.

Again. Again. Again.

Tara realized she'd made a grave mistake the moment her arm slid too high into the air. But this time, Aiden gave no reprieve. Twisting himself on the ground, he hooked his leg under her arm and shoved her face forward into the mat—her shoulder joint trapped by his powerful thighs. Tara's heart sped now. She knew the move, which was already making her trick shoulder scream in agony. The only escape was to roll, but Aiden was blocking that as well.

"Got you, Wildcat," he said.

"Like hell you do." Bracing her legs against the mat, Tara pushed with all her might, trying to force the flip. It wasn't happening. Not against Aiden. He had her trapped too well. Was too big. Too strong.

"Tap." An order. A demand for surrender.

*No.* She wasn't going to surrender to him. Blood rushed through her veins, determination and adrenaline pulsing through her. She moved, gaining a bit of purchase, a bit of breathing room for the trapped joint. The ligaments, already abused, screamed in protest, but a combination of genetics and a brutal training master had turned the shoulder into a trick joint. It dislocated easily, but came back just as well. It was never pleasant, but it was an option.

"I have you," Aiden snarled. "Tap out."

Tara shoved off the ground, committing every inch of herself to the roll. The joint shifted, throwing bolts of lightning down her nerves. Swallowing the shout of pain, Tara felt herself finally roll out of Aiden's hold and come to her knees on the mat. A jerk of her arm yanked the joint back into its groove, while her eyes never left him, her chest panting with harsh breaths.

"What—" That was as far as Aiden got before Tara launched at him, flattening the man to his back. Straddling Aiden's chest, she drew her fist back and punched the side of his head. Making him pay for toying with her. For demanding she surrender. Over and over and over. Until he tapped out.

Aiden sat back on his heels when she released him, his face devoid of emotion. Tara raised her chin. She didn't expect congratulations on her victory—in her experience, men were too self-loving to offer such a thing, but at least an acknowledgment of the score would have been nice.

Nothing.

Tara gave a mental shrug. She knew the truth. That would have to be enough. "Go again?" she offered.

"No. Thank you." Aiden rose to his feet, his voice tight. Grabbing the bottom of his shirt, he wiped the sweat off his face, exposing the solid six-pack of muscle beneath. "I'm going to take a shower before bed."

"Suit yourself."

Aiden's jaw tightened. "Tara—" He closed his mouth without finishing the thought and let himself out.

Alone in the sparring room, Tara put her back against the padded wall and slid down to the floor. Her shoulder hurt. A lot. And she had a cramp in her calf. She didn't know what she'd expected when Aiden coaxed her into a sparring match, but the pit of loneliness now gnawing her insides wasn't it.

The stupid thing was that Tara was actually surprised by the turn of events. Men thought they could toy with her, and when they discovered they couldn't, they walked away. She was well aware that this was the one and only time she would beat someone like Aiden, who could flatten her into a pancake if he wished. She'd won because he'd underestimated her and she threw everything into exploiting that element of surprise. He'd never make that mistake again. And she'd never make the mistake of agreeing to spar.

# 12

Aiden

Aiden stood in the shower, water pouring over his skin, and reminded himself that if he punched the tiles into bits, Staden would be very upset. And so would Aiden's knuckles. But it was tempting, because he had no idea what else to do with the pressure cooker of frustration that was building inside him—with Tara in the center of it.

She'd *dislocated* her shoulder. For what? To avoid losing a bullshit sparring match? Tara was very good, but they weren't in the same weight category, and she didn't have the years of special forces training behind her. So why did she feel she needed to win at any cost? At that cost?

Though she hadn't tapped, the match was over the minute she sacrificed her shoulder for it. Aiden had done his best to figure out just how much resistance he needed to offer to ensure that she believed her victory was well earned and gave it. But it wasn't fun anymore. Maybe for her it had never been fun.

He lifted his face toward the stream. What did it matter that some random bounty didn't trust him enough to enjoy a sparring match, to play and explore each other's styles? He'd wanted a conversation of the kind words couldn't offer, and he got exactly that. The conversation had simply come down to *fuck off, you bugger.* Tara didn't owe him more than that. Hell, she didn't owe him anything.

Without warning, the image of her in sweat-drenched clothes plastered against her skin filled Aiden's mind again. Maybe that was the crux of the issue. Tara was beautiful. The way her hair framed her face, the way her hips shifted as she delivered the blows, how her breasts drew the delicious curve of her chest. She wasn't the waiflike girl you could find parading down the catwalk, but real, with hips and curves and muscles and substance. The kind of woman he would enjoy holding. The kind who wasn't afraid to get into a sparring ring with him. The kind he could too easily imagine doing a lot of things he shouldn't with.

Aiden reached for the thermostat and twisted the shower to cold before his cock got too many new ideas. Tara wasn't interested in him. Tara didn't trust him. And that was that. What he really needed was to get her the hell out of his head.

After getting out of the shower, Aiden left Tara to fend for herself with dinner from the groceries they'd picked up on the way while he took over the apartment's sole bedroom to catch up on work. Liam was less than pleased about the choice of vehicle, which he let Aiden know in no uncertain terms, but otherwise was pleased to hear that they'd made the first leg of the journey without incident. A few other items from previous security assignments and upcoming assessments popped up in the inbox and were easily dealt with. The email from Jaz—Liam's fiancée and the new head of Trident Security's search and rescue arm—demanding that Aiden get into compliance with three certifications, he deleted.

And then undeleted and marked with a red follow-up flag. As much as he despised paperwork, he feared Jaz's wrath more.

Right. Closing the laptop, Aiden went to the kitchen to grab a sandwich—realizing as he approached the fridge that, despite bracing himself for it, he hadn't walked past Tara to get there. With a string of colorful curses, he put down the cold cuts he was about to grab and went to search the house. The alarm he'd armed once they got inside should have alerted him to any perimeter breach, but he put nothing past the wildcat.

Not even dislocating her own shoulder to win a stupid sparring match.

To his frustration, he found his charge in the garage, halfway under Wilfred's hood. From the way her back end tensed against her tight jeans, Aiden was sure she was aware of his presence. He waited a moment for her to acknowledge him and maybe explain what the heck she was doing to their already questionable mode of transport, but Tara remained buried in the engine.

Fine. He didn't really want to be talking to her anyway just now. Making a mental note to check under the car's hood before driving off tomorrow, Aiden turned back to the house. He didn't think Tara was rigging the car to murder him, but when it came to the wildcat, assumptions were dangerous. As he opened the door, a fluffy torpedo rushed past his legs. Apparently, Overlord—who hadn't consented to leave his chariot earlier—had come to the same conclusion Aiden had with regard to lingering about while an Obsidian Ops explosives expert toyed with wires.

Since there was only one bedroom, Aiden unfolded the living room futon for himself and made up the bed. Staden had gotten the couch from some European store, and instead of pulling out, the futon folded flat like a book. Years of use made it prone to folding up like a book too, but Aiden finally wrestled it into compliance. He ate some dinner while Tara finished up with the car, showered off, and called it a night, then got into bed.

He even tried to sleep. He really did. But every time he closed his eyes, his mind shuffled through a kaleidoscope of images. Tara on the sparring mat and Tara leaning over the car trunk, her curvy ass filling out the seat of her jeans, featured most prominently in the rotation.

*Bollocks.* Cursing under his breath, Aiden grabbed his phone and went to the bathroom, turning on the water to muffle any sound as he dialed a number.

"Aiden?" Despite the late hour, Dani's surprised voice came over the line on the second ring. "Everything all right?"

"I need you to get my bounty out of my head," Aiden barked into the phone. "She's taking over my bloody mind. I can't concentrate on my job. I need her gone."

"I'm not a priest, Aiden."

He made a confused sound at the back of his throat.

"Well, you seem to either be expecting me to perform an exorcism or prescribe some confessional penance to reset your moral compass. I fear I'm useless on either count."

"Verra funny. You're the head expert—and mine's currently under invasion. So can you please tell me how to put a stop to it?"

Dani sighed. "All right. Well, first of all, realize that it takes a lot more effort to prevent a mental action than it does to engage in alternative action that's incompatible with the original."

"I recognized what you said as English, Doc, but that's about as far as I got."

"If I order you not to think about pink elephants, you'll likely think about pink elephants," Dani explained. "Because not thinking about something is, as you put it, *bloody difficult.* If, however, instead of telling you not to think about elephants, I ask you to recite the multiplication table, keeping your mind elephant-free becomes much easier."

"So instead of trying not to think about Tara, you want me to recite the multiplication table?"

"You can use your fingers and toes to help if you need to." Her tone changed to one Aiden recognized as the serious voice. "Review the security protocols. Look for speed traps on your drive. Maybe actually get ahead and compose a report. It will help—but it's all a short-term fix."

"Thanks. I knew you could come up with something."

"I didn't! Aiden. It's a Band-Aid. When you get back, we'll—"

"Thanks again, Doc. Good night." Aiden strategically hung up, pulled out a laptop, and began typing up the standard security procedures he'd been putting off touching for the past three months. It wasn't perfect, but it helped. Mostly. At least until midnight, when the sounds of breathing in the adjacent bedroom dissolved into a quiet rhythm that finally lulled Aiden into sleep.

Three hours later, he woke up screaming, his belly, sides, and back blazing with stripes of pain and blood soaking his sheets.

# 13

## Tara

Tara vaulted out of bed at the sound of Aiden's scream. Grabbing the first thing that came to hand to use as a weapon—which turned out to be an ornate walking cane that had been attached to the wall by way of décor—she crept into the living room and flipped on the lights.

Aiden was on the futon, his bare torso bleeding from crisscrossed gashes as he writhed in combat with Overlord. As fast as Aiden moved, he was little match for the vicious feline whom Aiden appeared to have rolled on in his sleep. Making matters worse, a good clump of the cat's fur was stuck in the middle of the carnivorous couch.

"Come here, sweetheart," Tara cooed, holding her arms out to the cat.

With a triumphant meow, Overlord leapt from the fray into Tara's hold—though he continued to hiss at Aiden from the new high perch.

Aiden, now fully awake and blazing with a mix of fury and indignation, got to his feet. With the attack over, he looked like something from a slasher movie, each thin cut oozing blood down the grooves of his muscles.

"Rough night?" Tara asked.

"I'm going to kill that goddamn cat," he said.

"Meow," said Overlord. Now sitting comfortably in Tara's arms, the cat looked down at Aiden and snorted, as if to say, *you can try, silly human.*

Emitting a long-suffering sigh, Aiden strode toward the bathroom and turned on the faucet. Though he didn't know it, it was hardly the first time Tara had seen him bloodied, and the sight of his injured skin made bile and memories rise up Tara's throat. The funny-not-funny thing was that he'd rarely screamed in Afghanistan, but those few times he had were branded into her memory.

Setting down an indignant Overlord, Tara walked up to the bathroom door, making sure Aiden could see her approach in the mirror. One didn't have to be psychic to figure out that he might not like people coming up on him unaware.

Standing at the washbasin, Aiden lathered up a washcloth with soap, his face expressionless as he attacked the gashes crossing his abs.

"You know, this wouldn't have been an issue if you slept with a shirt on," Tara said. It wasn't exactly true, but it would have spared Tara the uncontrollable twinge of desire that sped from her sex to her toes at the sight of Aiden's half-naked body. Even bloody, the man looked too fit and chiseled and lethal for fairness. Especially when she was trying not to think of him that way.

*Enough gawking.* Grabbing a second washcloth, Tara went to dab at the cut on Aiden's back, the one he couldn't reach on his own. She could be professional about this.

Aiden twisted, grabbing her wrist in midmotion. "Don't."

Tara frowned. Was he serious? No, he couldn't be. "You got scratched by a cat," she said, waving her hand as if he was unaware of what happened. "There's only so much damage I can do to that with a washcloth."

Aiden shook his head, his hand still holding off hers. "Please."

Tara threw up her free hand. "Not only are you bleeding all over your friend's furniture, but I must now also inform you that Overlord's hygiene routine may have been less than ideal. By that I mean, he lived behind a dumpster." Tara sighed. "Seriously. You didn't survive—you didn't survive the military just to be beaten by a cat."

"I... I just don't like to be touched."

"I beg to differ." Tara pointed to another gash, this one on Aiden's shoulder and courtesy of her nails instead of Overlord's.

Aiden released her and rubbed his face, lines of tension and fatigue pulling at his eyes. "I don't like having my wounds handled by anyone," he said. "It's stupid and makes me the most delightful patient you've ever met. But it is what it is."

"It's—" Tara snapped her mouth shut, because suddenly, everything he was saying, everything he was feeling, made too much sense for comfort. Because they'd had this conversation before. Had it when she lashed down Aiden's restraints to force antibiotics into his veins as he thrashed and fought against the intrusion. It had been one of the few times he'd screamed. And the only time he'd begged. "It's not stupid," she whispered.

Before Aiden could question her change of attitude, she pushed past him to turn the shower on and pressed a bar of antibacterial soap into Aiden's hand. "Go and get de-catted," she said, pointing at the running water. "I'll make some tea and throw the bloodbath you made of the sheets into the laundry."

Tara tried not to think about the haunted look in Aiden's gaze as he asked not to be touched while she cleaned up the living room and put some water on to boil. She didn't know whether Aiden liked tea, but it was something she always drank when she felt off, and it was the best thing she could think to offer.

By the time Aiden came out of the shower fifteen minutes later, Tara had the offending futon cleaned up and two mugs of mint tea on the coffee table. She held one up as she turned toward him—and stopped. With a towel wrapped around his hips, Aiden was next to naked. And dripping wet.

"What is it with men and towels?"

He cocked a brow at her.

She pointed to the drops of water now plopping on the hardwood floor. "In most of the civilized world, the thing you've mistaken for a loin cloth is actually used to absorb moisture after bathing. Did you even make an attempt to dry your hair? Or any other part?"

Aiden frowned at his forearms, still glistening from the shower. "Fair point," he conceded. "In my defense, it hasn't actually bothered me before." Striding over to his bag, Aiden rifled through to pull out a clean T-shirt—which, of course, stuck to his damp body as he pulled it on, making Tara's hands tighten on the cup to keep from walking over and helping out.

"I have a bottle of Advil in Wilfred's glove compartment," she offered.

"I don't like drugs."

"I said Advil, not fentanyl and crack cocaine."

"Don't like anything in my system." He pulled on a pair of sweats, discarded the towel, and held out his hand. "I'll take the tea, though. And cat stew, if you can arrange it."

Overlord hissed.

Tara surrendered the mug, and Aiden settled next to her on the futon, tipping his head back. "I know it's hard to believe just now, but I'm worth my salt if Obsidian Ops comes to call." He touched her shoulder, the brush of his fingers sending a jolt of electricity through Tara. "You should go to sleep. I'm going to stay up for a little while."

She shrugged and reached for the remote, flipping the channels to a rerun of *Battlestar Galactica*. They sat quietly as cyborgs took over the galaxy and humanity went on the run in a vintage ship. Tara liked the show and was more than a little pleased to find Aiden of a similar mind. In the night's dimness, the heating ducts hummed with white noise while somewhere outside, something that sounded suspiciously like an owl hooted into the darkness.

"Why chemistry and explosives?" Aiden asked as credits rolled across the screen. He was sitting close to her, his legs on the coffee table and crossed at the ankles, his body relaxed against the futon's back. Given the thing's age, it was an unusually comfortable couch to sit on, and the soft veil of night had Tara more relaxed than she remembered being for some time. "I would have taken you more for a medicine type, actually. Either that or assassin, but those aren't mutually exclusive."

"I make a lousy medic," Tara said. "Serious injuries make me queasy. But as for the rest... I guess I ended up being a default alchemist of sorts on one deployment. Someone was injured, and we had an odd assortment of drugs and medical supplies on hand."

She didn't feel the need to add that the injured person was Aiden himself and that not all the drugs in the arsenal were legal.

"There was no end in sight, and I wanted to make the person more comfortable, so I started doing a bit of mixing. It was a less than ideal situation, to say the least, but it made me realize a few things about myself."

"And the explosives?"

She shrugged. "I had to make my education worthwhile for Obsidian. They aren't a research institution. So there you go."

"What happened to your patient after all that?" Aiden asked.

*That is an excellent question.* "He parted ways with Obsidian."

"I imagine he's grateful to you, wherever he is."

"I wouldn't bet too much money on that," she muttered. "In fact, I believe the last words he said to me were to the effect of a promise to cut my throat with a horseshoe. Which I didn't even know was a thing."

"Aye. That does seem an odd choice of a weapon."

"Yes, well, he might have been hallucinating a bit at the time. Like I said, I was learning as I went along, and I had limited supplies to work with. But just in case, I try to keep a healthy distance between any horseshoes and myself."

Aiden laughed. It was a rich, delicious sound that made his chest vibrate and constricted Tara's.

"Whether or not he thinks fondly of me, I'm forever grateful to him," she said softly. "In many ways, he saved my life." Before the admission could open her up to questions she wasn't prepared to answer, Tara grabbed the remote and started the next episode of

*Galactica*. As the opening montage played itself out on the large-screen television, she surreptitiously stretched her aching back. She really should have grabbed that Advil while she was working on the car. Tara considered stepping away to do so now, but the aftermath of the sparring match had left a bad taste in her mouth, and she didn't want to do anything to resurrect the topic.

It wasn't fair, she knew. Had Aiden won, he would have expected good manners from her and a congratulatory pat on the back. But because it was her victory, a girl's victory, she now had to avoid bringing it up just to protect his feelings. But those were facts of life that Tara had long ago learned to accept. And she didn't have the bandwidth to fight against it just now.

She realized she'd been staring off to the side when she felt Aiden's hands on her, his body shifting closer as he angled Tara slightly away from him. "What—"

"Shh. Just watch the show, wildcat," Aiden said, his thumb brushing over her shoulder where the abused muscles were wound tight as guitar strings. Pain and ecstasy spilled into her blood as Aiden worked at the knot, the muscles simultaneously howling and savoring the manipulation. She was sore. So very sore.

Aiden's next pass went deeper, and Tara clenched involuntarily, shifting her body away—only to be braced by Aiden's free hand across her abdomen, which was not nearly as rock solid as his. "Sorry, not sorry," he said into her ear, though the pressure from his fingers gentled as he coaxed another muscle spasm to ease. "You deserve it, after all. It was a stupid thing to do."

Through the haze of ache and endorphins coursing through her blood, Tara finally realized Aiden's focus on her bad shoulder was anything but accidental.

"I didn't think you noticed," she muttered.

"You think I missed you dislocating your own shoulder to keep from losing a stupid sparring match?" Aiden's voice hardened. "You can bloody well bet I noticed. I have opinions on that score too—ones that you should be grateful I'm keeping to myself."

"You aren't actually keeping them to yourself." Tara swallowed a moan as Aiden rotated her shoulder about, stretching the tightest spots with sniper-like precision. Tension gave beneath his touch, a deep, relaxing sensation. "Say what you will, but it worked."

"It worked, all right."

There was something about the way he said it that made her turn around to study Aiden's face. Warmth radiated from his large body, and stubble that he'd shaved off in the morning covered the angle of his jaw, but it was his guarded gaze that made Tara's spine tighten with suspicion. "Did I win our sparring match?" she asked.

"Of course you did," he answered a little too quickly. "I tapped. You won. I've got some bruises to show for it too."

Tara froze. He was lying.

"Aiden—"

"Turn back around and take your medicine, lass. I'm not done." He ran his thumb down the long muscle along Tara's spine, hitting knots that she didn't even know were there. The pressure continued to trace around her shoulder blade and up to her neck and the base of her head. God. It felt good. So dizzyingly good that it was hard to think through the sensation. But she pieced her thoughts together anyway.

Her whole read on the evening had been off by a hundred eighty degrees. She hadn't won the match—Aiden had staged the victory. And if he hadn't been upset about losing to a girl—he hadn't lost to anyone—then he'd been upset about her tactics. It didn't make sense. Nothing about this man made sense.

Tara pulled away from him, though it was a matter of will. "We should get some sleep. Long drive tomorrow."

Aiden was on his feet at once. "Of course."

She rose, and he folded the futon back flat, though there were no more sheets to be had. The instant the couch was flat once more, Overlord leapt into the middle of the space.

"Oh no, you don't, cat," he said with a growl.

Overlord flicked his tail and showed off a pair of sharp teeth.

"Off!" Aiden made a commanding gesture with his hand, that would probably have worked for a dog and would certainly have worked for most humans.

"Meow," declared Overlord, adding a bit of a hiss to the end of his statement before closing his eyes.

"You can sleep in the bed," said Tara. "It's king size—plenty of room. And it doesn't seem you're welcome here."

Aiden threw a frustrated look at the cat, then rubbed his side where tiny prickles of blood had already seeped through the white T-shirt. "I can sleep on the floor."

"I'll tell all your friends you got evicted by a cat. At least this way, they'll think you were trying to get into my pants."

He snorted.

Tara yawned, rubbing her face. "Come on."

He followed her reluctantly, slipping under the covers on the other side of the bed before turning off the sidelight. Despite being in one bed, he felt farther away than he had minutes ago, and Tara found herself missing the warmth and the touch as she closed her eyes and tried to sleep.

An hour later, Tara was still awake, listening to Aiden's uneven breathing. Though he lay still, he was as wide awake as she.

"Let me guess," she finally said into the darkness. "You're worried that a primal monster living inside you will overpower your self-control in the dead of night—so you're valiantly staying awake to protect my maidenhood from your werewolf self."

Aiden laughed. "How did ye know?"

"That you're awake?"

"That I'm a werewolf."

"Oh, that was easy. The yellow eyes, of course."

"My eyes aren't yellow."

Tara lifted herself up on an elbow. Now that she'd adjusted to the darkness, she could make out a good deal of Aiden's body beneath the covers. "Sure they are. I'm just the only one who can see the truth. Like a werewolf slayer."

"In that case, good thing I'm awake. Would hate to be killed in my sleep."

"I'd never do such a thing."

"Given that you've tried to in most every other situation, better safe than sorry."

Tara chuckled, but the humor disappeared quickly from her thoughts. From the path the jokes were taking. Laying her head down on the pillow, she stared at the ceiling for several heartbeats. "The things that happened to you when you were captured," she said quietly. "Are you glad that you can't remember them?"

For a moment, she didn't think he would answer, but then he shifted. "No. The not knowing is driving me crazy. I've read all the reports I could find, but there's little in them. I'll get there, though. It's all within me, deep in my head somewhere. Lying in ambush."

"But why try so hard?" she insisted, her voice a whisper as her hand tightened around the covers. "Nothing about that experience sounds pleasant. Why would you even want to take that walk down memory lane?"

"Isn't it obvious?" Aiden sounded surprised. "I need to remember who was there so I can hunt down and kill each and every one of the bastards who held me."

# 14

## Aiden

Aiden didn't know what surprised him more, the fact that he woke up feeling more rested than he'd felt in years or that there was a woman pressed against his side. Tara. He didn't remember them moving toward each other at night, but clearly they had, and now her soft, warm cheek was pillowed on his shoulder. Closing his eyes, he breathed in her apple scent. Not sweet, but tart —like those green granny apples. Fresh and cheeky.

Aiden's finger longed to brush along Tara's skin, to smooth out her short, ruffled hair and trace along the muscle spasms he'd started coaxing free yesterday. He was still cross with her over the shoulder stunt, but he hated her high tolerance for pain even more. She should never have felt she needed to do that. Should never have been willing to take that step.

He lay back on the pillow and closed his eyes, wondering why he'd told her as much as he had about his captivity. It was a topic he had trouble verbalizing even with Dani, yet when Tara asked the questions, he answered. Not only that, but he didn't mind answering them. Not with her. Maybe because, unlike the rest of the world, she managed to radiate compassion without pity, interest without intrusion. No matter how little or how much he told her, he got the strangest feeling that she understood him.

His attention shifted to a small weight on top of his thoughts, light and warm and vibrating. Lifting his head, he discovered none other than Overlord, curled up and purring atop him on the covers.

"Adding insult to injury, are ye?" Aiden demanded of the feline.

The cat opened one eye, blinked, then closed it and returned to sleep.

Shaking his head, Aiden extricated himself from beneath the covers, doing his best to disturb neither the sleeping woman nor the evil feline, then went down to the gym for a quick workout on the punching bag. Hearing Tara get up and move about upstairs, he popped into the garage for a thorough check over Wilfred—just to be on the safe side.

They were on the road in short order, the final leg to Denton Valley flying by in a series of changing landscapes and growing mountains. There was so much open space here that Aiden never got tired of the scenery, and the companionable silence between them as they drove made the time go by quickly. They made one stop for lunch at a sushi place that Aiden dared Tara to try, which somehow led to a discussion on chemical compounds and explosives that Aiden didn't know he would find fascinating. By the time dessert showed up, they were off schedule. And Aiden couldn't care less.

Liam, on the other hand, cared a great deal as it turned out a couple of hours later when Aiden called into Trident Security to give an official thirty-minute ETA.

"You're late," Liam informed him over the headset.

"I am," Aiden agreed. Having no good justification for it, he let the words hang.

"Well, get your ass back on track," Liam ordered. "Go to main directly. High-risk intake protocol."

Aiden's hands tightened on the steering wheel, and he felt Tara glance over at him from the passenger seat. She could only hear his end of the conversation, but his body language had plainly put her on alert.

"I don't think that's necessary," he told Liam. "She isn't a threat."

Aiden thought he heard Liam choking on something, probably coffee. "You're still bringing in Tara Northpoint, right? The Obsidian Ops explosives expert currently wanted for multiple homicides? Or is there another Northpoint you picked up somewhere?"

"I am, but—"

"We have a protocol for a reason, McDane. If you're unhappy with it, take it up with the guy who wrote it—which, if I'm not mistaken, was you." Liam's voice changed to emotionless command. "High-risk protocol. I'll see you in thirty—now twenty-eight minutes. Turn on GPS location. Rowen out."

Disconnecting the phone, Aiden turned on the GPS tracking Trident Security used. The start and end of a movement was always the most dangerous, so from now on, there would be a technician watching every turn of Aiden's car.

Despite the question in Tara's eyes, Aiden procrastinated with the specifics until he pulled into a car trap in the secure entrance of the Trident Security building. The guard checked Aiden's credentials, then waved him farther in, closing the gate behind him before opening the one in front to allow continued passage. As he pulled into the spot near the pedestrian entrance, however, and Tara reached over to undo her seat belt and then for the door handle, there was no more hiding.

"It's locked per Trident Security protocols," he told her. "There are some other things that need to happen too."

She looked at him warily. "Things like what?"

Aiden hated this. Reaching under the seat, he pulled out a set of handcuffs.

Tara flinched as if struck.

It was all Aiden could do to keep from flinching himself. He hadn't expected how much her betrayed look would sting. "It's standard procedure, Wildcat," he said softly. "I'm sure Obsidian Ops had them as well. But I have to take you in in cuffs."

"This wasn't our agreement," she said. "I came voluntarily. I could have walked out of that hotel, remember? I didn't."

"That doesn't change the fact that there still is a warrant out for your arrest for murder. I can't undo that at a snap of my fingers, lass. I have Liam's word that Trident will work with you. Protect you physically and legally. But right now, at this moment, you're a wanted fugitive. Giving you a free run through Trident Security is a step too far for Liam."

She glared at him.

He waited.

"The deal is off," she said. "I want out."

He swallowed and stayed put, allowing the situation to speak for itself. They were in a secure garage. Cameras, guards, and locks. There was no out.

"You fucking asshole," Tara snarled into Aiden's face. "I trusted you. It's a mistake I won't repeat."

He held up the cuffs. "These are going on one way or another, Tara. Whether it's me or someone else, they are going on. Let it be me."

Jaw so tight that Aiden could see a muscle pulsing along it. Tara held out her hands, the wrists pressed together.

He shook his head and made a turn-around gesture.

She twisted in her seat, bringing her hands behind her.

Aiden locked the cuffs into place, a small jolt of pain shooting through him as the metal teeth caught the lock with *click* sounds, and then again as he double-locked the mechanism to ensure it couldn't be beat. His hand hovered over Tara's shoulder, his fingers longing to run the length of her muscles, soothing the strain he knew the restraint added. But he knew better than to think Tara would let him touch her.

Getting out of the car, Aiden did a quick check in the back seat to ensure Overlord had water in his freshly acquired carrier, then opened Tara's door and helped her out.

With his hand in the middle of Tara's back, Aiden guided her into the barren receiving area where Liam Rowen was already waiting. Standing with his feet apart and his hands draped loosely behind his back, Liam Rowen could have been a model for a special forces recruitment poster—except that instead of an inspirational expression that art usually preferred, Liam's current look threatened to tear Aiden limb from limb.

"Liam, allow me to introduce Tara Northpoint," Aiden said, coming to a halt before him.

Tara lifted her chin, glaring at Liam in defiance.

Liam gave Tara a small courteous bow of his head and shoulders. "Welcome to Trident Security and Rescue, Ms. Northpoint. I understand that, given the situation, safety is a paramount concern for you, and I assure you that we're taking extra steps to prevent any Obsidian Ops operation from doing you harm."

Aiden doubted that anyone at Obsidian was reckless enough to try anything in the middle of a Trident stronghold, but he knew Liam wasn't just giving Tara lip service. If he said there were extra measures being taken, there were.

"I appreciate hearing that," Tara said tersely.

Lian nodded again. "If at any point you feel the security is not adequate or has been compromised, please talk to me directly, and the situation will be rectified. Meanwhile, we have some processing in procedures to go through and then I look forward to speaking with you about the events in the Denver Research facility explosion. I understand from Aiden that your recollection of actions substantially diverges from the ones in the court documents."

Without giving Tara a chance to reply, Liam gave a small signal to someone behind Aiden and Tara. At once, two female officers stepped forward to bracket Tara on either side. Liam turned on his heels. "McDane, my office."

Aiden hesitated.

One of the women politely cleared her throat. "If you don't mind, sir, we would like the intake room. Unless there is an operational reason otherwise, we prefer to keep all the strip searches to same-gender observers."

"You—" Aiden snapped his mouth shut. He knew better than to make requests or give orders that wouldn't be followed, and this whole thing had been decided before he ever pulled Wilfred into the garage. Tara wouldn't be mistreated, but she would be strip-searched and cavity searched before being allowed on. In cuffs. The high-risk procedure would be in place until Liam himself lifted it.

Not meeting Tara's eyes, Aiden walked to the elevator.

The Up button failed to light when Aiden pressed it. The Down arrow stayed equally dark. Aiden glanced at the security guards. They glanced away. Aiden snorted. Yeah. The elevator wasn't actually out of service—Liam had turned it off on purpose. Just now.

Turning about, Aiden headed to the stairs and up to the seventeenth floor, where Liam had his office.

Aiden took the steps two at a time, keeping up a healthy jog—not only because he needed to burn up some of the frustration that was pounding through him, but also because he knew Liam would notice anything else. He hadn't commented on it, not right away, but there would be hell to pay later. That was Liam's way.

On the final landing, Aiden allowed himself a few steadying breaths, then walked into Liam's office without knocking.

"Strip search, really?" he demanded, crossing his arms over his chest. "She was just in the car with me for half a day."

"Yes. *Her* car." The beat of silence that followed said everything Liam thought about having brought Wilfred. "You need to cool off, McDane."

Aiden rolled his shoulders back, struggling to reclaim his self-control. One thing he knew about his boss was that Liam was both smart and reasonable—which meant rationality and logic got a lot further with him than bullying. Taking a chair, Aiden turned it around and straddled it in front of Liam's desk.

"Northpoint has good information to offer," Aiden said. "Speaking out against Obsidian Ops is no short order. You're going to get a lot further by being her teammate than by being a warden."

Liam leaned back in his chair and steepled his fingers under his chin. "My problem is that Northpoint has been actively trying to flee the country. Frankly, I don't blame her one bit, and if I were in her shoes, that's exactly what I'd do too. Staying here, working with us—in many ways that goes against her self-interest. Plus, we have this." Liam flipped open a manila folder on his desk, the now-familiar-to-Aiden pictures of the explosion site at Denver Research spilling out. "She's an Obsidian explosives expert wanted for murder."

"I know all that. But she is more than that."

Liam flipped the pages. "In the last seventy-two hours, she also tried to rip out your eyes, kill you, and escape custody. If I'm reading the report from Las Vegas correctly?"

Aiden cringed. "It's a bit more nuanced than that."

"Glad to hear." Liam threw his hands up before closing the folder. "Northpoint will be treated with respect and will be provided with protection—both physical and legal. But in terms of freedom and what she's privy to, I have to go by what's in this folder. Past behavior is the best indication of future behavior. I don't need to be telling you that." Reaching into his desk, Liam pulled a second folder from the drawer and handed it to Aiden. "Your new assignment."

Aiden froze, his hand gripping the manila folder. "Tara is going to need someone assigned to her full time. I—"

"You're off this case."

"No." Aiden winced at his raised voice and checked it. "She's my assignment. I want to finish my job."

"You're too emotionally involved with this one," Liam said. "I don't know what's happening, but this isn't you. Get some space. Get some perspective. I'll put another operative on Northpoint."

Aiden swallowed, Tara's betrayed expression as she was taken away in cuffs to be searched burning into him. "Please," he said quietly. "She can stay with me. You don't need to keep her under lock and key, because she isn't going anywhere."

"Good God. Why, McDane? Why in the name of all that's logical would you think the Obsidian Ops fugitive is going to stay fucking put?"

"Because I already let her go!" Aiden's hand tightened on the back of the chair. "I know she's not going anywhere because she already did. And came back." He drew a breath. "The first night in the hotel room. I told her she was free to go. And she chose to stay. Because…because she didn't want me to lose my job, of all things."

Liam froze, his intelligent eyes piercing Aiden in that way he had that made you feel like he could see right into your mind. The room chilled, the seconds of tense silence ticking by at a crawl. "Why did you let her go?" he asked very quietly. Dangerously. As if he'd already figured out the truth.

"Because I had sex with her." Aiden's voice sounded too stoic to his own ears.

Liam blew out a long breath, his eyes closing. "You had her captive." He rubbed his face, turning away. "I know you well enough to know that you'd never force a woman, but the situation itself—it doesn't allow true choice. We don't do that. Not here."

Aiden's jaw tightened. He knew Liam was right. And yet… He motioned toward Liam's finger where a wedding ring would soon be. "Wasn't Jaz your protectee?"

"Protectee," said Liam. "Not a prisoner. Everyone should know the difference."

Aiden nodded, his chest tight. Reaching into the inside of his jacket, he pulled his gun from its holster, took out the magazine, and cleared the chamber. Locking the slide to the rear, he laid the weapon on the table between Liam and him, then added his Trident Security bounty hunting license to the pile. "I know," he told Liam. Despite the tight band around Aiden's chest, he kept his voice even, letting him know there were no hard feelings.

Liam looked impassively at Aiden's things, at his identity, then back at Aiden's stony face. Reaching out slowly, Liam picked up Aiden's weapon, examining the empty chamber. Then he turned its grip forward and handed it back. "You aren't fired," he said finally. "I'll punish you, but I won't fire you."

Aiden exhaled, his burning lungs finally taking in air. He hadn't realized how much the Trident family meant to him until now, when he stared at the abyss of losing it all. "I can't say I'm looking forward to that."

"I can't say I am either." Liam pinched the bridge of his nose. "With regards to Northpoint… I'm going to give her the choice. If, and only if, she wants to stay with you, I'll authorize it. But if I get even a hair of a sense that she's uncomfortable with such an arrangement, you take the assignment I just handed you and get your ass to California. Fair?"

"More than," said Aiden. He stood, reloading his weapon before sliding it into its holster. "Liam. Thank you."

Liam shook his head. "Don't thank me yet. This is going to get worse before it gets better."

# 15

Tara

Tara was exhausted. After being searched and processed like a criminal—which, in the world's eyes, she was—she was taken to a large conference room where several Trident operatives, including Liam Rowen, a forensics examiner, and an attorney with the unfortunate last name of Dancer, had her go over the events at the research facility. Over. And over. And over.

They went through everything in chronological order, then backward, then from different perspectives. They sped over some events and slowed time over others. They drew pictures, wrote out formulas, and did math calculations of blast radius. It was hard enough to get through when telling the truth. To keep lies straight would have been impossible. And they all knew this was only the start of the debrief.

Through it all, Tara tried not to look at the door through which Aiden never walked. At first, the harsh sting of his betrayal made her throat close as she searched out words to offer the Trident team. Then, as hours passed without his appearance, the pain morphed to anger.

"Is Aiden McDane going to condescend to join us any time soon?" she asked four hours into the discussion, as an assistant showed up with boxed dinners for the group. "Or will we be going over all this from the beginning for his benefit tomorrow?"

Liam Rowen, the head of Trident Security who ruled over the space with a quiet dominance, looked up from his notes. "McDane has been reassigned," he said matter-of-factly. "There's a witness in LA who needs some babysitting."

"What? Why?" The words escaped Tara too quickly for her to catch them. She didn't know what part of the news made her more unhappy—that she hadn't gotten to give Aiden a piece of her mind for the welcome treatment or that she hadn't seen him. Wouldn't feel his hands rub along her shoulder, quietly finding the sore muscles she was too proud to admit having.

Liam returned to his notes. "His assignment was to bring you in. He finished it."

She remembered the argument Aiden had with Liam in the car and the hard look Liam gave him on arrival. Now that she'd spent some with Liam Rowen, being on the receiving end of his wrath seemed even more uncomfortable. "But he isn't in trouble, right?" she asked.

Everyone at the table looked up at that.

Liam turned toward her. "Should he be? Is there something I need to know?"

"Only that I wouldn't be here if not for him."

"Yes," Liam agreed readily. "I find that is how bounty hunting usually works. Can we go back to the initial entry, please? What roads did you take to get to the research facility?"

Tara answered mechanically, the fury that was keeping her alert for these hours shifting to an emptiness. Everything logical inside her said that separation from Aiden was the best thing she could have hoped for. For all the memories lost in his conscious mind, the truth was there. In his sleep. And sooner or later, he'd recognize her.

*Isn't it obvious? I need to remember who was there so I can hunt down and kill each and every one of the bastards who held me.*

"Ms. Northpoint. Tara."

Tara blinked, realizing that Liam had been repeating himself. That she'd missed the last few minutes of the discussion entirely. "I'm sorry. Could we take a break?"

"Of course," said Liam, and everyone at the table rose at once. An operative stationed near the door stepped forward with handcuffs, as she did each time Tara moved locations—even to use the bathroom. This time, however, Liam held up a hand. "Can Tara and I have the room. Please?"

Though he worded the request as a question, it was truly a command, and everyone seemed to know it. A moment later, the room was empty except for Tara and Liam, who walked over to pour two glasses of water, sliding one over to her.

"It's been a long day," Liam said. "And I think it's time to turn in for the night, not just pause for a break. Before you go, though, I wanted to ask whether you'd like to press charges against Aiden McDane. It will in no way affect the protection Trident has offered."

Tara's hand closed around her glass, her shoulders tensing. "I'd love to press charges for false imprisonment, but given the warrant, I don't think the law is on my side."

Liam swirled his water. "I was referring to sex while in custody."

"I'm afraid I didn't see him have sex with anyone."

Liam lifted a brow. "The jig is up. Aiden told me he had sex with you."

Idiot. Big-mouthed idiot. "Aiden was clearly confusing wishful thinking with reality."

Putting down his glass, Liam focused all his attention on Tara and for the first time since meeting the man, she felt the full effect of his penetrating gaze. Though he wasn't moving, he seemed to fill her whole vision. The whole room. "Why are you protecting Aiden?" he asked.

She swallowed, the answers springing to the tip of her tongue fading away without being said.

*Because evidently, he's too stupid to protect himself.*

*There's nothing to protect him from, Mr. Rowen.*

*You know, there's little point in asking questions if you intend to ignore my answers.*

In the end, she went with the truth. "Because he makes me feel safe in a way that I haven't felt for a long time." Her words were quiet and not what she herself expected to utter, but Liam seemed unsurprised.

"Would you like me to reassign him as your warden?" he asked. "It would mean staying with him until the trial."

She nodded and felt a knot loosen inside her chest as Liam pulled his cell phone from his pocket and dialed a number.

Aiden was waiting outside the Trident Security building when Liam walked Tara out, her hands cuffed. Aiden stepped toward them. His gaze scanned Tara, then focused on Liam, who stood beside her.

Liam nodded.

The mist around Aiden's face thickened as if he'd sighed in relief. He turned to Tara, meeting her gaze for the first time. "You don't have to come with me," he said. "Liam explained that to you, right?"

"We had a chat."

"She's your headache now," Liam confirmed, giving a curt nod to them both before turning back toward the building. "I'll see you tomorrow."

As Liam walked away, Aiden reached into his back pocket and pulled out a key. "Turn around," he said softly. The first words since the parking lot of betrayal.

Tara did.

Aiden unlocked her cuffs with quick motions and stepped back while she turned around and rubbed her wrists.

"How long were you out here?" she asked.

He glanced at his watch. "Three hours, give or take."

"Why?"

A corner of his mouth twitched ruefully. "Because Rowen told me he'd get around to talking to you when he got around to talking to you. And that if I cared about the answer, I could wait here."

"Ah." She put her hands into her pockets. "So what now?"

"I keep you safe," Aiden said.

"And keep me from changing my mind and making a run for it?"

"Aye. That too."

She nodded, but made no movement, and neither did he. After wanting to slug him in the nose this afternoon, all Tara felt now was tired. And not certain of anything. "Shouldn't you keep me in cuffs, then?" She tried to sound businesslike. "Isn't that your protocol?"

"I have to secure you when you're inside our headquarters," he replied. "But outside the sensitive areas, the discretion is mine. As it was on the trip."

"Are you sure you're making the right choice?" There was a bite to her words.

"Tara." Aiden let out a long breath. "I should have warned you."

"You think?"

Reaching out slowly, he pressed a loose strand of hair behind Tara's ear, his fingers brushing along her cheek for the barest of moments. "Are you all right, lass?" he whispered.

"I…" Tara rolled back her shoulders. "I'm fine. It's all right. I understand. And really, it isn't a big deal either way."

He shook his head as if to say he disagreed, then pulled her toward him, his strong arms encircling her body protectively. Tara leaned into Aiden's solid chest. She let out a breath against him, and Aiden kissed the top of her head. "Let's get you home," he said softly. "Overlord too. I won't risk the wrath of Denton Valley, Colorado by letting that monster run wild."

# 16

Liam

"Wait, Aiden? Our Aiden McDane?" The last syllable of Jaz's question turned into a nasal moan as Liam pressed his thumbs into the arch of her foot. As he stroked up and down the muscle, Jaz's moan morphed into such a deep, satisfied purr that for a moment, Liam was unsure she remembered what they'd been talking about.

The past few months, as Jaz's pregnancy had taken a greater hold on her body, she'd alternately complained about no longer fitting into her best climbing shoes, and foot pain after she forced her feet into them anyway. Liam had tried suggesting that she abstain from climbing while pregnant. Once. The result—Jaz packing up her things and moving into his mother's apartment for a week—taught Liam to keep his mouth shut about what his fiancée should and shouldn't be doing with her pregnant body.

It didn't matter that her growing belly meant she couldn't actually get more than a foot off the ground, that she could demonstrate technique in sneakers, and that she herself was not going anywhere near a real actual mountain. He didn't get to have an opinion on her climbing unless he wanted to walk around carrying watermelons in his pants for the next four months. She also found his copy of *What to Expect When You're Expecting* and burned it.

Being a quick study, Liam had pivoted at once to fully embracing his new habit of fulfilling food cravings and making noncommittal sounds in response to all family-planning conversations. Suspend the cribs from the ceiling so that Jaz could get a little extra exercise? Climb Mount Monadnock with babies in backpack carriers on the twins' first birthday? Host a pediatric CPR and First Aid class for all friends and family every weekend?

Mmm. Hmmm.

Fortunately, so long as Liam didn't interfere, Jaz tended to course correct anxiety-induced planning a great deal faster than he could have in her shoes. And when it came to matters outside changes to her body, she had the sharpest mind Liam had ever had the pleasure of tangling with. A mind that was now once again focused on the Northpoint-McDane situation.

"It's a huge step," Jaz said. "Aiden has been spiraling. I've even noticed it on the rescue side. He keeps it together while focused on a job or an exercise, but you get him relaxed, and it's like ghosts come haunting."

Liam nodded. Aiden could take and dish out a great deal of pain in the sparring ring, but a friendly slap on the back made the man tense up like a cornered dog. And for everything he'd fucked up bringing Tara to Denton Valley, he'd been more rested than Liam had seen in the past six months.

"What's she like?" Jaz asked.

Liam considered their debrief. "She's a fighter. I have a feeling she's been a second-tier citizen at Obsidian her whole life, fighting for every shred of respect that everyone else got as a matter of course."

"Why?"

"Best I can tell, because Obsidian Ops recruits special forces operatives on contract. You're only as valuable as the skills you bring. She was picked up off the street as a kid—not a skill set a mercenary op needs, exactly. A charity case. So she was treated as if she owed everyone just for existing."

"She said that?" Jaz asked.

"Not directly." Liam snorted at Jaz's knowing look. Yes, he had a way of ferreting out what he wanted to know and he was not above using all resources at his disposal to do it. But hell, that was Liam's job, and Tara had somehow gotten into Aiden's confidence. Which meant he would be keeping an extra eye on the operative.

Jaz tapped her fingers on the side of the couch, her eyes sparking with mischief. "I can't wait to meet her."

"Why would you be meeting her?" said Liam. He knew better than to get into Jaz's professional way, but no amount of mental gymnastics put Tara into Jaz's search and rescue sphere.

Jaz lifted a brow in that way she had when she thought he was missing something obvious. "Well, she's going to be at the wedding, for one. Since I doubt Aiden thought to bring appropriate clothes, we'll need to go shopping for that. And two, because I want to."

Liam's thumb, which was still on Jaz's swollen foot, pressed into her arch a good deal harder than warranted.

Jaz yelped. "You did that on purpose."

"Of course I did that on purpose. I thought I heard you suggest that we invite an Obsidian Ops operative to our wedding."

"Well, Aiden is coming to our wedding, isn't he?" Jaz asked with suspicious mildness.

"Yes. Of course."

"And he's running Tara's protection detail?"

"Yes," said Liam.

"So what exactly is Tara to be doing while Aiden and the rest of the people you most trust are busy dancing to Coconut Joe at the North Vault?" She held out a finger. "And before you suggest locking her in some cell for the day, Aiden does get a plus one. And I, for one, am not going to deny him that if he's interested. Plus—"

"Plus you're a curious busybody," said Liam.

"That too."

"I think our guest list is full." Liam was reaching for straws, and he knew it.

"I'm happy to uninvite my parents." Jaz's voice turned serious. "I'm worried about Aiden, though. He doesn't talk to anyone except Dani, and frankly, the fact that Tara managed to have sex with a man who has a panic attack at the notion of intimate touch is telling. She can be good for him. And she can destroy him just as quickly."

Jaz was right. It was a point he himself had considered, though not as fully as or quickly as she had. For as long as Liam had known Aiden, the man had avoided relationships of any sort—hell, he changed continents to escape a loving family and was now successfully managing to be too busy to talk with his own cousins. The bond Aiden had with the Tridents had been forged through action and operations, but that wasn't how the rest of the world worked.

Liam was damn lucky he had a woman in his life who looked out for their whole family, and Aiden was a part of that. Liam picked up Jaz's other foot, aware that her demeanor had shifted again, as if she was reading his thoughts. Sometimes Liam wondered whether she didn't have an ability to do just that—usually in order to get under his skin in the most creative way possible. But now, Jaz's face was serious.

"How hard do you have to be on him over the whole unprofessional-conduct thing?" she asked.

Wasn't that the million dollar question. "He offered up his weapon and license," Liam said, not hiding from Jaz how much Aiden's readiness to run again had shaken him. "I can't turn the other way without the whole business feeling unfinished. Or worse, Aiden thinking I doubt his ability to handle what's dished out, that holding him to account is a pointless proposition not worth the time and effort."

"I've got awesome administrative work he could—"

"I'm not a sadist."

"Debatable," Jaz purred, shifting her thighs in a way that made Liam harden painfully despite himself. He didn't think he found pregnant women unusually attractive in general until his fiancée suddenly fell into that category, but Jaz was a game changer all around. It was truly a shame he couldn't bend her over the kitchen counter and warm her backside just now, but he'd have to come up with a creative way of hitting the right note tonight.

Jaz's free foot slid over his pulsating bulge.

Liam groaned, then pulled himself back together with herculean effort. "Aiden is one of us now. The whole of him, not just some perfect version. Sometimes that takes a bit of pain to sink in."

"Remind me to ask Dani if DSM-5 has a special diagnosis for military psychosis. Because—just for the record—normal human beings don't think the way you do."

"Noted." Liam's phone rang. He glanced at the caller ID and put it on speaker. A moment later, the voice of Sonia Dancer, Trident Security's new young attorney, came over the loudspeaker.

"The North Vault, that's your club?" Sonia asked by way of greeting.

"Yes," said Liam.

"And Cassey McKenzie, is he yours too?"

"Is there a correct answer to that question?" asked Liam.

"Let me ask it a different way. If he gets thrown in jail and North Vault is dragged through the mud, does that have an effect on your interests?"

"Right. We're on our way," said Liam. "Where are we meeting you?"

"Glad to hear it," Sonia said jovially, as if she had no doubt whatsoever on how the conversation would end. "I happen to be at the North Vault just now."

THE NORTH VAULT was unusually quiet as Jaz and Liam walked inside, mostly due to the lack of patrons. Empty except for the McKenzie twins and Sonia, the club seemed almost overwhelmingly large—a feeling that Cassey, sitting at his piano with a scotch in hand, didn't seem to share.

Unlike Cassey, Sonia sat at one of the tables, her hair pinned back into a bun and her briefcase open. Briar, being Briar, lurked in a shadow a few tables away.

"Good evening." Cassey beat Sonia to the greeting. "If you're wondering about the lack of strippers, that's because your gorgeous pit bull over there insisted we shut down until we have a few things sorted." He toasted Sonia as he spoke, his narrow Prada business suit flowing with the motions. "She utterly spoiled a threesome I was planning too."

The gorgeous pit bull in question gave Cassey a look that promised to rip him to bits.

Cassey took a sip of scotch.

Sonia turned to Liam and Jaz, the young attorney's body vibrating with tension. Liam had hired the woman for her drive and promise, and now he was about to reap the benefits—for better or worse. "I was reviewing your holdings and saw that you intended to host a wedding reception here. Having done my due diligence on the venue, I feel obliged to tell you that the North Vault's current proprietor is one breath away from jail. I instructed him to shut down operations before he can cause additional damage to your name and brand."

Cassey tilted his head, regarding Sonia with interest. "When you say jail, would there be handcuffs involved?"

"Yes," said Sonia.

Liam winced.

Cassey grinned. "Promise?"

A muscle ticked at the base of Sonia's jaw, and as much as Liam was enjoying watching the collision, the responsible part of him felt the need to pull the poor attorney out of the deep end before she quit on him. Sonia really was good—one had only to watch her in debriefs with Tara Northpoint—but she also came from a world where the written word of law ruled supreme. Cassey.... Was Cassey.

"I presume that resolving the issue with Mr. McKenzie directly proved less than fruitful?" Liam asked, pouring himself a drink from the bar and grabbing a juice for Jaz.

"It did. With both of them." Sonia pulled her briefcase closer to herself as if it were a shield. "One Mr. McKenzie has refused to talk to me at all."

Sitting in the corner, Briar snorted with derision. Though the McKenzie brothers looked identical, no one who was in the room with them for more than ten seconds could fail to tell the pair apart.

"And the other," Sonia continued.

"Wouldn't shut up?" Liam offered.

"Has been very verbal. Yes."

Jaz kicked Liam under the table and cleared her throat. "Perhaps we could go over the substantive issues, Counselor?" she said.

Sonia gave her a grateful look and opened her case. "To start with, Mr. Cassey McKenzie has been accused of bribing Denton Valley's liquor license inspector."

"Did I not give him enough?" asked Cassey.

Liam threw him a *shut up for a second* look and returned his attention to Sonia. "Please go on."

Sonia flipped to the next page of her notes. "Next, I have five reports from Denton Valley Memorial Hospital about slip-and-fall incidents at the North Vault in the past week. The fact that no charges have been pressed yet is a miracle. You have a hazardous environment lawsuit hanging in the wings, and I highly suggest we get ahead of it."

Briar extended his legs in front of him and crossed the ankles one over the other. Though he said nothing, Liam had little doubt that the quiet twin helped those slip and fall along.

Sonia Dancer, now on a run, flipped the page again. "Last but not least," she said, "is a review of North Vault's financial records since the operation has been turned over to the McKenzie brothers. Bottom line up front, the club is well on its way to a tax evasion investigation by the IRS." Sonia put the papers down and crossed her arms, her nostrils flaring delicately as if the assault on the law was personal.

Liam suspected that to her, it was exactly that. And that Cassey knew it. "Well?" Liam asked Cassey, turning toward the man.

"Oh, it's all true," Cassey said with no trace of remorse. "Incomplete but true."

"I recommend you evict Mr. McKenzie from the North Vault immediately," said Sonia.

At those words, all humor that hung around Cassey disappeared and he rose to his full height, his shoulders unfurling. "Ms. Dancer." Case put his drink down on the top of the baby grand piano and strode forward, adjusting his cuffs. "Where did you go to school?"

"Excuse me?" said Sonia.

"Your law degree. Where did you get it?"

"Yale."

"Yale, Colorado?"

"Yale Law School, New Haven, Connecticut," Sonia said.

"Ah. In fact, you only passed the Colorado bar a month before taking a job with Trident Security, is that right?"

"If you're trying to attack my bona fides—"

"Oh, I'm not attacking your qualifications in the slightest," said Cassey. "Simply your intelligence and common sense. Did you happen to call the Denton Valley head inspector or their legal department before coming here?"

"Of course not," Sonia said, her back straight and chin raised in the air. "My purpose is to protect Trident Security, not give other agencies ideas on how they can implicate us."

"Which explains why you don't know that my bribe was offered in support of their internal investigation," Cassey told her. "In plain terms, they asked me to do it."

"I see." Sonia regained her composure with admirable speed. "And I imagine the slip and falls were also sanctioned by a cleaning company?"

"Of course not. That would be absurd." Cassey picked up his drink again. "Nobody slipped. They did fall, though. At least..." He turned to his brother. "I forget, did we smash those bastards into the floor or a brick wall? I don't know if it counts as a fall if they were upright during the smashing."

"Your defense for a hazardous environment is that you were actually involved in felonious assault and battery?" said Sonia.

"Oh, I'm not defending anything. I can tell you right now that anyone who doesn't take a woman's no for an answer at the North Vault will be finding themselves in the very same emergency room that those five assholes who cornered a seventeen-year-old girl in the bathroom last Friday did." His jaw tightened. "I expect you will find no slip and fall lawsuits to be filed on that night's account, Counselor."

Liam made a mental note to talk to Cassey about accepting fake IDs to get into the Vault, but this wasn't the time.

Sonia, meanwhile, looked a shade paler than she had a few minutes ago. Still, the young woman only swallowed and turned the file over to her last set of notes. "The accounting—"

"Could I see that?" Cassey took the stack of sheets from Sonia's hand and pulled a Mont Blanc pen out of the inside pocket of his suit. "You know, you're right," he said, scanning through the ledger. "There are several errors in the accounting here." Correcting several digits, he handed the stack of sheets back. "I filed to have the North Vault marked as a historical building with the Denton Valley preservation society. The status grants tax relief, but the administrative setup of the accounts is more arcane than the society itself."

"So what's looking like double-book accounting is actually a transition," Sonia finished for Cassey, rubbing her face with her hands. "Why did you not tell me any of this when I barged in here two hours ago and demanded you clear out the place?"

Cassey grinned. "Because I knew you'd call Liam eventually—the wee bastard has been avoiding me for two weeks. We've got some wedding planning to do."

"Oh God." Whatever color remained in Sonia's face now drained completely. "Mr. Rowen—"

Liam shook his head. "Welcome to Denton Valley, Counselor. Where the inmates run the asylum. Your head was in the right place."

"The kind of place doctors need a flashlight to check," said Cassey.

Liam shot Cassey a murderous look and turned to Sonia. "Since we're having an impromptu business meeting, I sent you some more paperwork about the Denver Research explosion that I meant to brief you about."

Sonia nodded, all business. "Yes. I've been going over the affidavit Colorado's state attorney filed regarding Northpoint's murder charges."

"Right. My interest actually goes beyond Tara herself. Specifically, I'm interested in Tara's employer—Obsidian Ops. I'd like you to talk to Denver Research. Trident Security would be happy to represent them pro bono in a wrongful death civil suit against Obsidian."

A corner of Sonia's mouth lifted in a comprehending smile, reflecting the quick mind for which Liam had hired her. "Colorado is going after Tara, but Obsidian Ops is getting off scot-free. You want to drag them out into the open. And if the state won't do it, then we will. Show their warts to the world."

"Exactly. Once you get Denver Research on board, get with the public defender's office and talk to the state prosecutor about delaying Tara's criminal trial until after she testifies in the civil one. The public defenders are overworked and understaffed, so you'll be de facto doing their job for them, but I'm all right with that. Anyway, explain to the prosecution that they might get bigger fish with the info that trial brings out. Depending on how forthcoming Ms. Tara Northpoint is, she could get a good deal out of this as well."

"On it," Sonia said.

"Will you be able to squeeze what's basically an organized crime case around all the important work you're doing to ensure the North Vault isn't sued for slip and falls?" Cassey asked. Of course he did.

Sonia pulled her briefcase to her side. "I feel confident I can do both."

"No doubt." Cassey took a pious sip of his scotch, but at least he kept his mouth shut while Sonia gathered her dignity and walked to the door. With her hand hovering above the door handle, Sonia turned back to Cassey.

"What exactly did you do before taking over the North Vault?" she asked.

"Ran around doing pull-ups and shooting things."

"I see. And did you by chance have any auxiliary duties during your military service?"

Cassey gave her a piercing look that actually bordered on respect. "Aye."

"And what branch were those duties in?" she asked.

A corner of Cassey's mouth twitched up. "Judge Advocate Corps."

"You're an attorney," Sonia said flatly.

"Not in Colorado. That's all you." He toasted Sonia and set his sights on Jaz and Liam, who suddenly felt the full force of being trapped in the man's snare. "We've got a wedding in three weeks. Let's get to it, shall we?"

## 17

### Tara

Aiden didn't seem like himself Saturday morning—and after a week of staying with him, Tara had a pretty good notion of what his usual self acted like. They'd gotten into a routine of sorts: Aiden woke up first and did a body-weight workout on a nifty little chin-up bar setup he had mounted to a doorway. By the time Tara got out of bed, he had coffee brewing, and the smell of Arabic beans filled the small kitchen. Breakfast was up to Tara, lest she wanted to eat cereal with chocolate milk, which seemed to be the primary staple Aiden stored in the place. To his credit, Aiden did attempt to buy muffins from one of the three bakeries within a block of the building, but anything more imaginative—like eggs—required someone else's intervention.

And a skillet.

The two-bedroom apartment Aiden rented not far from the Trident Security complex was large enough to host a military regiment, but furnished little better than a college dorm room. Worse, actually—dorm rooms usually had two chairs, and, at the point of Tara's arrival, Aiden only had one. They'd gone out to the store to grab a second one just so the two of them could sit at the breakfast island together. In short, the setup left little doubt that its owner was ready to leave at any time.

The few things Aiden did acquire, however, were of good quality. A sharp cooking knife. One. A coffeemaker. A blender. And, with Tara's appearance, a skillet and two pots.

After breakfast, they typically went to Trident Security for the ongoing debriefs. Since Liam insisted on not letting Tara wander the halls unrestrained, Aiden would put cuffs on her just outside the first security door and remove them the moment they stepped into the conference room. Though they never talked about it, Tara noticed that Aiden was never far from her while she was restrained. A hand splayed across the small of her back as they walked down the hallway, a touch on her shoulder as they turned a corner, his solid body pressed against her back in the elevator. *I'm here. I have you. You're not alone.* For the first time in her life, Tara felt like someone was on her side, rooting for her.

After the day's debrief, she and Aiden went to Liam's gym for a full workout and then ordered takeout dinner to bring home. A search of Aiden's kitchen had proved that while he owned a microwave, he'd never bothered to replace the stove the apartment's previous tenants had, for some reason, taken with them. So takeout it was, eaten on the couch in the living room while *Battlestar Galactica* unfolded on the large-screen TV.

Sleeping arrangements had proved to be a moving target. Despite having two bedrooms, Aiden had only one bed—but had acquired an air mattress for Tara's stay.

Overlord punctured that within the first hour of its inflated existence.

The second, extra durable, airbed lasted one night.

Given the two dead airbeds, the fact that the recliner couch was ill-suited for sleeping, and that the cat appeared to be part shepherd and threw a fit any time his humans chose to occupy different rooms, they went back to the shared-bed arrangement that worked out fine at Staden's place.

Though they always fell asleep on opposite sides of the king bed,

Tara woke up as often as not in the middle of the night to find her body pressed against Aiden's hard muscles. It never went further than that, though, and by the time she awoke in the morning, he was always already up, starting his morning routine.

Except for today.

Tara first noticed that Aiden had made only one cup of coffee—hers—while he stared glumly at a green-colored nutrition shake in front of him. Then there was the lack of sweat he typically worked up on the pull-up bar. Last and not least was an air of tension that hung thick in the air as he nodded good morning.

"No morning exercise today?" Tara slid onto the chair near the coffee.

Aiden pushed the cream and sugar her way. "Oh, there'll be plenty of exercise." He sipped his concoction and grimaced. "For the record, when Dani said that green apples drown out the kale, she lied through her teeth."

"And why are you drinking kale?"

"In theory, it's supposed to help with energy and muscle recovery." He took another sip, cringed, and dumped the concoction down the sink. "Fuck theory." Striding to the fridge, Aiden pulled out the half gallon of chocolate milk and drank it right out of the carton. "I've been summoned to Liam's gym."

"The one we go to every day?"

"That very one." The way Aiden said it made it clear that this trip was going to be different, and Tara's gaze narrowed as her mind flipped through the possibilities of what this meant.

"Would this have anything to do with the fact that you were dumb enough to tell Liam Rowen we had sex en route to Denton Valley?" she asked bluntly.

"Aye."

A shiver ran along Tara's spine, the morning suddenly taking on a different color altogether. She didn't know how such things worked at Trident Security, but at Obsidian Ops, the penalties for disobedience were harsh enough to ensure no repeat performance. More importantly, whatever was going to happen clearly had Aiden concerned.

"I told Liam it wasn't true," Tara said, leaning forward. "Liam asked me whether we had sex, and I said no. I'll tell him so again. If both of us deny—"

"I'm not going to lie to Rowen." Aiden's gaze cut to her over the chocolate milk carton. "I highly recommend you never do it again either, by the way."

"What are they going to do to you?" Tara tried to sound cool and logical, but the thought of seeing Aiden be hurt because of her made nausea rise up her throat. "What can I do?"

"You'll be having lunch with Trident operatives. I'll catch up with you after I take my beating." He grinned at her, but the smile didn't touch his eyes and the milk carton crumpled in his grip as he spoke. "It will all be over in a few hours."

She shook her head. "I'm not going to lunch," she said, leaning forward. "I'm going with you."

"To enjoy the show? I can't say I blame you."

"Stop it," Tara snapped at him, her mood for jests gone altogether. She'd seen what punishment in mercenary units was like. Felt it herself. And whatever she could do, she would. "If I'm there as witness, there's a better chance Liam won't cross the line."

Aiden seemed like he was about to say something, then stopped himself, his intent gaze penetrating Tara. After putting away the chocolate milk, he walked around the kitchen island to stop right in front her. With his legs slightly apart and his hands on either side of her, Aiden seemed to bracket her in a cocoon of safety. "The Trident men are not going to cross the line whether you're there or not," he said. "I'm fretting over how well I'll fare in their eyes, but I'll walk out with injuries to nothing but my pride. But that's not how Obsidian treated you, is it?"

Tara shook her head, a tiny motion, but it was enough.

Aiden brushed his thumb over her cheek, then tucked a stray lock of hair behind her ear. "What did they do to you, Wildcat? What happened when you broke their rules?"

Images flashed unbidden in Tara's mind. A conference room. The click of a gun. The slap of Raymond's hand across her face as she pleaded not to be made to hurt Aiden. The ruthless beating that came when they discovered she'd injected him with drugs. Not her first at Obsidian, and not the last either.

Tara drew a shaking breath, wishing she felt anger flowing along with the memories. But instead, her body echoed the fear and shame she'd felt at the time. The bone-deep belief that she'd deserved it all. A stray who should have done better.

"Tell me, Wildcat," Aiden whispered. "I'll understand more than you think."

Tara shook her head. She couldn't tell him. Obviously.

The burn mark she'd left on Aiden's biceps stared at her from between the ink lines of his tattoo. She reached over and brushed her fingertips over it.

Aiden tensed at once.

She pulled her hand away. "I'm sorry," Tara said, without specifying what she was sorry for.

"Don't be. My demons have nothing to do with you." Aiden squeezed her shoulder, then kissed the top of her head before pushing away.

WHEN AIDEN and Tara arrived at the gym, the place was empty but for four military-looking men. Liam, Tara recognized at once, and the others introduced themselves as Cullen, Kyan, and Eli—the latter with a British accent that seemed too polite for whatever was about to happen. Kyan, who had burn scars along one side of his face and neck, touched Tara's shoulder.

"I had a short tangle with Obsidian Ops," he said softly. "I'm not going to pretend to know what it's like to grow up there, but I probably get it more than most. If you need someone to talk to, Aiden knows where to find me."

Tara thanked him absently, her attention on Aiden, who'd already moved away to begin a warm-up routine. The gym was neater than she remembered seeing it, the scent of cleaner and the vinyl rising from the wall-to-wall mats. A scent that Tara knew would soon change to salty sweat and, very likely, the copper tang of blood.

Liam cleared his throat. "Tara, you're more than welcome here usually, but today's training session is a private one. I'll call someone to—"

"She wants to stay," Aiden called, interrupting Liam's words.

Liam turned, clear doubt in his gaze. "And you're all right with that?"

Aiden stretched his back, "Aye," he said, not looking at anyone.

"Your call," Liam told Aiden, then circled the other men around him. Tara waited for him to say something along the lines of letting this be a lesson to everyone, but that wasn't what came out of Liam's mouth when he rocked back on his heels. "Watch yourselves, because God knows McDane won't, and I've no desire to discover just how high his pain threshold is. Enough to say it's higher than any of us are comfortable with."

"Shark bait endurance run?" asked Cullen.

"Yes. Three minutes on, thirty seconds off."

"How long are we keeping him in the penalty box?" Eli picked up a pair of fingerless gloves and secured them around his wrists. With his unruly hair and animated face—that was the polar opposite of Cullen's—he looked the least military-like of the bunch, but the way he moved left little doubt of his skills.

"Twenty rounds," said Liam, loud enough for Aiden to hear.

Aiden nodded.

Eli winced.

Tara put her arms behind her back, not sure what to make of the whole ordeal. No one in the room seemed particularly excited for what was about to happen, but for reasons as different from Obsidian Ops' as everything else the Tridents did. Before she could dwell too much on the situation, Eli started toward the sparring ring. Aiden secured his headgear and ducked beneath the ropes as well.

The men touched gloves.

"Three minutes," Liam called, and started the timer.

# 18

Tara

Aiden moved first, setting a deadly tone for the bout, which Tara thought was utterly against his self-interest.

Rule one of discipline—don't piss off the person inflicting the discipline.

Eli grunted at the force of the first blow, then came back at Aiden with a combination that was smooth enough to belong on a set of a Hollywood film. As Tara sat at the edge of the mat, she saw the plot play out before her, Aiden's deadly blows against Eli's more water-like style, both men utterly present in the fight. Kick. Block. Move. *Thump. Thump. Thump.*

Aiden's breath stayed steady through the round, his eyes alert and motions lithe and deadly and too beautiful to be real. Except they were. Hell, they were real enough to have knocked most men unconscious several times over. Aiden's skin glistened with well-earned sweat as the timer signaled the end of the round. Eli bumped his glove in encouragement and ducked out. So far, so good.

Cullen went into the ring next. Then Kyan. Then Liam. Aiden

met them all with everything he had, the deadly grace of the exchange echoing throughout the quiet gym. Kick. Block. Move. *Thump. Thump. Thump.*

By the end of the first rotation of all four men, the even match of the pairing had begun to wane. Unlike Aiden, the others were coming in fresh every round, and the thirty seconds of rest he got seemed to rush by quicker with every rotation. Aiden braced his hands on his thighs at first, then stayed on his knees for his break. The water from the bottle Eli threw to him started missing his mouth.

Tara bit her lip as she noticed the changes creeping into Aiden's fighting tactics as well. Blows that he'd sidestepped easily earlier in the fight, Aiden now started to take against large muscle groups, the energy required for that extra quick step no longer worth it to expend just to save himself a little pain. Sweat soaked his shirt and flew onto the mat in slippery streaks.

On round ten, Aiden stumbled, missing his footing at just the wrong moment as Cullen sent a vicious roundhouse toward Aiden's ribs. Liam's curse before the blow even landed made Tara's stomach tighten with dread. On the mat, Cullen threw himself backward to try to pull the blow, but Aiden's grunt of pain as Cullen's foot cracked against his side said the man had only partially succeeded.

The room, already quiet, went more silent still as Cullen held his hand out to help Aiden up. Aiden ignored it and climbed to his feet alone.

"Fuck," Kyan said under his breath.

Tara glanced at the time, seeing the round was only halfway through. On the mat, Cullen hung back, moving and blocking, hesitating to attack until Aiden found hard-won breath to curse him out for it. The morning conversation with Aiden came back to Tara, his gripping fear over failing to demonstrate some phantom level of strength in the eyes of men he respected. In that twisted looking glass, Cullen's mercy looked like disappointment, and Tara could see Cullen realize that as he picked up the offensive again.

It was a catch-22. The men couldn't spare Aiden physical pain without inflicting an emotional one he himself had created. God.

Tara rubbed her hands over her face and made herself keep watching the no longer amusing show.

Aiden had just finished his fourth go with Eli when he dropped to all fours, wheezing to get air into his abused lungs. The nearly healed gash Tara had put on Aiden's forehead when they'd first met had reopened, and blood trickled along his face into his mouth and eyes. More blood came from his nose, where he must have taken a hit at some point.

"Let me take a look at you, mate." Eli crouched next Aiden.

Tara tensed.

Eli reached forward.

Aiden slugged him.

Tara jumped to her feet. She didn't care how big or trained or deadly Eli Mason was. If he retaliated—

Kyan grabbed Tara's arm, the moment of delay enough for her to see that instead of being angry, Eli raised his hands in surrender and was speaking to Aiden in tones too soft for her to make out. Aiden shook, and Tara felt each one of his trembles hit something inside her soul.

Her fault. This was all her fault on so, so many levels.

"I know what Obsidian does for punishment," Kyan said into Tara's ear. "I've a scar or two to show for it. That isn't us. But that doesn't mean it's fun to watch either." He pointed with his chin toward the office door. "There's a fridge with Gatorade over there. The orange may look radioactive, but it tastes decent. Maybe Aiden will be able to drink some if we offer."

Tara gave Kyan a hard look. They both knew the Gatorade mission was invented for Tara's benefit. And at least one of them knew that she deserved no benefit whatsoever. More importantly, Aiden had allowed her to stay—and hell would freeze over if she walked away from him just to soothe her nerves.

Aiden needed the ropes to climb to his feet when the timer went off again, and he fell hard at the first blow offered. Cullen, who was in the ring, stopped hitting Aiden after that, tossing him down onto the mat in throw after throw after throw. *Thump. Thump. Thump.* Sometimes Aiden climbed to his feet. Sometimes he fell on his own midway through. His gaze was unfocused now, as if struggling to anchor in a shifting world.

It was the final move of the round that made bile rise up Tara's throat. After tossing Aiden about like a rag doll, Cullen threw a roundhouse kick that was slow and high, and aimed at where Aiden's hands were already raised for a block. Tara had no idea what went through Aiden's mind as he dropped that hand, turning into the kick instead of away from it.

The surprised look on Aiden's face as the blow landed said he hadn't done it on purpose, and, as the timer went off, Cullen cussed out a storm as Aiden blinked like a deranged owl.

"That's enough," Liam said, turning off the timer. "We're ending this."

"I'm fine," Aiden snarled.

"Like hell you are," Cullen snarled right back at him.

Tara wondered if the men could see the look of desperation and failure that filled Aiden's eyes. The pleading for another chance that he shouted silently to deaf ears.

"We. Are. Not. Done." Aiden was on all fours, gasping for breath. "Four more rounds."

Walking up to Liam, Cullen threw his gloves to the mat. "I'm done."

Aiden flinched.

Tara stepped forward, her heart quickening as she raised her voice. "I haven't had a turn," she announced to the group, knowing how insane she sounded. Because this whole plan of hers, it was insane. "You can't end it because I haven't had a turn. And if Cullen doesn't want his, I'll bloody well take it."

The men turned to her, the fury in their gazes enough to burn her to the ground. But she'd spoken loudly enough for Aiden to hear, and the man was already climbing to his feet. Short of holding both Aiden and her down, the men knew they couldn't stop them. Not really.

Tara picked up Cullen's gloves.

As she did, Liam leaned down to whisper in her ear, the fury now saturating the air around Tara so thick that it threatened to choke her. "You injure him, and I swear I'll put you through a kind of hell Obsidian Ops hasn't yet invented."

"I don't think there is a hell we've not yet tried," Tara told him coolly and, snatching Cullen's discarded headgear, walked into the ring.

The beep of the starting timer sounded faintly in the distance as Aiden lifted his hands into a fighting stance. His glazed eyes met hers and through the sheen of exhaustion, she could see the gut-wrenching gratitude there. Not that it would last long with the plans Tara had for him.

She let him move forward first, then sidestepped and swept Aiden's legs out from behind him. He landed hard on his back, and she followed him down. Gripped his arms and...and instead of pinning Aiden to the floor, hauled his head and shoulders onto her lap. Gathering the bottom hem of her shirt, she pressed it against his bleeding forehead.

Aiden's reaction was as predictable as it was fast. He balked, his remaining strength focused on shoving Tara away.

She batted his hands away with too great an ease.

Liam's menacing growl was more difficult to ignore. "He doesn't like that."

"No kidding," Tara snapped back at Liam before turning her attention to Aiden. Capturing his eyes with her own. "Listen to me. You have a choice to make, Aiden, and you're not going to like this next part no matter what you choose. But you can either let me take care of you for three minutes and gather the strength you need to stay in the ring with the Tridents, or you can surrender now. Because no one will keep fighting with a rag doll. So what will it be? Will you tap out to me, or will you trust me for just a few minutes?"

Aiden swallowed, trembling in Tara's arms. He didn't nod, but he didn't tap the ground either, and that in itself meant the world. Tara stroked his hair and gathered a fresh corner of her shirt to wipe the sweat and blood off Aiden's face. Small, gentle strokes that made Aiden tense, then slowly, so slowly, loosen.

Tara didn't realize Eli had come beside her before the man slipped a bit of ice wrapped in a wet towel into her hand. Kyan was right behind him, handing her a water bottle with diluted orange Gatorade and a straw. Liam and Cullen had magicked a set of Steri-Strips from somewhere, talking her through closing the gash on Aiden's head, Liam's small nod carrying all the gratitude in the world. They had three minutes. And everyone was determined to make the most of it.

"It's time," Liam said quietly.

With a small hint of a smile at Tara, Aiden rose to his feet, his gaze focused as he took his stance. "Let's finish this, Liam," he said.

"Let's finish it," Liam echoed and climbed into the ring.

# 19

## Aiden

Adan knelt on the mat, his knees pressed into the sweat-slicked vinyl, his hands braced on his thighs as he looked up at the Tridents' faces. Eli was grinning, but the rest nodded to him with approval and acceptance that meant more than Aiden could explain. His gaze shifted to Tara. Locked with hers. For a moment, all he could do was stare at that beautiful, strong face that had been his lifeline. Then she nodded too, like the others had, and Aiden realized he had forgotten to take a breath.

Closing his eyes, Aiden gasped lungfuls of sweat-laden air. His lungs burned, his body ached, and several of his muscles were trembling from overuse. But it was a good kind of ache, the kind that seeped into his bones and—for the first time in a long time—put him at peace.

"Thank you," he said, then lifted his face to Tara, his mouth suddenly dry. He didn't know what to say to her. How to express his gratitude for what she'd done.

"You're supposed to be calling us all sorts of arseholes, not thanking us," Eli informed him. "I think someone wacked you too hard."

"No, think he was this dumb to begin with," said Kyan.

Liam rolled his eyes and turned to the locker room. "I need a shower. Tara… We train on Sunday morning and during the week as schedules allow. You're welcome to join."

Tara jerked in surprise, staring after the men as they filed out the room. Once the mat was empty but for the two of them, however, the woman's demeanor seemed to shift. Wrapping her arms around herself, Tara hung back at the edge of the mat as if uncertain whether now that they were alone, Aiden's gratefulness might shift to something different. Something angry.

Aiden beckoned her closer, his stomach tightening at the reluctance in her steps. With an effort of will, he forced himself to climb to his feet so that when she got close enough, he could pull her toward him the rest of the way. God, she was beautiful. From the way her leggings hugged her curved hips to the way a tiny wisp of her hair fell over her right brow.

"Wildcat," Aiden whispered, hugging Tara tightly against him. He felt her tense, then mold into him, her breath hot against his chest, her body fitting perfectly against his. "God, Tara. I don't know what to say,"

When she said nothing, Aiden pushed her away slightly, just enough that he could see her face. Taking it between his hands, Aiden ran his thumbs along her cheekbones.

"You aren't mad at me for pushing you?" she asked.

"I'm grateful to you for saving me. For knowing that I needed saving, when I didn't know it myself." He tilted his head down, unable to look away from Tara's big hazel eyes. She had the longest lashes he'd ever seen. And, if he looked closely, he could make out a smattering of a few freckles dusting the bridge of her nose. A matching set to his own.

From somewhere beyond the mat, the dull sound of running shower water penetrated the walls. A car honked at another at the intersection outside the gym. But here, with Tara, all Aiden could focus on was the steady beat of his heart, the soft whisper of her breath. The crinkle of her hair between his fingers.

He leaned forward until their breath mixed, the moist air around them rising like steam. God, he wanted her. Not the way he'd taken her in the shower, hard and fast and angry, but soft and deep. Intimate.

Slipping his hand along Tara's forearm, Aiden brushed along her shoulder and neck until his fingers braced her head. He brought his mouth toward hers, slowly, carefully, though every fiber of his body wanted more, though his nerves vibrated with a fear that she'd pull away.

When Tara leaned into his kiss, it felt as though an explosion of sensation shot through Aiden's core, coating his nerves and muscles in tingling energy. He felt himself harden uncomfortably, but didn't shift his feet for fear of breaking the connection between them. His whole body sang at the kiss, and now that Tara had answered it, Aiden's luxurious strokes deepened and tangled with her own. He savored her taste, the energy of her body, the wholeness he felt as time stopped moving.

God he'd never met anyone like this lass. Someone who grounded him, made him stronger just by being beside him.

Aiden was out of breath by the time they finally pulled apart, his heart pounding as hard as it had during the sparring rounds. His hands, unwilling to leave Tara's skin, rested on her biceps. Aiden had never kissed anyone like that before. Never been kissed that way in return.

He was still staring at her when, in the corner of his vision, the door to the men's locker room opened and Eli came out fresh from the shower.

"Seriously?" Eli called and threw a boxing glove at Aiden's head.

Unwilling to let Tara go even for the split second it would take to fend the projectile off, Aiden shifted his weight to take the blow on his back.

Eli snorted. "Well, I guess since you already paid the dues, might as well continue with the crime."

Tara laughed, picked up the glove, and launched it right back at Eli—who ducked out of the way at the last second.

"You have good friends," she told Aiden.

"Aye, I do," Aiden agreed, hoping she knew that he included her in that statement.

"This is a terrible idea," Tara said, standing at the entryway to Aiden's bedroom while he flipped through the closet in hopes of locating his tuxedo. Before working for Liam, Aiden wouldn't have been caught dead in the monkey suit, but with Trident Security, Aiden found himself wearing a black tie at least as often as he wore Kevlar. Poor innocent Tara, however, was still in denial about reality. She reached for a reasonable tone. "The last thing anybody connected to Trident Security wants is an Obsidian Ops operative at their friend's wedding."

"Considering that the head of Trident Security and his fiancée invited you, I think you need to rethink your argument." Finding the suit he was looking for, Aiden pulled it out and grimaced at the fancy fabric. Wearing it always made him feel like a polished fraud, a perfect page hiding damaged goods. "Look, lass, I would absolutely love to go to the gym instead of a party at the North Vault, however, this particular event happens to be for Liam and Jaz. I can't talk my way out of that one. And if I have to go, you have to go."

Tara rubbed her arms, a tell that Aiden noticed she had when she was uncomfortable.

Tossing the tux back into the closet, Aiden strode up to Tara and pulled her into him. He did that unabashedly now, the feel of her against his chest filling a void inside him that he hadn't known existed. "You've trained with us three times in the last week. Liam didn't have to invite you to the mat, he chose to. You aren't a stranger with the Tridents anymore."

In truth, Aiden had been worried the first time Tara joined them for practice, but Liam had spotted her tendency to avoid tapping earlier than Aiden first had and told her in no uncertain terms that if winning meant that much to her, she could go find another gym. It was a rocky path from then, but with Eli trying out a new move that had him on his ass more often than not, the atmosphere of the training was starting to sink in. The Tridents were brutal, but preventing injury was everyone's responsibility.

"Fine," Tara sighed, rubbing her forehead against Aiden's chest. It felt good. Strangely good. "But I'll be wearing my pajamas. I think that's the only clothes I have that Overlord hasn't put a rip in yet."

"Yeah, about that. You really don't have the right clothes—"

Tara gave him a triumphant smile. "Enjoy the party without me, I guess."

"Which is why Jaz and the bridesmaids are taking you shopping."

Tara's smile faded. "No."

"Go ahead and tell that to Jaz. I dare you." Aiden pulled out his phone and held it out to her. "She's on her way over right now. And she's bringing reinforcements."

Tara pushed away from him. "This wasn't a discussion—this was an ambush."

"I never claimed it was a discussion," said Aiden. "More of a briefing on your upcoming schedule. Or, our upcoming schedule."

Tara's face shifted, realization filling her intelligent eyes. "Wait… If I have to go shopping with bridesmaids, does that mean *you* have to go shopping with bridesmaids?"

Aiden put his phone away. "Aye. And I value my skin too much to stand up to Jaz on this one."

"In that case, we should totally start with bras and underwear. Build the outfit from the inside out, you know. You can carry the bags."

"I'm carrying a gun," said Aiden.

"You can bring that too."

# 20

Tara

Standing in Aiden's bathroom, Tara tried and failed to give herself a pep talk. She didn't do shopping. Hell, she disliked the sight of her own reflection most days—the notion of trying on clothes in company and twisting before a mirror voluntarily made her long for an extra session of Liam's push-ups. At least that, she had control over. Unlike the fact that most of the world's clothes were made for people who belonged on the runway.

Or the price tags. The clothes Aiden had gotten her to get by in the hotel room cost more than Tara dreamed of spending. She still owed him for that. How much would something appropriate for a black-tie wedding cost her?

"Hello, hello!" Jaz's jovial voice echoed from the front foyer, announcing the arrival of Tara's executioner. She knew Jaz by occasional sight from when the bride-to-be had stopped by the gym or Trident Security, but that was a far cry from having a conversation. She drew a deep breath, hating the way her hands clenched around the windowsill at the thought of walking out into the hallway.

"Where is Tara?" someone asked. Not Jaz.

"We're going to take the Suburban, Aiden. And you've been voted driver." That was a third voice. Good God, this wasn't a shopping trip, it was an invasion.

No. *No, no, no.* Tara closed the bathroom door and turned the lock. She was not going out there to be a whole bridal party's object of entertaining ridicule. At least with men, insults were direct. Tara was so used to being told what an idiot piece of stray crap she was at Obsidian Ops that the words hardly registered anymore. Women, on the other hand, were sly and insidious.

*I don't mean to be mean, and I'm only telling you this because you're my friend but…but no one wants you here. You're a little big-boned. He only talked to you out of pity.*

The voices inside Tara's memories echoed through her mind. When she'd been twelve, she'd naively believed them to be a plague of childhood, but she knew better now. Adult women were the same sixth grade girls, just more sophisticated in their torment.

"Tara?" Someone knocked on the door. A fourth someone. "Are you here?"

Tara closed her eyes.

"Listen up, McDane." Jaz's authoritative voice, coming from somewhere near the living room, rang through the apartment. "I was promised a dress-shopping trip. So either you produce a female in need of a dress, or you're going to be the one trying on dresses. Can I make it any clearer than that?"

"No, ma'am," said Aiden. The coward.

A moment later, something clicked in the lock, and Aiden unceremoniously pushed the door open.

"Sorry." He didn't sound the least bit sorry. "But in case you didn't hear, it's either you being tussled into a dressing room or me. Throwing you to the wolves is really a no-brainer on this one." He raised his voice. "She's in here, Jaz. And she's hostile."

Tara was right. It *was* an invasion. And the entire assaulting force of four women and one guy looked like they'd walked right off the cover of a magazine. Even Jaz, who was halfway through her pregnancy with twins, looked photo-shoot gorgeous. Before Tara could draw breath, the energetic swarm had encircled tightly around her, the tall guy in their midst weighing her with his eyes.

"Couture," he said, snapping his fingers. "Look at her gorgeous eyes. We can play off those, I'm telling you."

*Cou-what now?*

"We're going to be at the North Vault, not a catwalk," Jaz protested.

"We could put a catwalk into the Vault. Now that Cassey is running the place, it wouldn't be too difficult. Fine. Cache. This body was made for Cache's clothes. There is the most delicious top I've ever seen in the window, and it goes with her skin."

"You think Cache is the answer to everything," said Jaz.

"And am I wrong?"

"What about Gucci or Chanel?" the blonde, who Tara was pretty sure was Cullen's wife, Sky, suggested.

*What about the discount rack at Walmart?*

"Has anyone asked Tara what she actually likes?" one woman asked, setting the gaggle into a sudden silence that was as strange as their conversation had been.

Tara shifted from foot to foot. Fuck it. When all else fails, try the truth. "Fatigues are nice. Or a lab coat."

Silence took the room as the invasion force stared at her. Then at each other.

"I think she just lost her right to vote," said the guy.

The woman who'd spoken last elbowed him in the ribs. "I think we should maybe start this again. Hi, I'm Dani." Turning to Tara, she extended her hand and offered a firm, friendly shake. "These two ladies are Ivy and Sky, and the big oaf is Bastian. I think you probably remember Jaz—I say that because there is no one within a hundred miles who doesn't remember Jaz."

Dani. Ivy. Sky. Bastian. The names found little shelves in Tara's mind. "Good to meet you."

"Eli has been telling me about you joining morning training. You impressed him," Dani continued. "Not an easy feat."

Heat touched Tara's cheeks. That was unexpected. And nice. And… She tensed, suddenly realizing that Eli's wife might feel less than charitable toward a woman who *impressed* her husband on a training mat. Before Tara could think of something disarming to say, however, Dani continued.

"I was meaning to ask you if you would be willing to be a guest self-defense instructor at the women's shelter. Many of the ladies are not comfortable taking direction from a man yet."

"You want me to teach vulnerable women?" Tara cleared her throat, trying to keep up with the tide. Dani and her invite both seemed genuine. But surely… "Did Eli happen to mention my background?"

"Unless Aiden has several women stashed at his apartment, we presume you're Tara Northpoint," said Sky, inserting herself into the conversation. "The Obsidian Ops operative who came over from the dark side."

"Not a bad description, actually," said Tara.

Sky grinned. "And I hear we need to get you dressed for a wedding. Hence this whole swarm."

"Right. About that." Tara twisted toward Jaz. "I just wanted to say that I appreciate Liam's invite, but I don't imagine you actually want an Obsidian Ops girl at your wedding. So, I'm—"

"Liam's invite?" Jaz frowned. "Oh no, that came directly from me. I mean, he'd love to see you too, but I'm not about to give him any more credit than he is due. Anyhow, potato potahto. We should get going."

As if Jaz's declaration was some kind of signal, the crowd around Tara swarmed back into motion and she barely had time to pull on a pair of sneakers before being herded into the seven-seat Suburban. Aiden dutifully took the driver's seat while the others returned to arguing over Tara's shoes, dress, and makeup—none of which she actually owned. By the time they pulled into the Denton Valley Mall and headed to Saks Fifth Avenue, Jaz had declared that everyone would get two outfits for Tara to try on, with the winner being decided in the dressing room.

As Tara stood by helplessly while the entire bridal party put things for her into a dressing room that was fancier than most hotels, Aiden settled on a chair and stretched his legs out in front of him, his feet crossed at the ankles.

"You're enjoying this," Tara accused quietly.

"Oh, aye," Aiden agreed. "I'm thinking stilettos for you, if you want my opinion."

"I don't want your opinion."

Aiden smirked.

The first dress Tara was ordered to don was a royal blue number that hugged her breasts and hips before flaring out in a mermaid cut. Despite the gorgeous shape of the piece, the restrictive material made Tara feel vulnerable, and she ventured out of the dressing room with a frown.

"No," Sebastian declared, walking around Tara critically. "The dress brings out her chest beautifully, but we need to show the legs more."

The others agreed, and Tara was sent back inside to try on a pantsuit, a high-waisted chiffon gown that seemed to change and flow as Tara walked, and a long black dress with a slit that crawled sensually up her thigh.

Each time Tara stepped out of the changing room, she felt like she climbed the stage with an eager audience determined to get a better look. Or maybe a red carpet with reporters discussing what she was wearing to the premiere. Either way, the energy was contagious, and even Aiden sat up straighter each time the changing room curtain opened.

Aiden's gaze in particular stayed on her the longest, his eyes still burning into her shoulders as she disappeared back into the dressing room after every outfit. As if he wanted to follow her there. The picture-perfect, muscular, lethal warrior gazing after *her*.

A few hours into the trip, the mall started to get more crowded to the point of a young woman knocking into Tara as they fought their way to Nordstrom. They were on their fifth store, with Tara thoroughly exhausted and the bridal party showing no signs of slowing, when Aiden grabbed a dress off the rack and pressed it into Tara's chest. "This one," said Aiden.

"What is it?" Jaz asked.

"A dress."

"That's not nearly as helpful an answer as you think it is," Jaz informed him. "And did you even check the size?"

"It's her size." The self-assurance in Aiden's voice heated Tara's cheeks.

Before Aiden and Jaz could take the discussion further, Tara disappeared into the dressing room to appease Aiden—to put on the dress choice she was certain he'd made blindly—and froze before the mirror. The gown was a deep red that hugged her neck before opening over her breasts. The oval was just large enough to be sensual without being crude. The silk continued down, hugging the tops of her hips before swishing down with an asymmetric skirt that was both liberating and gorgeous.

As Tara stared at her reflection, she tried to understand who this woman looking back at her was. She was beautiful. And feminine. And strong.

"Holy mother of God," a male voice said behind her as Aiden unceremoniously pulled back the dressing room curtain. The tip of Aiden's tongue darted out between his lips, his usually stoic face suddenly taking on color. "That's, eh..." He cleared his throat, his legs shifting. "That looks acceptable."

"That looks absolutely stunning," said Sebastian, inviting himself into the conversation, the others agreeing with enthusiasm. Instead of being sore losers to Aiden's lucky choice, they quickly shifted course toward makeup and towed Tara to the Sephora counter.

There, Jaz elbowed the makeup artists out of the way and made Tara up herself with a basketful of sampler goodies she'd quickly assembled. "My parents are in Hollywood," she explained over her shoulder. "I grew up with makeup artists."

Twenty minutes later, Jaz had managed to put more products on Tara than she could count, yet the results somehow looked invisible—as if Tara's eyes, lips, and skin glowed with natural potent beauty. This time, Aiden didn't even pretend to play on the phone as he stood at the wall, watching her reflection intently.

Trickles of pleasure crept along Tara's skin, the unusual

sensation of being seen, or being beautiful, filling her chest. Suddenly, she didn't mind paying the coming check, even if it was going to take most of her savings along with it.

As she came up to the counter to check out, however, the woman behind the register waved her off. "The bill is covered."

"By who?" Tara's chest tightened. There was no such thing as free.

The cashier pointed behind Tara, to where Aiden was now busily speaking on his phone.

Tara pulled out her wallet. "Well, can you uncover it?" she asked the cashier. "I'm paying myself."

The young woman shifted uncomfortably. "I'm sorry, that transaction already went through. We would need the gentleman's ID to issue a refund."

"You want an ID?" said Tara. "Fine. I'll get you an ID."

Marching over to Aiden, she took the phone out of his hand and hung up on whoever he was talking to on the other end. "Give me your wallet," she demanded.

"What? Why?"

"Because you clearly can't be trusted not to go around sticking your things where they don't belong."

"Debatable. But please do detail what I stuck where." He cocked a brow in a way that made no secret of his thoughts—especially given the hardening bulge in his parts. Stepping closer, he ran his thumb over Tara's chin. "I'm all ears."

Tara batted him away before her own traitorous body could follow down the path Aiden was laying. "You stuck your credit card into my bill. And you're going to pull it back."

"What do you mean your bill?" For once, Aiden sounded genuinely confused.

"My clothes and makeup and—"

"And stuff that you're going to wear to a party that I pretty much forced you into attending? That is the most absurd notion I've ever heard." Plucking his phone right back out of Tara's hand, he pressed redial and held it up to his ear.

Tara put her hands into her pockets, readying for the next attack

—but as she did, her fingers brushed along a smooth piece of paper she was certain hadn't been there before. Excusing herself to use the restroom, Tara pulled out the small sheet and felt her heart stutter.

The sheet itself was made of smooth stock, the kind restaurants often used for printing menus and flyers. It was as unsuspicious as the pizza printed on the front. Except for the fact that Tara never took a pizza menu. Even if she had, she wouldn't have folded it into the precise pattern of creases and squares that was staring back at her.

A message. Put into her pocket by someone in the mall—likely the woman who'd knocked into her at Nordstrom. It was in no way surprising that Obsidian Ops was keeping an eye on her and knew that she'd gone shopping. But making contact, that she hadn't expected.

Tara's heart quickened as she examined the paper closer, rereading the clear message coded in its folds. *Call Lucius.*

Jaw tight, Tara crumpled the paper before flushing it down the toilet. Whatever Lucius wanted to say to her, he could keep to himself.

"Everything okay, lass?" Aiden asked as she walked out of the restroom.

Forcing her panicked thoughts into the back of her mind, Tara summoned the bit of good-natured snark that Aiden expected. "It depends on whether you've come to your senses about payment," she said.

# 21

Aiden

[Note to self: add the women coming down the aisle and their respective men's facial reactions. Possibly Aiden's thoughts on their happiness. Maybe some of the vows. It seemed a little short wedding wise.]

"You clean up nicely." Coming up behind Aiden, Tara ensured he could see her in the mirror as he adjusted the black bow tie on his tux. It was something Tara did a lot—making sure that any touch or approach was telegraphed ahead of time. How many women would make that kind of effort, especially after the grueling hours of debriefs Trident Security was putting her through? Tara traced her hand over his shoulder, no doubt feeling the strap of the leather shoulder holster beneath the fabric. "You going to the wedding armed?"

Aiden nodded and flashed his weapon. Given the nature of the event, he'd compromised to a baby Glock on his shoulder, and a similar one strapped to his ankle.

"Mmm." Tara cocked her head to the side. "I think somewhere down the line, you confused a Glock with a security blanket."

"I hate weddings," Aiden said, looking at Tara through the reflection in the mirror. "People seem to feel at liberty to ask personal questions they'd usually keep to themselves." That went double for Aiden's family, whose propensity to stick their noses into other people's business was probably a result of some genetic mutation. The fact that Cassey and Briar were now not only in Denton Valley but actually in charge of the reception venue was cosmically unfair.

"Be grateful they only do it at weddings," said Tara, her gentle smile taking the sting out of the words. Her hand brushed Aiden's shoulder, turning him toward her. "On the bright side, you've got me to draw away fire today. I imagine more people will want to know about Obsidian Ops than when you're planning to have babies."

Aiden took Tara's face in his hands, tilting it up toward his. Though he knew she'd meant the words lightly, the notion of her drawing fire made him nauseated. It was his job to protect her, damn it, and that meant more than not letting the woman get kidnapped by Obsidian. "New plan," Aiden said. "We protect each other. Hard to ask questions if we're dancing, aye?"

"Dancing," Tara echoed, her lips parting slightly in invitation. She was yet to dress for the wedding, but Sky had stopped by earlier to help with makeup, and Tara's already large eyes seemed to capture all the light in the room. Her short hair played off impossibly long lashes and, as she shifted her weight, her full breasts brushed against the thin cotton shirt she still had on.

Aiden lowered his mouth toward hers, the last few millimeters of distance destroying his self-restraint. Threading his fingers through her hair, he pillaged Tara's warm mouth, swallowing her moan of pleasure. His free hand slipped under her shirt to cup that amazing breast of hers. God, she felt good. Tara's body pressed into Aiden's touch, sending a wave of pleasure through him, and when his thumb brushed her erect nipple, Aiden's cock responded in kind.

The alarm on Aiden's phone went off, reminding him that they were about to be late for his already-planned late arrival. Still, it took an effort of will to pull away.

Aiden swallowed, watching a shudder run through Tara's thighs. Yeah. She could have done without the alarm as well. *Behave, McDane.* "Aye," he said finally, his breath catching. "Dancing."

AIDEN TIMED his and Tara's arrival at the ceremony to the last moment—a valiant effort to attract as little attention as possible. Thirty seconds into their arrival, however, Aiden gave up the lost cause. With Tara in that red gown of hers, she gathered attention like a target gathered bullet holes.

She strode forward confidently, her dress swooshing from her hips in a tantalizing dance. It made Aiden long to rip the silk off her then and there. Tara herself might be oblivious to the effect her body had on the male population, but Aiden was sure as hell aware of it. Just as he was aware of how most every male they passed stared at her with various degrees of appreciation, condemnation, or both.

It was irritating.

Finally, giving up pretenses, Aiden laid his hand on the small of Tara's back as he guided her inside. Yes, he felt possessive. But he had a right to be possessive, damn it. Tara was under his protection, so everyone else could keep their eyes to themselves. The logical side of him knew the flaws in that lizard-brain reasoning, but it little mattered. With Tara beside him, the world felt more stable, and it had been a while since he'd enjoyed that luxury. Six years, to be exact.

Catching sight of Sonia, the attorney working Tara's case, Aiden felt his chest tighten. The case was going to trial soon, and one way or another, Tara would have no need for Aiden any longer. Don't mistake forced proximity for a relationship, he reminded himself. He knew better. More to the point, he was self-aware enough to know that he was too damaged to ever get the happy journey they were here to celebrate for Liam and Jaz. Square pegs, round holes, and all that.

But for now, he and Tara enjoyed each other—and Aiden was determined to savor every moment of it.

Aiden had just managed to navigate to the last pew when two identical-looking men bracketed them on both sides. Cassey and Briar.

Swallowing an internal groan, Aiden gave his determined-to-stick-their-noses-into-everyone's-business cousins a cursory nod and made a show of focusing his attention on the front. Liam was already on the dais, waiting with his groomsmen, Eli, Cullen, and Kyan. With a bit of luck, the ceremony would start quickly.

Sitting beside Aiden, Cassey stretched out his legs and crossed them at the ankles, showing off a pair of Italian loafers. Aiden wondered if the man owned a single pair of shoes that cost under five hundred dollars. Probably not. "Nice as this looks, just wait until you see the reception at the North Vault. We've transformed the place."

"Hmm." Aiden made an acknowledging sound with his throat.

"Though given your poor attendance record, I'm not sure you'll notice."

Aiden shrugged "Sorry, mate. Work. Plus, I'm not a social kind of guy. From what I hear, though, you're social enough to make up for me and stone face both."

Sitting on the other side of Tara, Briar snorted. If Cassey wouldn't shut up, Briar held words at a premium and was careful not to go over some daily allowance. It was amazing how two men could look so identical, yet emit such different vibes.

"Aren't you going to introduce us to your lady friend?" Cassey asked.

"She isn't my lady friend," Aiden snapped back on some juvenile instinct.

Cassey grinned. "Excellent. Then move over. She can be my lady friend."

Aiden's hand tightened into a fist.

Tara elbowed him in the ribs and leaned forward to look between Aiden and Cassey. "You two will not start a brawl in the middle of Liam's wedding ceremony."

"It's not the middle, technically speaking." On the other side of

Tara, Briar joined in reluctantly. "They haven't started. Kid's still working up courage."

Looking closer, Aiden spotted the kid Briar was grumbling about. In a poofy pink dress, Ella—Dani and Eli's preschool daughter—held a basket of rose petals like a shield. Crouched beside her, an exasperated Dani in a bridesmaid's gown made encouraging noises as she gestured toward the aisle.

Aiden cracked his knuckles and returned his glare to Cassey—only to find his cousin's gaze now covertly weighing Tara. As Cassey's eyes brushed over her face and gown, his body stiffened for a moment, and he made a small hand gesture to his twin.

Briar grunted, his face unreadable.

What in the ever-loving hell was that about?

Summoning a cocky smile, Cassey extended his hand to Tara. "Clearly, McDane is leaving us to fend for ourselves introduction-wise. I'm Cassey McKenzie, from the better side of the family."

Tara shifted uncomfortably. "Enchanté."

Throwing caution to the wind, Aiden put his arm around Tara's shoulders and pulled her into his side.

Meanwhile, at the front of the church, Liam looked paler than usual as the pianist started up the same march for the third time.

Ella the flower girl took one step, turned, and ran back to bury her face in Dani's leg.

The music stopped.

Liam exhaled.

A soft chuckle rippled through the audience.

"Forget this." Standing up, Cassey vaulted over the back of the pew and strode up to the piano. Brushing away the penguin-tailed pianist, Cassey slid onto the bench and launched into a jovial tune that sounded like the opening credits to a children's show. *Power Rangers,* maybe. Or *Paw Patrol.* Aiden had no idea—but Ella clearly did.

Emboldened by the familiar sounds, Ella grinned and skipped down the aisle like a champ. She was already at the dais when the realization that she'd forgotten to throw the flower petals stopped her in her tracks. After a moment of thought, she tossed the entire content of the basket right at Liam.

With the soft petals clinging to Liam's tux, Eli quickly swung his daughter onto his neck, which seemed the safest place for her under the circumstances. Liam looked down at himself ruefully, a chuckle escaping his chest. Refusing to relinquish the piano, Cassey changed the tune to a bridal march, and then the entire room came to its feet as Jaz walked down the aisle.

Liam stared at her as if in a trance, the entire lethal intensity of him focused on the petite woman walking down the aisle. She was five feet away from the front when Liam's resolve broke apart and he jogged down the three-step dais to make the walk up together.

"Smart move," said Jaz, the mic picking up her soft words. "I was just considering making a break for it."

Liam's hand slid down to his bride's pregnant belly. "Someone in there is certainly trying." The wonder in his voice was almost boyish, showing a rare side of the hard commander Aiden knew.

A lump formed in Aiden's throat. He might have run from his overbearing family back in Scotland, away from questions he didn't want to answer after Afghanistan, but he missed the *before* time dearly. As the oldest of five boys, he'd always been the one to hold his infant siblings, and he envied Liam the soon-to-come sensation of cradling a warm little being in his arms. But there was no man better, no man more deserving of the joy Liam was venturing into. Hard as it was to believe, he and Jaz were perfect for each other in every way.

In the front row of the church, Liam's mom, Patti, and sister, Lisa, sat together. Patti wiped away tears, but Lisa, as if feeling the weight of Aiden's eyes, turned around to lock gazes with him. It was because of Lisa that Aiden had started seeing Dani, and because of Aiden that Lisa went into drug rehab. Neither would have happened if not for the presence of Liam and Jaz in their lives.

This union was a celebration not just for the bride and groom, but for all of them.

For a moment, Liam and Jaz just stood together, forehead to

forehead, oblivious of the church full of people gathered around them. Cassey quieted the music to a temporary interlude, only picking the pace up again once the couple was ready to share their bond with the rest of them.

THE WEDDING RECEPTION at the North Vault was, admittedly, well done. Cassey had had the tables rearranged to create a larger dance floor while the soothing blue lights provided a feeling of intimacy. The superb sound system he'd upgraded to let music into every nook and crevice of the club. Although Aiden didn't have pitch-perfect hearing like Briar and Cassey, he could judge sound well enough to know premium when he heard it.

The bridesmaids quickly swept Tara up into their gaggle, leaving Aiden torn between feeling oddly naked with Tara's absence and content over seeing her laugh. The woman didn't laugh nearly enough. For all the grief that Aiden's family had caused him, he'd always felt loved growing up. Always felt himself a part of a clan—too much so sometimes. To think of Tara being cast away as a child, an Obsidian Ops stray—Aiden's jaw tensed at the word—who had to fight for every scrap of dignity… It made him want to destroy them all bare-handed.

Leaning against the wall, Aiden crossed his arms over his chest and tried to look unapproachable. His best efforts aside, he still quickly lost count of the number of people who felt an unholy calling to make small talk at weddings. Yes, he liked the Colorado mountains. No, Edinburgh looked nothing like Denton Valley. No, he didn't know whether he'd be going back to Scotland anytime soon; for now, he was content right where he was.

"If you enjoy yourself any less, I'll have to start calling you Briar." Scotch in hand, Cassey leaned on the wall beside Aiden. "The two of you turn brooding into an art form."

Aiden made a noncommittal sound, then caught Cassey's hand midmotion when the man tried to clap his shoulder.

"Sorry," said Cassey. "Slipped my mind."

Aiden released the wrist he held and turned to watch Tara toasting with the women. At least one of them was having a good time. For that, Aiden would put up with however long this wedding reception took.

"When did you meet?" Cassey asked, following Aiden's gaze.

Aiden raised a brow. Tara being his assignment was general knowledge. "When Liam sent me to Las Vegas. I'll happily arrange for you to be sent somewhere too." Antarctica, for instance.

"I'm wounded."

"Is it fatal?" Aiden asked hopefully.

Cassey snorted, but still stayed put. Aiden sighed. He liked his cousins well enough, but in the past decade, they'd not seen each other for more than a family dinner or two. Cassey and Briar had surfaced briefly—and intrusively—after Aiden was rescued, but otherwise, most of their time in the Delta Force was shrouded in darkness. Until now.

"How much do you know about her?" Cassey took a sip of his drink. When Aiden ignored the question, Cassey settled himself in more comfortably against the wall. "I should warn you that silence only encourages me. A hazard of being Briar's twin."

"Noted."

"Come on, mate. Put yourself in my shoes," said Cassey. "If your little cousin was drooling over a woman, wouldn't you have questions too?"

"I'm not drooling."

"Noted."

Aiden rolled his eyes and gave in. "Northpoint is a former Obsidian operative," he offered, in case Cassey really didn't know. "Trident Security is prepping her testimony against the parent company." It was easier to talk business than personal shit, and Aiden was pleased to discover that when he wasn't being a pain in the ass, Cassey asked competent questions.

"So, Rural Minnesota," Cassey said, returning the discussion back to Las Vegas. "That's where you first saw her?"

"And where she tried to take my head off the first time." Aiden grinned despite himself at the memory.

Before Cassey could press further, a waltz came over the club's sound system. Separating from the group, Tara strode toward them, her sensual dress flowing like liquid around her hips. Cutting in front of Aiden, she held out her hand. "Could I have this dance?"

# 22

Cassey

Cassey strode through the reception, smiling suggestively at the women—and some men—and nodding to the others, but never slowing until he reached the back booth where Briar was nursing a scotch. Sliding into the seat on the opposite side of his twin, Cassey leaned forward and braced his forearms on the edge of the table. "Aiden says he met her in Las Vegas. A few weeks ago."

"He's wrong." Briar's jaw was tight enough to make the vein throb around his temple. They had both taken Aiden's rescue badly, but Briar had been the team leader, the one who'd made the decision to check another location first. They'd lost three days on the detour—three days that Aiden spent being tortured. "It's her. I remember the eyes."

Cassey blew out a long breath, the shock of seeing Tara's face at the wedding ceremony still vibrating through him. A face that he hadn't seen in six years. Cassey remembered the rescue vividly. The first surprise had come when the team discovered that the bastards holding the Scottish hostage were not Afghan natives. Cassey remembered catching sight of Caucasian faces and hearing

American accents as they scattered like cockroaches when Delta made entry.

Briar's orders demanded the team confine itself to extracting the prisoner, so when the captors scampered like cockroaches, Cassey had been powerless to give chase. With his legs or his bullets. If Cassey had known it was Aiden being held, he would have disobeyed and taken the fucking court-martial.

But he didn't know, not yet, and none of the assholes gave him a reason to shoot them dead. The men fled, disappearing into the sandbox with practiced ease. The one operative remaining looked paralyzed with fear. A girl, not more than seventeen or eighteen, bruised and cowering against the wall as Briar pointed the muzzle of his M4 at her head. The fear rolling off her had made Cassey wonder about the validity of the intel. Was the victim female? Were there two?

Walking up beside Briar, who still had the woman at gunpoint, Cassey had weighed the young woman with his gaze. With his face covered by a balaclava and tactical gear, he knew he looked frightening, but he extended his hand and kept his voice low. Friendly.

"It's all right. We're here to help. Are you here against your will?"

The girl's hand slid toward a knife sheathed at her calf.

That would be a *no*. Cassey's compassion faded. "Touch it, and you're dead."

Her hand froze, and Cassey's teammate came to relieve the woman of her weapons and zip-tie her wrists. A temporary restraint unless she gave them reason to kill her.

Cassey's headset crackled. "All clear, back room. One friendly. Badly injured."

"All clear, front room," Briar's voice came through the set. "One hostile. Controlled. Scene secure. Bring him."

That was when Cassey first saw Aiden's limp, battered body, his chest barely moving with labored breaths as his eyes stared unfocused at the ceiling. Though he knew better—though Briar was yelling at him to get back to position—Cassey had wheeled on the girl again.

"Did you do this?"

The guilt written all over her face was answer enough. Rage pounded through him, and the red dot of his sights appeared between her eyes, though Cassey didn't remember pointing his weapon.

"Stand down," Briar hollered at him. "Hold your fire. Hold your fire."

Cassey's finger tightened on the trigger, taking up slack. He prayed that she would reach for a knife. Would so much as look wrong. He prayed she would simply shift her weight. That would be enough for Cassey. He wouldn't feel the need to give her a warning.

But she didn't reach for anything. She just stayed frozen as Briar ordered the team to take Aiden out of the cave to the extraction point. With no justification for putting a bullet through the woman's skull and no permission to take her captive, they'd just left her. Zip-tied, shaking, and unjustly alive. Cassey never expected to see her again.

Yet, there she was. Not a scared teenager any longer, but a glorious woman in a sensual red dress, dancing with the man she'd tortured. And Aiden? Only a blind fool could miss the heat in his eyes, the vulnerability, the protective possessiveness that rippled from him as he looked at Tara.

Tara Northpoint. Yes, the femme fatale now had a name. And, no doubt, an agenda.

"What the fuck is she doing here?" Briar asked. "In Aiden's mind, I mean."

"She's the Obsidian Ops protectee he's babysitting for Liam." He tapped his fingers against the table. "I was paying little attention, but I think Liam's pit bull is trying to cop a deal for her in exchange for testimony against Obsidian."

"Rowen needs to know who he's harboring."

"I'm not letting her gut Aiden again." Cassey gripped Briar's gaze, knowing the fire blazing in his own. If Briar hadn't pulled him off target then, if he'd tightened his finger on the trigger a hair more… Cassey's teeth ground together. "Figuratively or literally."

They'd come here to make things right for Aiden. Cassey just wished he bloody well knew what *right* looked like.

"Talk to her," Briar ordered. Sometimes the fucker forgot he wasn't in charge anymore. A small growl escaped his throat when Cassey stayed right where he was. "You want me to talk to her?"

Cassey shook himself back to the real world. "We'll save that for when we need her to commit suicide."

Briar toasted him with his scotch.

"Run interference," said Cassey, but as he turned back toward the reception crowd, he saw someone he wanted to speak to first. Signaling his brother to wait, Cassey strode off to intercept Sonia Dancer.

"May I have this dance?" Cassey asked, snagging Sonia's hand just as the woman tried to skirt around the dance floor to where she probably had her briefcase and several law books set up for a quick read before dessert. Unlike the rest of the women in attendance, the pit bull lawyer was wearing a white pantsuit, her hair having been harassed into a tight bun at the back of her head.

"No." Sonia tried and failed to pull her hand away. "Thank you."

"You can't mean that." Cassey swung Sonia around, capturing her slender waist in his right hand. "Everyone wants to dance with me."

"Then you must live in an asylum."

"Key word being 'live.' Have you tried it?" Cassey spun the pair of them to the upbeat music and watched Sonia try and fail to swallow a squeak as she realized they were past the point of no return. "Much as I'd like to inquire about the origin of the sound you just made, I'm afraid this is a business dance. Tara Northpoint. What's she looking at?"

"Currently? At Mr. McDane's shirt collar."

Cassey spun them again. "Come on, Counselor. Murder one. You think you can get her off? I mean in the boring, legal way."

Sonia closed her eyes, and Cassey swore she was counting

breaths. When she spoke again, she enunciated each word as if speaking to someone slow of mind. "I do not discuss my clients out of court."

Cassey smiled in a way that didn't touch his eyes. "We can chat in court if you prefer. You'll find me at the table on your right." The prosecution.

Sonia went rigid in Cassey's hold, but—to her credit—made herself move along with the music again as her intelligent eyes rebalanced and recalculated the situation. "What don't I know?" she asked.

"Well—" Cassey cut himself off. The song was going to be over soon. "Let's say, theoretically, I had firsthand witness testimony that cast Northpoint in a negative light. How much of a difference would that make?"

"How negative?"

"Negative enough that your actual client, Liam, would likely draw down on her himself. Unfortunately, I have no way of playing that card without hurting people I care about very much."

"You want to bury Northpoint, but would rather avoid Aiden and Liam becoming collateral damage."

"She's not…a good person."

Sonia's gaze narrowed, that mind of hers spinning behind big brown eyes. "The public defender intends to file for full immunity."

"Fuck."

"You aren't my type."

"The public defender probably hasn't even bothered to talk to Northpoint, much less drafted a motion," said Casey. "Anything that's happening is because you're doing it for them. Maybe you should remember who your real client is."

"My real client wants Obsidian exposed, and Northpoint's testimony and good will aligns with those goals." Despite the ongoing music, Sonia extracted herself from Cassey's hold. "If you want a shift of course, you'll need to lay your cards wide open for a change."

Left alone on the dance floor, Cassey ground his teeth, then turned to snatch a scotch from a waitress's tray. The woman protested on behalf of the drink's intended recipient, but Cassey waved her off.

"I need it more than he does just now." Walking away from the waitress, Cassey signaled to his twin and set his sights on the evening's main event. It was time for a chat with the femme fatale herself.

# 23

## Tara

Tara stood, slightly breathless, at the side of the dance floor, trying to make sense of the divine happiness that pulsed through her blood. Hell, she didn't need to make sense of *it* as much as make sense of how *it* was possible. How Aiden was possible. The feel of his hand on her back, the thorough and ridiculously public thank-you kiss, the slow-rocking dance that made everything inside her sing. They'd be dancing still if Briar hadn't thrown down the gauntlet of darts, the challenge laden with Black Watch vs Delta sauce.

Given Briar's lack of propensity to talk, Aiden seemed willing to defend his military honor, and Tara was glad to see him spend time with his family without flinching. Even if that time involved grunting and throwing sharp things.

"The view is better up there." Scotch in hand, Cassey appeared at Tara's side. He motioned toward the mezzanine that ran the perimeter of the North Vault's main floor, the spiraling stairs at both ends of the space decorated with climbing rope in honor of Jaz's expertise. "Come."

There was a note of command in Cassey's voice that put Tara on edge, as if the invitation was more than casual. The bliss-induced fuzziness cleared from Tara's mind in a moment, her senses on full alert as she followed Aiden's cousin. Despite his easy-seeming nature, there was a lethal darkness that shimmered below the surface in Cassey's face and in the way he'd startled when he saw her in church... It made a shiver rush along Tara's spine. Whatever he wanted, she needed her full wits about her.

Not an easy feat when, on the open floor stretching below them, Aiden had taken off his tux jacket and left the ironed white shirt to contour his muscles. As Tara and Cassey stood in silent observation, the other Tridents came to join the game, with Eli rousing the guests for bets.

"They are a family, aren't they?" Cassey was looking at the game. "My little cousin is stuck with Briar and me by blood, but with the rest of them—that's a family in the truest sense."

"I was just thinking the same thing." She rested her fingers on the railing. "And are you here in the role of dad, incidentally, cleaning his gun in front of the new boyfriend?"

Cassey snorted. "Yes. Though I thought I was being discreet."

"You were," said Tara. "But I have a sixth sense when someone doesn't like me." She'd had a lifetime of practice.

He didn't deny it. Not even to be polite. "Where did you and Aiden first meet?"

"The Rural Minnesota. It's actually a diner near Las Vegas." Surely, Cassey knew as much. A man like him would have done some homework.

"No, it wasn't."

Ice gripped Tara's chest, but she kept herself in check. Kept her stance easy. Cassey could mean a number of things by that. Plus, an injured prey only encouraged a predator. "I wouldn't take my word for most anything either. You should ask Aiden."

"I don't know that I want him to remember the truth." Turning his back to the reception below, Cassey rested his forearms on the railing. "Tell me, have you been back to Afghanistan? I lost my taste for the sandbox since we last met, to be honest."

The ice in Tara's chest turned as cold as frostbite, piercing her bones with deadly shards. Her mind raced, the memories she'd tried to unsee now playing over and over inside her. Afghanistan. Who had she met in Afghanistan? The rescue team that had descended upon them out of thin air had worn no insignia. Gio Welch and the other men had sounded the scatter alarm, but Tara had been too frightened to move.

And none of them had bothered to take her along.

She'd looked so pitiful that a soldier on the entry team thought *she* might be the victim. She had been. She just didn't know it back then. She was young and proud and blind. And so full of shame. "I've never been to Afghanistan."

Cassey's smile didn't touch his eyes. "Seven fractured ribs. Enough torn ligaments that it took seven surgeries to put him back together. Burns covering twenty percent of his body. Some had shapes. Other just looked like someone had amused themselves with a pot of boiling water. We thought he'd lose his kidney for a while there, but it was the pneumonia that bought him a ventilator for a while."

Nausea rose up Tara's throat.

"He'd been beaten so badly, one of his ribs had actually punctured a lung. He was full of drugs too. A juvenile chemist's attempt at a truth serum, perhaps?"

That was what she told the men. But it hadn't been. At least not on purpose. She'd been experimenting, trying to dissociate Aiden from the pain. By the end, she would have given him most anything so long as it didn't stop his heart.

"Even some antibiotics in there. I remember, after Aiden was carried out, that I saw a little defibrillator on the floor. How many times did the assholes bring him to the edge of death and revive him just to do it all again, you think?"

Nausea rose up Tara's throat, choking her, and she felt all the blood drain from her face. She turned around lest anyone below caught sight of her pallor and leaned back against the railing for support. Her hands were clammy, the sweat probably leaving stains where she gripped the fabric of her dress. "Stop," she whispered.

"Please stop."

"There was water in his lungs as well. Waterboarding, you think? Or did they just use the same bucket for cold water as for hot?"

Tara's mouth tightened to swallow bile. "Stop."

Cassey raised a brow at her, his face serene. "I seem to have upset you."

Tara's hands curled into fists, her heart pounding through the sludge of nausea and terror and dread. "What do you want?" she whispered.

"I want to wrap my hands around your neck and shake you like the rabid cur you are." Cassey appeared to be dropping all hints of politeness for the sake of expediency. "But unfortunately, you seem to have gotten yourself lodged into my little cousin's heart, so I can't do that without hurting him in the process. So here is what we're going to do. First, you're going to break up this absurdity with Aiden. Then you're going to withdraw your immunity petition. I don't give a fuck what reason you give Sonia Dancer. Claim that you've grown a conscience if you think you can pull it off. Do what you have to—but if you come out from behind bars in less than ten years, I'll make you wish you hadn't. If you make one wrong move, I'll take you for a walk down memory lane. I think I saw enough paraphernalia left behind in that cave to ensure the experience is genuine."

TEN MINUTES LATER, Tara stood in the North Vault's spacious bathroom washing bile out of her mouth. She stared at her reflection in the mirror, the overhead lights revealing the shiny layer of sweat covering her skin. Her heart still pounded in her ears too loudly for thought as Cassey's words repeated themselves.

*He knows, he knows, he knows.* Tara had no idea how she'd held it together enough to tell Cassey he was insane, how she managed not to break her neck on the spiral staircase when the whole world was spinning about, how the entire club didn't hear the *bang bang bang* of her heart against her rib cage.

The truth Tara had naively thought was forgotten had come back to bite her in the ass. More like to rip her throat out with its bare teeth. And Cassey… She couldn't even bring herself to hate the man. They'd tortured his cousin. Held him in a hellhole for a month. The only reason Cassey hadn't slit her throat then and there was to keep from ruining Liam's wedding and North Vault's floors.

Despite its generous size, the walls of the restroom seemed to close in around her. Like a cage. Like a cave. With her testimony, Obsidian would get to her in jail. And if she clammed up, told the Tridents to go fuck themselves—Tara ignored the pang of pain the thought brought her—and refused to testify? Did she trust Cassey not to drag her off for a chat with a knife and a bucket of water if she was no longer useful to Liam's cause?

Outside the bathroom window, the Colorado landscape stretched in the distance, a lake reflecting the full moonlight. That was where they'd drop her body. Dead body, if she was fortunate. Still alive if not. Would Aiden be there, helping Cassey along?

The thought of Aiden learning the truth made Tara's eyes sting. The thought of him hating her. Maybe it was karma. Cosmic justice. Maybe he deserved to pay her back. Hell, he'd told her as much himself—his need to kill his tormentors.

To kill her.

Tara didn't think she could face that. Not from him.

The door to the bathroom opened, Ivy coming inside. The petite doctor started to smile at Tara, but quickly changed the expression to a frown. "You don't look well."

"I might be a lightweight when it comes to a flute of champagne," Tara said, gripping the washbasin for balance. Whatever she was going to do, she needed to get herself together before her own body turned against her. Filling her hands with cold water, she splashed it over her face and ordered herself to pull it together. Survive. She needed to survive. If Obsidian Ops had taught her nothing else, it had taught her to survive. "Don't tell the others, all right? It's a bit embarrassing."

Ivy made a locking gesture by her lips and tossed away the key.

As Tara walked out of the bathroom, she forced her analytical chemist's brain to list out possibilities. She had guesses of what could happen if she went one way or another, but not the real lay of the land. She couldn't afford the uncertainty, not now. Couldn't afford missing any piece of intelligence. Her hand went into where a pocket would be on normal clothes. The dress had nothing, but her fingers remembered feeling a smooth piece of paper. A picture of a pizza that was so much more than a pizza.

*I don't know what you're thinking, Lucius, but you might be the lesser devil.*

She had one tactical advantage with Obsidian—they didn't know Cassey had figured her out. So long as they believed the whole force and protection of Trident Security was behind her, Tara had some advantage. And the threat of what she could say in court was a double-edged sword. Her testimony was deadly, but her silence, that was worth something.

Taking another breath, she reached up and fixed her hair as she walked back to the reception. Composure. In no other time in her life did keeping her composure mean the difference between life and death. But today it did.

By the time Tara cleared the restroom corridor, she knew she looked put-together. She waved to Aiden, who was still playing darts, gave a big keep-playing, all-good-here grin, and wove a path between guests, chairs, and discarded coats.

Soon enough, she found what she was looking for—an older woman with a phone showing pictures to somebody sitting nearby. Memorizing the unlock code the woman entered each time she picked her phone back up, Tara waited until her mark got up to go to the buffet. With all the chatting and trusting guests, taking the phone off the table was painfully easy.

Making the call was anything but.

Hidden in a bathroom stall, Tara dialed the number.

Lucius picked up on the first ring. "Ralf's Pizza."

Tara's mouth opened, but no sound came out.

"Hello? Can I take your order?"

*Get it together, Northpoint.* "Yes. A stray rat with—"

"I expected a faster response," Lucius chided as if he hadn't been the one to knock her to the curb when she last called. But it was always like that. She didn't get to ask, but when Obsidian called, she was expected to answer.

"I was busy," she said. "Or more accurately, I wasn't sure I wanted to talk to you again."

"What changed your mind?" Lucius sounded genuinely curious. He probably was.

"Guilt. I didn't like how we left it."

"Neither did I." The sincerity in Lucius's voice made Tara's eyes sting all over again. Lucius wasn't perfect, hell, he was probably not even passably all right. But he was the closest she'd ever had to a father. He cleared his throat. "Your new documents along with a plane ticket to Argentina and fifty thousand dollars have been prepared."

Tara's breath caught. An exit package. "What? … How?" She forced herself to sound professional, as Lucius would expect from her. "I didn't think I was in anyone's good graces."

"You aren't." But Lucius was. "I didn't do it for you. I just didn't like watching the train wreck that we both know you were heading for." He cleared his throat, sounding gruff. "This would have been easier if you had fucking called when you were supposed to." There was a pause, and she could almost see him pulling out his phone to check the details before relaying them in code. A time. An address. And then the line went dead before she could say thank you.

That hadn't been an accident either. The old man was getting sentimental. Swallowing, Tara whispered her thanks to dead air anyway.

Quickly deleting all traces of the dialed numbers from the phone, Tara left it near the buffet table, where its owner would likely dismiss the phone's absence and relocation to absentmindedness. It was safer than trying to return it to the right table. Then it was all smiles and jokes as Tara joined Jaz and the women she had dared to start thinking of as friends at the pool table. The bride was kicking her brother's butt, wedding gown, pregnant belly, and all.

Coming up behind Tara, Aiden wrapped his arms around her hips. His hard body pressed into her back in a way that made her sex awaken with need, even as her chest and throat closed. "Do you play?"

"I do." Tara twisted in his grip to face him. "But if you want to know whether I'm better than you, that will cost you."

"Arg, lass. What are the stakes?" Aiden asked.

Rising onto her toes, she whispered into his ear exactly what she planned to do to his already pulsing cock if she won. When Aiden made a small mewing sound in response, she knew victory was already hers.

Whatever Cassey demanded, Tara was going to make her and Aiden's last night together worthy of a lifetime of memories.

# 24

Tara

Tara looked hungrily at Aiden's reflection in the bedroom mirror. The pair of them had come home from Liam's wedding, the intensity of the night still hanging around them, albeit in different ways. Need clung to them both like perfume, though only Tara knew that this would be their last time to give each other pleasure. Now, she drank in his reflection, trying to memorize every glorious line of him. Still in his tux, Aiden gave any James Bond a run for his money.

Tara reached around from the back to undo his bow tie. Aden met her gaze through the mirror and lifted his chin to give her access. The silk cloth felt smooth and soft in her hands, smoother than Aiden's shaved jaw that was already showing the first signs of prickly growth. Tara's thighs tingled, the sensation from her fingers traveling all the way to her sex.

Aiden started to work on opening the buttons of his shirt, revealing his muscular chest beneath. Tara stood back to watch, not willing to spoil the perfect last evening by trying to help. That would be too much for him, and she wanted this memory to be perfect. He smiled at her and let the cloth fall to the ground in a whoosh of fabric, his musky masculine scent caressing her nose.

God. He was taking his time on purpose. She could see it in the mischievous spark in his eyes. And damn it, the torment was working. Tara's damp panties were proof of that.

Aiden removed his cummerbund. Unbuckled his pants. When he lowered the zipper however, she'd reached her limit of waiting. She twisted him about and closed her hands behind Aiden's large neck. Fire sparked in his eyes as he hoisted her up on his hips at once, her dress riding up enough that Aiden's hand caressed her thigh.

Tara inhaled sharply, locking her ankles around his waist.

Their sexes rubbed against each other, Aiden's cock already engorged and perfect and waiting. Tara's own sex was ready for him as well, and she knew he could feel as much with his hands under her backside. Along her moist thighs. Need rose inside her with every moment of delay, her hips already undulating against the remaining barrier between them—a set of Tara's now-damp-with-arousal panties.

Aiden flicked them out of the way and entered her with a long single thrust that filled Tara all the way to her core. Ripples of pleasure rolled through her body, the sound of his breathing and her own hammering heartbeat drowning out the gentle hum of the furnace and the occasional honking of the outside cars. With each thrust, everything but the sensations going through her became irrelevant.

*Thrust. Thrust. Thrust.* The great size of him filled her channel. He supported her weight as he moved her up and down the length of him in a rhythm that was a perfect harmony to Tara's pulse. Every fiber inside her body woke to the sensation. Her breasts ached. Her channel clenched. A moan of need escaped her throat.

*Thrust. Thrust. Thrust.* The abyss of pleasure approached with every powerful stroke. Her heart quickened, her hands tightening around Aiden's neck. The need growing inside her became so powerful, it edged on pain, and her vision tunneled to see nothing but Aiden's face. The drop of sweat along his hairline, the glassiness of his eyes, as pleasure rose inside him to match her own. She was close. So close.

Aiden's fingers dug into her backside, powerful and strong and promising to keep her steady, and the *thrust thrust thrust* grew harder still. Pleasure. Need. Inevitability. Oh God.

"Aiden!" she called out.

He pressed his mouth against hers, pillaging with possessive strokes that sent a blaze through her, meeting the heat already coming from their joint sexes. The twin forces sent Tara over the edge of pleasure. Her channel tightened around Aiden's pulsing cock, and she moaned against his mouth as the orgasm filled her completely.

It came like a storm, sweeping away everything in its path. Everything, from her toes to her sex to her lungs, clenched hard enough to make her head swim before swaying back to glorious satisfaction. Tara shook as she slowly returned from her high, a trickle of sweat snaking down the groove of her spine while Aiden held her up. It was only after a few heartbeats had passed that she slowly became aware that while she'd had her release, he'd held himself back.

"Forgot. Something." His words were ragged, and he struggled for every bit of control as he slowly slid free. Setting Tara on the edge of his high bed, he reached for the dresser where he kept the condoms.

Tara grabbed his wrist. "No, wait."

He cocked a brow. "Have we forgotten eighth grade health education?" The words were strained, and his engorged cock twitched with every beat of his heart.

Tara shook her head. She hadn't forgotten, but that velvety cock right in front of her was too great a temptation to resist. Sliding off the bed, she crouched in front of him and let her hands brush up his powerful thighs. His rock-hard muscle made her want him all over again, and her mouth was already watering at the sight of the glistening moisture at the head of his shaft.

Aiden inhaled sharply when she cupped his balls.

Tara stopped. Letting him adjust to the change. Waiting for him to give her permission to take the kind of control that what she longed to do entailed.

"I reckon you're going to be the end of me," Aiden muttered, settling his hands on her shoulders for support.

With a grin, Tara slid her tongue along the full length of him, swirling around the top as with a delicious ice-cream cone. It was glorious, and she did it again and again to fully savor the velvety texture. Aiden's thighs were trembling as she finally took him into her mouth.

His hands moved from her shoulders to grip her short hair.

Tara sucked. God, it felt good to have the length of him inside her, to feel his muscles contract beneath her ministrations. She sucked again, taking him deeper.

"Tara!" Aiden threw his head back, panting. Arching.

She worked his shaft in every way she could, savoring the feel and taste and unconstrained open need he let her see. God. She should have done this earlier. She should have done this every single day that she'd had the chance. Back when there was no expiration date.

Aiden tried to pull out before his release, but she held him tight and swallowed his essence. The hot, thick taste of him made her sex clench with need all over again. She pressed her cheek against his thigh as they both regained their breath, then he lifted her onto the bed, and they fell backward onto the thick down comforter.

"You know, I was fully intending to remove that dress of yours." His voice was tipsy with satisfaction. "I've been looking at those little hooks. I think I can do it."

Tara laughed, then laughed again as she realized that she was, in fact, still in her dress.

"I mean it." With a deft flick of his hand, Aiden flipped her onto her belly. She had only a moment to indulge in the feel of the fluffy down against her cheek before he straddled her from behind. He began unhooking each little metal contraption of her dress, working with determination until her back was exposed to the cool bedroom air. Then he slid the gorgeous gown that Tara would never wear again off her and let his hands roam free along her skin, leaving little footprints of prickling sensation everywhere they touched.

Aiden's thumbs ran down the length of her back, pressing on either side of her spine. Kneading out knots in her shoulders. Sliding around to stroke between her folds and tease her clit. Each motion was slow and luxurious now, and despite her exhaustion, despite wanting this moment to last forever, Tara felt arousal gripping her uncontrollably all over again.

Before Aiden—now sheathed in a condom—could take her from the back, Tara rolled over and put her thighs onto his shoulders. This would be their last time together, and she wanted to watch and remember every line of his gorgeous face as they found release together.

# 25

## Tara

The potent pull of guilt and soul-ripping sadness twisted Tara's gut as she held herself up on her elbow, watching Aiden's sleeping form. It was one of those rare precious moments when his beautiful body looked relaxed, his muscles sunk deep into the down pillows. She tried to memorize every detail of the moment. The fresh, musky scent. The way his lashes, so long and dark for a guy, brushed his cheeks. How his chest moved up and down with deep, even breaths that sounded like rustling paper.

Her hand reached out toward him, stopping just before touching his skin. In her imagination, she tried to pretend this moment was natural. That Aiden's deep slumber had come from sex and celebration and trust. But of course, she knew the truth—that she'd helped things along with a finger dipped into a mild sedative, brushed over Aiden's lips. The old ladies at the wedding truly carried enough drugs in their purses to make a pharmacist blush. Getting them was no harder than getting to the phone had been.

It had been a risk. Worse. It had been a betrayal of his trust. But Aiden's instincts were too well honed for Tara to get by him otherwise. Her fingers longed to touch him, to feel his skin just one more time. She couldn't risk it, though. Just as she couldn't bear to imagine what Aiden would do, what he would think, when he awoke to find her gone. At least she was getting to say goodbye. Aiden would not be afforded that luxury.

Aiden would certainly try to look for her, but with her out of his life, nothing would hold Cassey back from revealing the truth to him. Then this man, the one who made her soul sing, would hate her with every fiber of his being. He'd be right too. Karma in action.

Tara realized her cheeks were wet and quickly scrubbed her face. It was time to go. With one last silent apology and goodbye to Aiden and Overlord, she got up from the bed and picked up his gun from atop the nightstand—right where they'd left it in last night's hurry. Another mark of his trust in her that she was breaking.

After slipping out of the bedroom, Tara stopped at the bathroom to turn on the water. If Aiden did rouse enough to sense an empty bed, the sound would provide a temporary decoy. Then she was in her clothes and out the back door, quietly jogging down the steps to where Wilfred was parked in the building garage.

Making short work of the lock—Aiden had the key on his keychain, and she couldn't risk going for that—Tara hotwired the car she knew so well. Wilfred rumbled to life with a purr not unlike Overlord's soft snoring. A moment later, she was rolling into the darkness.

Despite the late hour, the interstate was alive with cars and trucks, and she made short work of blending herself into the traffic. The coordinates for the safe house Lucius had given her put the place about two hours' drive from Denton Valley. With adrenaline pumping through Tara's blood, the time passed in the blink of an eye.

Taking the exit for Crows Landing, Tara found herself grateful for the darkness that hid Wilfred's poor condition in the upper-class suburban neighborhood. The houses here were larger than any family could possibly need, with large yards and privacy fences to ward off unwanted eyes. Here and there, a soft decorative light brightened a stucco façade or bay window, but overall, the street remained dim and quiet. The kind of street where nothing ever happens.

She continued down Crows Landing for several miles until she spotted the peach-colored mansion with a FOR SALE sign in the front lawn. The driveway was so long, it actually hugged behind the house to end in a small private parking lot. One other car was already there, a chalk mark on the tires verifying it was sent by Lucius.

Tara parked Wilfred and made her way to the side door. She was proud to see that, despite the fear filling her body, her fingers were steady as she found the lockbox and entered the combination. The door was actually unlocked, but Lucius would have ensured a token was left inside the box as a secondary signal. If the box was empty, or held only a key, Tara was to turn around and leave.

Breath still, she eased open the box. Three pebbles. Three people inside. Standard. She closed her eyes. God. This was happening. The point of no return. Obsidian wouldn't force her to take the package, but once she started down that road by walking through this door, she couldn't turn back. What if taking the exit package was a mistake? It was set to get her out of the country, but after that…

*Come out from behind bars in less than ten years, I'll make you wish you hadn't. If you make one wrong move, I'll take you for a walk down memory lane. I think I saw enough paraphernalia left behind in that cave to ensure the experience is genuine.*

Tara shook her head. The life she'd been living with Aiden and the Tridents these past weeks was as real as a smoke dragon. Either way, it was over now, and the only choice she had was how to make her exit. Better to do it on her own terms.

Maybe in another life, she'd have gotten to teach that self-defense class for Dani, and hold Jaz's babies, and fall asleep with Aiden to reruns of *Battlestar Galactica*. But she'd been dealt a different hand. She only hoped that Aiden, at least, would find someone who made him whole. Yes, that was the silver lining. Aiden would go on and find someone who was better than her. He would be happy. Holding on to that thought like a lifeline, Tara turned the handle and let herself inside.

SHE WAS IN A MUDROOM, cleaned spotlessly by the seller's crew. Drawing her—Aiden's—gun, she continued forward. Trust, but verify. The kitchen came next, then a corridor with a turn toward the living room where a small lamp was lit. Though she couldn't see it from her current position, the high ceilings and staircase suggested that the living room was connected to some kind of second-story landing. That was no doubt where Obsidian's cover team had stationed themselves—not that Tara was likely to see them.

SHE WALKED TOWARD THE LIGHT.

"SO, YOU SHOWED." The voice came from the shadows on the other side of the living room, where the lamp was lit. With her eyes adjusting to the change of light, Tara could now make out a familiar female shape that belonged to the equally familiar voice. Katie May, one of the operatives Lucius trusted most.

"I came," said Tara.

Katie May strode forward, her hips sashaying beneath her short skirt. Unlike Tara, Katie May had the body to pull it off. "Don't look disappointed. You didn't actually expect *him* to come personally? For a stray?"

"No, of course not," said Tara. It was a lie, but now that Katie May had said as much aloud, Tara felt stupid for getting her hopes up to begin with. Lucius wasn't really her father. The fact that he'd pulled strings for this package, it was more than she had a right to hope for. "Thank you for coming. I know it's a risk."

"I'm not doing this for you. Frankly, I advocated finishing this with a bullet in your skull to put everyone out of their misery. You don't warrant an exit package. You don't come shoe-licking close."

*Please, tell me how you really feel.* "And yet here we are." Tara holstered her weapon. Katie May was snooty and self-important, but she was as close to a right-hand man as Lucius had. She wouldn't go further off script than a few insults. Not with a team watching. "Let's get this over with."

Katie Mae scowled, but reached behind her and tossed a backpack onto the coffee table. "Your papers. A change of clothes. Hair dye. Two passports, UK and Argentina. Plane tickets. A key to a safety deposit box in Buenos Aires. The cash is in the credenza behind you, top left drawer. Mixed denominations. Twenty thousand—but you should count it. That gets you started. The safe deposit box has the rest."

"Got it. What else?"

"That's it," Katie May said.

"You're lying." Tara's heart hammered so loudly that it was a wonder the neighbors couldn't hear the pounding, but she knew Lucius. He'd have a redundancy built in. He couldn't help being thorough.

"Why would I lie?"

The list of reasons was too long to enumerate and hardly a good use of anyone's time. Suffice to say, Katie May, who *had* been in the military, little approved of Tara's place at Lucius's dinner table. "Are you willing to risk Lucius discovering his instructions weren't executed?" she asked instead. "Unless you think the cover team up there is likely to choose your good will over Lucius's?" Wanting to please Lucius had always been Katie May's weak point. The possibility of losing his trust got her attention.

Katie May's lips pulled back in a snarl. "You have a backup account at a Swiss bank," she said, reciting the number and access code.

As the operative uttered each number, Tara created a picture for it in her head—a memorization technique she'd learned early on.

She made Katie May repeat the sequence twice more just in case, then nodded. "That's four digits too short."

Katie Mae snorted. "Of course it is."

Right. The last four digits would come from a number that had meaning to Lucius and Tara alone. Insurance to make sure no one got tempted to pocket the funds. Not that Katie May would, but there was the cover team to consider, and it was standard procedure anyway. Once Tara sat down to think about it, she was sure she'd come up with the right digit combination.

Good enough.

Tara grabbed the backpack from the table and headed to the credenza for the cash. For all her snottiness, Katie May had placed the bills in competent piles, allowing Tara to easily see how much she had of each currency while she was in a safe space.

As Tara went over the money, a sound and scraping movement upstairs cut into her hearing. Glancing up, she found Katie May likewise frozen in place. It was probably nothing, the cover team just choosing a very inconvenient moment to stretch. But then again, there was a reason Obsidian brought guns along with cash.

Katie May tapped her earbud. "Report."

Watching Katie's troubled face, Tara drew her gun. Her breath halted.

"Anything—" Tara cut off at a crashing noise coming from the floor above. Twisting, she grabbed Katie May's arm and pulled the woman down behind the couch just as shots rang out through the living room. One. Two. More. A vase shattered in a rain of glass.

They'd been compromised.

"Fuck." Katie May's curse came through clenched teeth. Even in the dimness, Tara could see the woman's sleeve turn wet with blood. Katie May tapped her earpiece again and again. "Rollo, report. Rollo!"

Fear rushed through Tara's blood, making it hard to think. She ripped off the hem of her shirt and wrapped it around Katie May's arm to stanch the bleeding as she surveyed the route to the door. Whoever had come after them was upstairs, with a clear shot down. Fish in a fucking barrel.

"We need to move." Katie was panting. "I'll cover you. Go for the door."

Tara shook her head. She was a dead woman anyway, and Katie May had a chance. "You first. Don't argue." She braced her gun on the top of the couch and fired blindly into the darkness. "*Go go go!*"

As Katie May ran for the door, Tara continued firing into the darkness of the upstairs foyer, another crash the only indication that a bullet had found a target.

# 26

## Aiden

As Aiden rolled off Tara's sweat-slickened body, he tried very hard to not overthink the sex. Tonight had been… passionate. Mind-blowing. Even now, with both their climaxes settling, the pleasure still coursed through his veins and penetrated his core. That was a good thing. Probably a carryover from watching the pleasure and affection that radiated from Liam and Jaz all evening. If those two had glowed any brighter, they'd be radioactive.

And yet… Yet something about the whole thing felt *off*. It was probably Aiden's imagination, but as they coupled today, he thought he caught an occasional trace of sadness behind Tara's big hazel eyes. Oh, there was pleasure too. A hell of a lot of pleasure. But sometimes, he thought hers had been laced with desperation. Even now, as Aiden held her against his side, she felt more tense than the rag-doll relaxation her body had dissolved into after their first lovemaking.

Stretching like Overlord, Tara picked up a water bottle from the nightstand and took a long drink before kissing him again. Thoroughly. Then she traced his mouth with her fingers.

Aiden chuckled. "Should I give up my plans for sleep today, lass?" he asked. "Not that I mind. Just good to know."

"No," Tara yawned, covering her mouth. "That would probably be irresponsible. Sonia wants to go over a few more things." She snuggled against his side. God, was there anything better than a woman pressed up against him?

Aiden licked his lips, hoping the taste of her had lingered there. Licked—and stopped. The tip of his tongue tasted something mildly bitter. The taste was faint enough that if he hadn't been on alert already and obsessively paranoid about any substance entering his body, he would have missed it completely. In fact, he wasn't truly confident he tasted anything at all.

But hadn't Tara touched him just there a few minutes ago?

Just in case his paranoia was right, Aiden surreptitiously wiped his mouth clean on the pillow and closed his eyes. Fatigue beckoned him like a rocking boat promising the wonder of sleep. There had to be an explanation, but it wasn't a question one asked politely. *Excuse me, but did you happen to roofie me a few minutes ago?*

Aiden felt stupid. Paranoid. Yet what was it he'd told Dani the other day? *Just because I'm paranoid, doesn't mean no one is out to get me.*

She'd chuckled. *Agreed. Can we talk about vetting the potential threat before reacting to it?*

A soldier, Dani was not. But neither was Aiden on a battlefield just now. He was in bed with a lover. *Vet before reacting.* Yes, he could afford to do that. Could feign sleep and stay alert until morning, when he could ask the beautiful chemist at his side to help him ferret out the source of the strange taste.

It wasn't long after that Aiden felt the bed shift beside him, the feeling of being watched tickling his skin. A quarter hour later, Tara was up, making a few common noises as if to test Aiden's slumber.

Fuck.

It took all of Aiden's will to keep feigning sleep as his heart raced with dread and pain as Tara quietly picked up his gun. His whole body longed to leap out of bed, to grab her and shake her and demand answers. Had something happened? Did she not feel safe with him watching over her anymore? Or was there more?

Only one way to find out, and it wasn't one Liam would ever approve of. Aiden's brain didn't approve of it either, but his heart was another story. It needed to know where the woman he'd fallen in love with was headed and everything else be damned.

From a small creaking sound, Aiden figured Tara went out the back door. He was up with his next breath, slipping into a pair of pants as he grabbed his leather jacket, gun, and keys. Then he was racing down the fire escape to his motorcycle, his stomach clenching with dread as Wilfred pulled out of the garage onto the interstate.

Keeping cover behind delivery trucks that littered the night highway like ants, Aiden easily kept pace with Tara as she headed out of Denton Valley. He tried to think. To understand. But all he felt was numbness. As if he was trudging through sludge that threatened to suck him under. Things became trickier when she turned off onto a suburban street where an extra vehicle would bring notice. Especially a particular Harley-Davidson motorcycle that the lass knew well.

He did his best to parallel her along the adjacent street at first, then pulled over and ditched his bike. Whether his mind liked it or not, it had to get to work. Pulling out his phone, Aiden called up the map of the neighborhood. Tara was at the tail end of a dead-end street. Big houses. Rich people with security systems. So where would she go?

Aiden jogged out onto Crows Landing, looking for a house with lights. If someone was up and waiting for her, they'd likely have lights on. Nothing. A sleepy street.

And a large FOR SALE sign. A smart place to meet if you wanted to draw little attention to unusual people's comings and goings. Spotting a large tree growing near one of the side windows on the second floor, Aiden quickly scaled the trunk and saw Wilfred parked in a small lot.

*Bingo.*

With his target thus confirmed, Aiden made his way along the branch to the window he'd spotted earlier. Whoever Tara was here with had conveniently disabled the security system before letting themselves inside. Sending a mental thanks to Lady Luck, he pried open the window and let himself inside what turned out to be a bathroom. The night light illuminated beige walls with dancing pink dolphins.

He crouched beside the door to listen. Two women's voices, coming from downstairs. One he didn't know, and the other... Aiden's heart, which he thought had lost all feeling hours earlier, shattered as the reality of the situation hit him full-on.

It had all been a lie from the very beginning. Tara hadn't come over to the good guys. She wasn't going to testify. She'd been biding her time, waiting for a way out of the country. Exactly as she'd been doing when Aiden found her. He'd been a pawn she'd played like a tuned violin.

The blow of betrayal hit so hard that, for several heartbeats, he found himself unable to draw breath through the pain. His hands tightened on the door just to keep himself steady.

The door shifted under his weight. Creaked.

"What was that?" The soft inquiry snapped Aiden from his haze. In his initial shock, he hadn't paid enough attention, but now it was clear that the house held more than just the women below. Light steps sounded along the second floor, and Aiden heard the telltale sound of a long gun being taken off safety and brought to bear.

Shit. Adjusting his hold on his gun, Aiden aimed at the door.

"The bitch is just going for the money. All clear," someone responded.

"Understood."

Aiden let out a breath, his thoughts racing. First shoot-out disaster avoided. But he had at least two armed men on the second floor. Two women, at least one armed, on the first. Whichever way this ended, it wouldn't be with Tara dead. Or Tara leaving.

Sending a prayer to whoever was listening, Aiden eased open the door. His steps were silent as he panned the corridor, marking the two black-clad shadows on the top landing. Long guns. M4s. One was trained on the floor below, probably covering the front entrance. The other was moving about, probably charged with keeping an eye on the rest of the house. Fortunately, he was doing a piss-poor job.

"This is fucking bullshit," the guy covering the front muttered. "All this trouble for a stray when I can get this corrected with a bit of lead." The man's finger twitched toward the trigger.

Aiden didn't think. He lunged.

Coming up from behind, Aiden grabbed Trigger Happy's weapon. The metal felt cool and familiar in Aiden's hands. Trigger Happy grunted in surprise but managed to hold on. They spun together, fighting for control of the gun.

Aiden saw the wall a moment before they crashed into it, but a moment was all he needed. He twisted, putting the wall at his back, taking the impact as the price of keeping Trigger between his partner and Aiden.

The move paid dividends a moment later as Trigger's partner fired despite close quarters.

Aiden threw Trigger at the shooter, and the man's next shots went wild. The pair fell in a tangle of limbs.

Aiden's heart beat a steady rhythm now, his senses awake. Alert. Following his victims to the ground, he knocked the top man out with a blow to the temple.

The bottom operative reached for his handgun.

Aiden stepped on the man's wrist, then grabbed the gun for himself. Without missing a beat, he twisted the weapon and used its butt to knock the operative out beside his partner. A quick but thorough sweep of the other rooms assured him the second floor was now secure. Part one accomplished.

Stopping just long enough to ensure both men's chests were still moving, Aiden switched his attention to the action below.

Tara was still there. Still alive. Unhurt. Taking cover behind a couch as she argued about something with the other woman. Four seconds, five max and he could get to her. Tara motioned to the front exit.

As Aiden started for the stairs, Tara leaned out from behind the couch and fired.

The shots rang through the darkness and then in his ears as he was suddenly falling backward, his chest moist with warm, viscous liquid.

# 27

Ivy

"Excuse me, Dr. West-Keasley?" Nancy, one of the emergency room nurses at Denton Valley Memorial Hospital, tapped Ivy on the shoulder. "Mr. Keasley says to tell you that he knows your shift ended thirty minutes ago and that if you're not ready to leave in five minutes, he's going to go and get coffee…and leave your son in the ER."

Ivy's eyes widened. "He wouldn't." No, no, Kyan bloody would. At almost two, their son, Bar, was deeply into the "me do!" part of toddlerhood. This determination coupled with intense ingenuity and more precociousness than any pint-size human being should possibly possess, turned life into a series of disasters interrupted by naps. Left to run free in the ER, the kid was guaranteed to leave a wake of destruction that would take a week to undo.

How did it get to be 7:00 a.m., though? Last Ivy remembered, it was barely six and she was just sitting down to tweak her write-up for getting Mrs. Johnson into a clinical trial, and then… She stood, her cramping muscles confirming that an hour really had passed.

Nancy gazed at her watch. "Just to let you know, it's only three minutes now. And when I was leaving the staff room, Bar was trying to stick the end of some oxygen tubing into an electrical outlet."

Ivy pinched the bridge of her nose. "I don't understand how the male of the species survives to adulthood."

"At least it was oxygen tubing and not scissors," the nurse added, clearly trying to be helpful. Ivy made a noncommittal sound. It had probably been scissors about forty-five seconds earlier. That was another fact of toddler parenting—life was divided into forty-five-second increments, after which a change of activity type would be demanded.

Ivy glanced at the screen and clicked Save. It had been an uneventful night, and if luck held, she'd get time to finish the application that evening. "Can you please tell him I'm on my way and stand guard, lest—" Ivy cut off as a familiar tone sounded over the ER loudspeakers, sending all the staff into attentive silence.

"MedFlight Bravo to Denton Valley Memorial. We're enroute from Crows Landing with thoracic gunshot trauma. Patient is awake and disoriented. Heart rate one-twenty, respiration thirty, BP one hundred over eighty and falling. ETA ten minutes."

Ivy waited for the rest. When the medic stayed quiet, she picked up the phone and dialed into the call.

"MedFlight Bravo, do you hear sounds in both lungs, please? Was a fluid challenge initiated?"

"Negative, ma'am. The patient is combative to intervention. We're trying to keep him as calm as possible for transport."

"Understood. Fly safe, MedFlight." Ivy disconnected and looked up at the nurse. "Change of plans. Please go tell Kyan to suit up and meet me in trauma one. I think Dani is in today. She may be able to watch Bar."

Eight minutes later, Kyan walked into the trauma bay and pulled a gown and gloves on over his clothes. The way the former SEAL filled out even the glorified paper bag was downright unfair. He shook his head at her. "If you had left on time, you wouldn't be here."

Ivy snorted. As if Kyan didn't absolutely live for trauma response. Ivy was in medicine to make people feel better. He was there for the adrenaline of fighting off death.

Once, she'd mistakenly thought that a military medic could bring nothing to her Harvard-trained surgical background. She knew better now.

Ivy looked at her watch. Two-minute ETA from MedFlight. "Any trouble finding a babysitter?" she asked. "Check the rapid sequence intubation setup—I thought I saw someone from anesthesia pilfer a Miller blade."

"All here." Kyan was already in motion, clicking open the instruments. "Dani was checking in with the women heading to the shelter. She was happy to reverse course. I swear, the moment Bar sees her, he turns into a perfect angel."

"It's part of his mastermind plan to ensure that all our friends think we're crazy. This may be a good time to tell you that Yarborough is out. If this guy goes into surgery—"

"You're going with him," Kyan finished for her.

The double doors to the ER opened to let in two men in flight suits wheeling in their gurney. Even from afar, Ivy didn't like the amount of blood she was seeing. "Nancy, let's get him typed as soon as—"

"It's A positive," said Kyan, his voice suddenly so calm that it set off alarm bells in Ivy's mind. Cold calm was Kyan's combat mode. "He's A positive."

"How—" Ivy froze, finally seeing what Kyan's greater height had allowed him to mark earlier. "Aiden," she whispered.

"Yeah," Kyan said as Aiden took a swing at Nancy, who'd come too close too quickly.

Shoving the nurse out of the danger zone, Kyan held Aiden down while he and the medics manhandled Aiden onto the trauma table. Ivy's heart broke. In the best of times, Aiden panicked at being touched. There would be a lot of touching in his future.

"Aiden." Ivy leaned over to ensure her face filled the entirety of Aiden's vision. He looked like hell. His face was pale, his shirt bloody, his eyes glassy and filled with pain and devastation. From the way he'd fought, he could move all four limbs, though, and beneath his soaked shirt, his chest seemed to show equal rise and fall bilaterally. Trachea was midline, no deviation. More likely than not, he still had two functioning lungs and the bullet had missed his heart. "Aiden, can you look at me? Do you know who I am?"

His upper lip pulled up in a snarl. "Tara."

Ivy exchanged a glance with Kyan, who was clearly torn between staying in trauma and stepping away to contact the Tridents. Desperate as Ivy was to know what had happened and whether Tara was safe, right now she had to force herself to stay in her lane. Her job was to keep Aiden alive. Nothing else. In the periphery, she saw Kyan jerk his head toward one of the staff and issue orders—no doubt to get Liam and the others on alert. Ivy didn't listen. She couldn't. Taking out her penlight, she shone it into Aiden's eyes, grateful to see him flinch away. Pupils responsive.

"I'm Ivy. What's your name? Tell me your name."

Aiden gritted his teeth and glared at her as if she'd asked for his bank account number and access code.

"All right." Ivy made her voice even. "Do you know where you are?"

"Go to hell."

"Small pinch," Nancy warned on the other side of Aiden. Ivy didn't think Aiden heard her, but he certainly felt the needle prick his skin, because this time, his blows connected. Nancy grunted and stumbled back from the impact of Aiden's kick, her tray flying into the air. The tech approaching with the portable X-ray screamed and jumped away. Kyan took a punch to the jaw as he tried to get a grip on his friend's arms without doing more damage.

Security rushed inside.

"Can you settle him down?" Ivy asked Kyan.

He shook his head. "Tara is the only one I've ever seen do it."

A band tightened around Ivy's chest. She hated doing this to Aiden, but there wasn't a choice.

"Restraints," she ordered the orderlies, and tried her best to ignore Aiden's screams as his limbs were Velcroed to the bed. The moment it was safe, the trauma team rushed back into action, using shears to ruthlessly cut off Aiden's clothes, prodding him for vitals and looking for IV access.

"Aiden, listen to me," Ivy said, her voice too calm and reassuring for the pounding in her ears. "I'm going to talk you through everything. All right?"

The small nod from him felt like a victory.

"Someone shot you."

"Tara," Aiden whispered.

"We'll find Tara." Ivy hoped to hell she wasn't lying, but she needed to keep him calm as she filled a syringe. "We'll make sure Tara is safe. Right now, I need to check your chest to see where that bullet went. You aren't going to like it, so I'm going to give you something to help you relax—"

"No. Please." Aiden's gaze gripped hers, his desperation making Ivy's eyes sting. Despite the futility of beating the restraint, he tried to jerk his arm away. "Don't…don't play with my head. Don't make me not know."

Ivy glanced up at Kyan. There was no good option; she was going to be hurting him one way or another no matter what she did. Though it made her feel like a coward, Ivy wished this was another week, one when Dr. Yarborough—the other trauma surgeon at Denton Valley Memorial—wasn't on vacation.

Anger shot unbidden through Ivy's blood. No one should have ghosts like Aiden's. It wasn't fair. Wasn't right.

"He can take the pain, Doc," Kyan told her softly. "And I'll make sure he doesn't hurt anyone or himself while you look. Remember, you weren't the one who shot him."

Ivy put away the drugs, and Aiden slumped against the bed in relief. He made no sound as she examined the wounds, her gloved hand slickened with his blood.

"Who the hell shot you?" Kyan muttered to Aiden. "You better tell me when you come to."

"I may be able to tell you sooner than that," said Ivy as she ran her hand along his chest. "No exit wound. The bullet is still in there, and I can feel it. Once I have it out—"

"We can run ballistics," Kyan finished for her. "See if we can find whose gun this was."

# 28

## Aiden

Aiden sat on the hospital bed a few feet away from the window, staring at Denton Valley sprawling outside. He wasn't wearing a hospital gown by virtue of having ripped the thing off the moment he had enough coordination on his good side to wrangle himself into a pair of scrub bottoms he'd located in a cupboard. Ivy had done her best to keep him awake, but in the end, surgery was unavoidable to repair bleeding near his lung. Even now, Aiden had trouble taking a deep breath and had to keep his left arm splinted against his chest to prevent too much pulling on the wound site.

The door opened, and he turned gingerly, getting to his feet when he saw who entered.

"Are you going to take my head off if I check your incision?" Ivy asked.

Aiden snorted softly. "No. I know who you are and what you're doing. Hard as it is to believe, I do have several modes between uncomfortable and homicidal."

Ivy gave him a smile that was much kinder than he deserved,

her hands gentle and efficient as they peeled back the dressing for a few moments. "I'm sorry I couldn't keep you out of the OR."

Aiden felt like the greatest asshole in the world for making her imagine he'd be anything but utterly grateful. Leaning down, he kissed the top of her head. "Thank you for saving my life. And for… everything else." Since the doc had honored his plea to keep the drugs away, he remembered almost everything that had happened. Including watching Ivy sob into Kyan's shoulder after Aiden made her work on him without sedation for as long as he had. "I'm sorry for what I put you through."

"You should be," she fired back at him. "If you don't want to be in here, don't go getting yourself shot, you bastard."

A corner of his mouth lifted. "Noted."

Ivy cleared her throat. "So, fair warning—Liam is lurking outside the door like a hungry wolf waiting to pounce. I can run interference a bit longer if you'd like."

Aiden shook his head. "Unlike wine, putting off that conversation isn't going to get better with time. Let him at it. Do you know if anyone has seen Tara?"

"No idea." Ivy pulled out her phone, then hesitated. "I do know that ballistics matched the slug I pulled out of your chest to your own gun, though."

Right. While Ivy called Liam to give him the green light, Aiden tried to drape his arms behind his back the way he usually did. Quickly realizing the impossibility of that with a sling, he settled for just one. He'd barely managed it when Liam strode into the room like a force of nature.

"Liam. I fucked up. I lost the subject. I'm sorry," Aiden said, trying to get in front of his boss's ire even as his own soul pulsed with pain. The *subject.* Aiden wasn't certain he could say Tara's name aloud without his throat closing. He'd been such a fool, had let his heart get ahead of his brain. Now, because of him, because he'd stupidly trusted the wrong person, everyone was in a world of trouble. "I'll correct this. I'll bring her back in."

"What you're going to do is stay in this damn hospital until everyone and their mother signs off on it," said Liam. "What the hell happened?"

Aiden tried and failed not to wince. "The subject tried to drug me and took off from my apartment in the middle of the night." He still couldn't make himself say her name. "I followed her to a temporary Obsidian location in Crows Landing. I observed an Obsidian team delivering money and documents to facilitate her fleeing the country. I tried to stop the transaction. I failed."

"Did you now?" said Liam. "And when *your subject* was leaving your house, you didn't think you should call anyone before driving to Crows fucking Landing?"

Aiden knew a rhetorical question when he heard one and kept his mouth shut. Liam was just building up steam.

"Do you know how recklessly unprofessional that was? This is a team sport, McDane. Do you understand me?"

"Yes, sir."

"How did you get shot?" Liam demanded.

Given Ivy's heads-up about ballistics, Aiden suspected Liam had already figured out the likely answer to his own question. And he was going to do nothing to make it easier. In Liam's defense, Aiden deserved it.

"After I neutralized two gunmen at the Crows Landing house, Tara…" He made himself say the name, though it punched as much as he expected. "Tara and another female initiated cover fire to get themselves to the exit. One of those shots struck me. Tara shot me."

Liam moved closer. "And what did she shoot you with?"

"My gun. The one she took before she left my apartment."

"Goddamn right she shot you with your own weapon. Because any idiot who decides to single-handedly chase an armed operative with everything to lose into the heart of their safe house and then, *then*, instead of calling for backup barges in with his ass hanging out of his pants deserves to get fucking shot."

Aiden flinched. Ivy did too.

Liam turned to her, his voice gentling with the kind of control that Aiden envied. "My apologies for upsetting you, Doc."

"It's all right." Ivy tried and failed to put on a brave face. "It's one of the hazards of having military friends."

Aiden turned as well, going so far as to walk over and squeeze her elbow. After everything that Ivy did for him, he felt extra protective of the little doctor. "You might want to wait outside for a bit," he said. "I have it on pretty good authority that Rowen won't be done yelling at me for some time yet."

"That is a very good presumption," Liam confirmed, blading his body to let Ivy by. The moment the door closed behind her, Liam twisted back and stepped so close that Aiden could see every furious line in the SEAL's face. Then Liam laid into him with a ten-minute tirade that was impressive by anyone's standards.

Aiden took it all in silence, standing as much at attention as his injuries allowed until his boss finally ran out of steam.

"Well?" Liam asked. "Anything to say for yourself?"

"I think you covered it all rather thoroughly, sir."

Liam sighed and scrubbed his face.

"I'll make this right," Aiden said softly. He would. Somehow.

"You're going to do no such thing." The quiet, measured tones hurt more than the yelling. "Consider yourself suspended. Cassey and Briar are going after Northpoint."

Aiden jerked, regretting it a moment later as pain zapped along his side. "What? Why them? They aren't even part of Trident Security."

"Because they gave me a very convincing reason," said Liam, something dark passing over his face.

A shiver ran down Aiden's spine. "What aren't you telling me?"

"I'm not telling you a lot of things," said Liam, putting up his hand to ward off Aiden's protest. "If the neighbors hadn't called 911 when they did, I would be telling those things to a corpse. So, here's what's going to happen now: you will stay here following everything the medical folk tell you to do to the letter. And frankly, the less you like it, the happier that will make me."

Aiden knew better than to ask when he could come back to work and waited until Liam strode out of the room before sinking back to his bed and rubbing the side of his chest. Everything hurt. His soul most of all.

"That sounded intense," said Ivy, slipping back into the room. Clearly, she hadn't gone far enough.

"Oh, aye," said Aiden. Given that the doc had already seen him at his worst, being around her felt easier. Kyan was a damn lucky bloke. "All deserved, though."

"I'd have been a puddle on the floor if someone yelled at me like that," she confessed, surreptitiously checking Aiden's vitals. Yeah, he'd learned to tell when she was secretly counting respirations.

Saving Ivy the trouble, Aiden held out his good arm to let her palpate his pulse. "Aye, but I imagine you wouldn't have chased a honeypot who'd just tried to roofie you *and* stole your gun, all because you were thinking with your cock instead of your head either." He realized what he'd said and winced.

Ivy just clicked her tongue. "I'll admit that is a very unlikely scenario." She hesitated, her demeanor changing. "Listen, for what it's worth… When you came into the ER and I ordered you restrained, you kept calling me Tara. I don't know that it means anything beyond the reality of being at the edge of shock and not thinking clearly, but given that I was the one hurting you at the time, it was a strange association."

"She'd just shot me," said Aiden, though Ivy's words struck something he couldn't put his finger on.

"True," Ivy agreed. "Plus, like I said, you were hypoxic. That's probably it."

Yes. That probably was.

Except Aiden didn't think so.

# 29

Tara

Tara stood in the darkness and looked through the window of a well-lit suburban home. Beyond a pair of roughhousing boys and a dog constantly chewing on a toy, the large-screen TV showed the news—with Tara's face pasted all over the blue background.

*Manhunt continues for Tara Northpoint, the woman suspected in the shooting in one of Crows Landing's upscale on-market homes three days ago.*

Tara knew how the rest of the story went, had seen it the night of the disaster at Crows Landing when she'd ducked into a twenty-four-hour convenience store to buy some supplies for Katie May. The news hadn't had her picture back then, but they did have a close-up of the MedFlight helicopter loading up the unidentified patient to be flown to Denton Valley Memorial Hospital. Unidentified to the news, but not to her.

Aiden.

Tara's hand flexed as if she felt the recoil of the gun all over again. She remembered the shadows moving upstairs, throwing down cover fire, the knowledge that she'd hit someone. She hadn't known it was him. Not until later. She wondered briefly what had become of the two Obsidian operatives who'd been upstairs. The news said nothing, so the men must have been well enough to get themselves out before the police got there. Aiden hadn't been so fortunate.

Another gust of wind ruffled her hair, but Tara stayed where she was, waiting for the announcers to give an update on the patient. To say whether he'd lived. Whether Aiden had lived.

They didn't. The story spun off toward the manhunt going on in a sleepy suburban town, with experts coming on to discuss the dangers of living next to houses up for sale, police response times, and—of course—the fugitive now being sought on two warrants.

Tara touched the documents in her pocket—useless at the moment as she couldn't go near a McDonald's restroom, much less an airport with everyone and their mother looking for her. No hotels either. She'd managed to find a store where the staff spoke no English and kept their televisions set on Spanish soap operas. A few hundred dollar bills got her basics, including a tarp and some blankets. Trash day in the rich neighborhood also provided a few discarded coats. But that was as close as she dared to go to civilization for now. Maybe for a long time still.

With three days since the shooting, the chances of the news returning to the John Doe who'd been MedFlighted was slim to none—yet Tara couldn't make herself stop coming out of the woods where she made camp to watch news in other people's living rooms.

The echo of a dog barking at the other end of the street snapped Tara away from the news. She could barely see the animal and its owner making their way down the night street, but she walked away quickly nonetheless. She felt numb. It had been like that for the past three days, absolute numbness interrupted by peaks of panic and valleys of being too chilled to think.

She'd just turned the corner when a group of less-than-sober young men stepped out from a party house onto the street, one of them running right into her. Tara's stomach plummeted, her heart jumping into a gallop. She was wanted. Hunted. She should never have gone to the street.

"Well, hello, missy." He made the *m* long, as if entertaining himself with the sound. "What's your name?"

Tara spun away from him and sprinted down the sidewalk.

"Awww, don't be like that!" one of the men—teens, really—called after her.

She ran faster, blood pumping hot. She didn't slow until she turned into the woods where she'd set up her shelter—a tarp on the ground and another for a roof cover—and slid into her sleeping bag. Curling up into a shaking ball, she pulled out a PowerBar and ate her dinner without tasting it.

She swallowed the last of the PowerBar and closed her eyes. She was alone. More alone than she'd ever been in her life. No friends, no Wilfred, no stray cat to keep her company. Even before Lucius had taken her off the streets, Tara at least had had those streets. Now she didn't.

It might not have been so bad had she not tasted love just so recently. Even in her short time with them, the Tridents felt like family. And Aiden... She'd fallen in love with him despite herself. Despite knowing that if he truly knew her, he'd kill her.

But being alone and scared, that wasn't the worst of it. Knowing that she'd betrayed Aiden in the worst of ways was. That, and not knowing whether he was still alive.

In the deeper parts of the woods, a coyote howled, and Tara felt its song vibrate through her. Coyotes weren't welcome around here. They ran unchecked and hunted small dogs who strayed too far from their owners. But at least they owned up to their nature and announced it to the night.

Shame choked her, making her eyes sting. The coyotes were better than her.

Swallowing, she drew a deep breath and found the last bit of her courage. She could never be good, could never erase the stain on her soul from six years past, but perhaps she could at least find enough honor left in herself to match the coyotes.

Before she could lose her resolve, Tara climbed out of her sleeping bag and gathered up what she could carry. The drive to

Denton Valley to Crows Landing had taken two hours. The walk back, moving by shadows and night, would take two days.

It was nearing dawn after the second night of travel when Tara reached her intended destination and knocked gingerly on a heavy door.

No answer.

Tara huddled down on the front steps of the North Vault and closed her eyes.

The first indication she had that she was no longer alone was the feel of a gun barrel pressed against her side. At any other time in her life, she would have seen it coming, but the truth was that she had no fight left. If someone wanted to shoot her and could spare the bullet, they were welcome to it.

Opening her eyes, Tara looked up toward the gorgeous harsh face that hovered above her. Briar or Cassey. She couldn't tell. But obviously, they had no trouble recognizing her. The man—whichever one it was—hauled Tara roughly to her feet and shoved her inside the empty club.

"What the hell are you doing here?" the second twin, who'd followed behind, asked. He turned to his brother. "What the hell is she doing here?"

Tara's jailer grunted.

Well, at least she knew who was who now.

"I thought you might be looking for me," she told Cassey, her voice shaking slightly. "I thought I'd save you the trouble."

"If you wanted to save me the trouble, you would have turned yourself in to the police," said Cassey.

Tara tried for a smile. "Didn't want to deprive you of your moment of vengeance." Her bravado faltered, then broke. "I wanted to know whether Aiden was all right before I got locked up. Or thrown in a ditch. Same difference."

"The latter's more efficient," said Cassey.

Tara shrugged, then nodded. "True." She closed her eyes, the plea coming in a whisper. "Aiden?"

Silence.

Her chest tightened.

"Alive," said Cassey.

Relief so powerful that Tara nearly lost her balance rushed through her. "Does he know about me? The whole truth, I mean."

"No."

She forced her chin up to meet Cassey's gray eyes. "You should tell him. Please. Tell him everything."

# 30

Aiden

"Are you in on it?" Aiden asked Dani without turning to look at her when she came into his hospital room. It was day five post-op, and Aiden knew full well that he should have been discharged by now—except someone was blocking it. While Ivy would usually be his first suspect, he read enough of the doc's body language to know she wasn't the culprit.

"In on what?" There was the sound of a chair being moved. "The plot to keep you caged?"

Aiden stiffened, but didn't turn away from the window. "So it's true."

Dani snorted. "That's my personal conclusion. Ivy is a terrible liar, and yesterday, it took her over an hour to finish your chart. I think she was changing *happy* to *glad* and back again the entire time to make sure everything was technically correct. Who do you think is behind it?"

"Liam," Aiden said without hesitation.

"Do you think he's right to do it?"

Aiden squeezed the ball that Addie, the physical therapist, had attached to the sling holding his arm. "Are you always in shrink mode?" He still couldn't see her, but in his periphery, the hospital room sprawled in all its glory. A Styrofoam cup with ice water and a plastic straw stood precariously on a kind of wheeled table that people who couldn't get out of bed used, and there was a constant smell of disinfectant and plastic everywhere. Yeah. He couldn't even pretend that he was just chatting with a foodie friend at a coffee shop.

"Aiden. McDane." Dani sounded like she had repeated his name several times. She probably had. He hadn't been listening.

"McDane." This time, his name sounded neither gentle nor the way Americans tended to pronounce it. "Snap out of the bloody pity party."

Aiden turned around to find Eli standing behind his wife.

The large Brit put his hands on Dani's shoulders. "And that, luv, is how one gets attention," he said in much kinder tones than he'd just used to bark at Aiden. Eli had the most easygoing temperament of the Tridents, but beneath that lay a steel-hard core and background as an instructor in the brutal course on surviving interrogation.

"I'm not having a pity party," said Aiden.

"Oh yes, you are. You've been partying hardcore there for a while now. And if you don't know it, you're a bloody idiot."

Dani touched her husband's wrist. "Maybe you could stop helping?"

"If you say so." Eli held up his hands in surrender. "I just stopped by to say I've checked in with my TSA contact again this morning. None of the departing flights took off with a woman matching Northpoint's description, though. So she's still on the continent, at least."

As Eli left, closing the door behind him, Aiden leaned against the wall. "He's right about the pity party, isn't he?"

"You're allowed," said Dani. "But I think that's wishful thinking. I don't think you're feeling sorry for yourself. From where I sit, it's more disorientation. It's how you act after an especially vivid dream, but magnified."

Now that he heard Dani say it, Aiden realized that she was right. Taking a chair, he turned it around and straddled it. "I called Ivy, Tara."

"You've told me. Ivy says hypoxia will do that."

"That's just it. I remember being confused and foggy. But later, when my limbs got strapped down, it wasn't foggy anymore. It was clear. Sight. Sounds. Everything."

"A flashback."

Aiden nodded. "Except Northpoint was in it. Which doesn't make any sense, but there it is. I feel my memories bubbling so close to the surface now, they're like an itch I can't quite reach." He took a breath, steeling himself. "What if we try to recreate the situation? Restrain me, cause a bit of discomfort." He tried to soften the notion for Dani's sake. "Trigger a flashback on purpose."

"Let me get this straight. You would like to get retraumatized in the most disturbing-to-you way possible in order to trigger a psychotic incident—all with the goal of recalling every detail of your torture?"

"I need to remember what happened," Aiden said.

"And you will. In a way that doesn't shatter your sanity." Dani held up a hand stopping Aiden's protest. "Aiden, it's been six years since some unknown bad guys captured and hurt you. It's been five days since the woman you fell in love with did the same. Forgive the bluntness, but from where I sit, this sudden need to resurrect Afghanistan at any cost seems more like a way to escape Colorado than anything else."

Aiden's mouth snapped closed. He didn't bother denying Dani's claim of his feelings for Tara. He did love her. Stupidly, blindly, deeply. There was no point in denying that to himself, and especially not to Dani, who knew it anyway. But that didn't mean he liked it. Hell, he fucking hated it. Hated how right Dani sounded. How much what she wanted him to do would hurt.

"I saw the way Tara looked at you when she thought no one was watching," Dani said gently. "And Eli told me what she did for you on the sparring mat. Whatever else, I don't believe her feelings for you were feigned."

"Because nothing says *I care* like a lead projectile to the lungs?"

"Sometimes people do things for reasons utterly unrelated to us," said Dani. "The reality is that we have no idea what spurred Tara's actions."

"We have a pretty damn good guess, though," said Cassey, walking into Aiden's room without bothering to knock. Briar, who strode quietly beside his twin, weighed Aiden with his gaze. The pair looked grimmer than Aiden remembered ever seeing them, but that didn't stop Cassey from grabbing the record of Aiden's vital signs and flipping through it. "How are you feeling?"

Aiden swallowed what he really wanted to say to his intrusive family. "Never better."

He didn't expand on the statement, hoping the silence would drive his well-meaning cousins out. Instead, Cassey and his mirror image looked at each other for several heartbeats until Briar nodded, as if answering some telepathic question from his twin.

Cassey put his hands into the pockets of his well-tailored suit. He was the only person Aiden knew who wore suits the way others did jeans. "The first time you met Tara Northpoint—"

"I was at the Rural Minnesota in Las Vegas," said Aiden. "We've been over this."

"The first time you met Tara Northpoint was six years ago in Afghanistan," said Cassey.

Aiden froze, waiting for the punch line of the very-not-funny joke.

Silence. Just the twins' eyes, boring into him.

"What the hell are you talking about?" Aiden said finally.

Briar closed the door and leaned against it. "I led the team that pulled you out of that shithole, McDane."

The world, which had been staying relatively put a few moments ago, shifted under Aiden's feet. He'd never learned how exactly he was extricated as neither his memories nor the documents he could get his hands on contained that information. He'd assumed it had been an American team since that was who Aiden's unit had come to train with, but his guesses ran toward SEALs. Either way, Americans were not forthcoming with classified documents, and at the end of the day, the identity of his mystery rescuers seemed less important than that of his captors.

Not that he'd been able to get to the bottom of either. Except… except the answer had been there all along. In his own family. Watching him.

The twins' intrusiveness now took on an entirely different note.

"Why?" Aiden demanded, his lip curling into a snarl. "You knew I was looking for answers."

Cassey opened his mouth, but Briar answered first. Hard and unapologetic. "I was the one who gave that order. You had no need to know. Nice to know and need to know aren't interchangeable."

Aiden was on his feet in a heartbeat, nose to nose with Briar. A snarl rose from Aiden's chest, the fury so palpable, it energized the air between them. "You want to try lecturing me again on who needs to know what?"

Briar struck Aiden's surgical site with the palm of his hand, sending Aiden into the seat of the chair behind him with a muffled scream. Pain shot through him, taking his breath, and, despite everything, all he could do for a few moments was rock through the agony until he could draw oxygen into his lungs again.

"Yeah," said Cassey with a good-natured shrug. "It's generally unwise to threaten him. Once you get your head on straight, though, the question you want to be asking is…?" He looked at Aiden expectantly, but all Aiden could see were stars and fury.

"What made you tell him now," said Dani. "That's the question we want to be asking."

"Very good," said Cassey.

Dani gave him a cool smile, then a cooler one to Briar. "Meanwhile, the question you want to be asking is how long you have until I call security and have you banned from Denton Valley Memorial for life." Her voice was sweeter than honey as she glanced at her wristwatch. "Three and a half minutes is fair, I think."

Briar's jaw tensed. Cassey snorted a laugh and toasted Dani with one of the stupid Styrofoam cups. Taking a sip of ice water, he frowned at the contents and dumped it back into the pitcher before pulling out a flask of something from the inside pocket of his jacket.

Pouring a splash of the amber liquid—whiskey by the smell of it—into the Styrofoam, he handed the cup to Aiden.

"Trust me, you'll want this." Cassey took a sip directly from his flask. "So, in answer to Dani's more relevant question, the reason we're having this conversation now is because Tara showed up at the North Vault this morning."

Aiden's hand closed around the Styrofoam so hard, the cup started to crack. He drank the whiskey before it spilled, the warm burn of it trickling along his throat. It was high-end stuff. "What did she want?" he asked.

"To turn herself in. We obliged." Cassey took another gulp from his flask, his face hardening. "We didn't know Obsidian was behind the interrogation until we smacked into Northpoint at the church. But now that we do, there will be a reckoning."

"Where is she now?" Aiden asked.

"Makeshift holding cell at the Vault," Cassey said.

Aiden drained the rest of the whiskey and crushed the cup in his fist. "I want to see her."

"You can't leave—" Dani started to say.

"Alone," Aiden added, an ice-cold darkness settling into his bones. "And I want the cameras turned off."

"Consider it done," said Briar.

# 31

## Aiden

Aiden pulled on the sweatpants and button-up shirt that Cassey and Briar had brought for him, letting the left sleeve hang over his sling. Thus dressed, he stalked out of the hospital room with purpose, leaving Dani and the nurses a choice between calling security and getting the hell out of his way. Fortunately, they chose the latter.

The twins followed Aiden out. They flanked him on either side until they got to the car. Cassey slid silently behind the wheel. They said nothing during the drive to the North Vault, which was locked up as usual for this time of morning.

But there was nothing usual about it at all.

Cassey pulled the keys to the club from his pocket and tossed them to Aiden, who caught them with his good hand.

"All yours," Cassey said, making it clear that they were not going to follow him in.

Aiden got out without thanking them. Walked to the door. Let himself inside and closed the dead bolt behind him. The North Vault looked strangely empty. No dancers on pedestals, no Cassey at the piano, no bartender in front of LED-lit rows of top-shelf liquor. Even chairs had been turned up onto the tables to allow for cleaning.

But the music was on. The volume turned up.

It didn't take long to find the back corner where they had stashed their captive, a small, faint light giving away her location behind a visual barricade of moved furniture. Aiden was numb as he walked between the tables to…her. He couldn't make himself say Tara's name even in his head.

She was sitting on the floor, the twins having somehow rigged two sets of chained shackles to attach each of her wrists to the wall. Aiden didn't want to think about whether they had such supplies on hand or obtained them that morning, but he had a damn good guess as to why they positioned Tara that way specifically. His own wrists and his shoulders and back all cramped in distant memory.

As he walked closer, he noticed a chalked line on the floor. A demarcation of how far the restraints let Tara move about. He stopped two steps short of the chalk.

Tara looked terrible. Stripped to pants and a wet short-sleeved shirt, she sat with her head down, her hair matted and her arms covered with scratches that spoke of trekking through the woods. Where the shackles bit into her wrists, however, the skin was rubbed raw and bloody. The twins hadn't been gentle when they cuffed her.

"Look up," Aiden ordered.

She did. Her face was scraped up with the same patterns as her arms, her full lips cracked and bleeding. She was cold, and her body shivered beneath the thin wet shirt. As Aiden's gaze moved about her face, he realized that he'd managed to look her over without ever looking into her eyes. He did so now, finding them dull with a mix of discomfort and resignation. And shame.

They weren't the kind of eyes he remembered Tara having, but certainly the kind she deserved. After a few moments of silence, she shifted her gaze back to the floor.

Aiden thought that he'd know what to say once he saw her, but he couldn't think over the roaring in his head. So he started with the irrelevant basics.

"When did you first know who I was?" he demanded.

Her answer started softly, and he interrupted her.

"Louder, Northpoint."

Tara nodded and started over in a louder voice. "You looked familiar at the Rural Minnesota. The more time we spent together, the more certain I became. Both of who you were and of the fact that you didn't remember it."

"So it's true. All of it."

"Yes."

"Why?" he asked.

She shrugged.

"That's not an answer!"

She flinched at his shout. "It was a job," she said, as if that explained everything. "I don't remember who hired the Obsidian team—the client wasn't important to me at the time. It was someone who cared about details of the Scottish special forces, and you were a target of convenience."

Convenient for them. It hadn't been very convenient for him. "Who else was there? How many of you?"

"Four. Giovanni Welch led the team. I was…extra."

Four people. Yes, that sounded strangely right.

"What did you do to be allowed to come?" Aiden asked. His voice was wooden.

Tara's face jerked up. "I wasn't *allowed*, I was ordered. I'd just turned eighteen, and there was a wet work requirement to fulfill. It helps Obsidian keep control of the operatives."

Aiden pulled off his sling and then his shirt, leaving his upper body bare. "Which of these marks are you responsible for?" he asked quietly. In the silence that followed, he realized he was holding his breath. Holding on to hope that Tara would say "none," would tell him she was nothing but an observer, an unwilling prisoner in all but name.

She pointed to Aiden's bicep. "The star-shaped scar. I left that."

It felt like she'd punched him. "How?"

"Don't make me describe it." For the first time since he'd entered, pleading entered Tara's voice. "Please."

"You did it. You'll survive saying it aloud."

She closed her eyes. "It's a burn. From heated metal."

Aiden's throat closed, phantom pain rushing over him. "Did I scream?"

"Stop it," Tara shouted at him. "What good is this doing anyone?"

"Did I scream?" he yelled.

"Yes!" She shook. "Yes, you screamed. And I didn't stop. Is that what you wanted to hear, Aiden? Does that make you feel better? Do you want me to describe other details? What it smelled like? Felt like?"

Bile rose up Aiden's throat. He couldn't move. Couldn't breathe. For so, so long he'd wanted nothing more than to find the people who'd hurt him and hurt them back. Make them scream as he knew they'd made him. Worse. And now that he had one of them in his grasp, it was Tara.

Aiden twisted around and spotted a metal, wall-mounted first aid kit hanging near the supply closet. Yanking open the cover, Aiden pulled out the bottle of alcohol inside. He opened it with his teeth and spit out the top. Walking back to Tara, he crossed over the chalk line on the floor and ruthlessly emptied the clear liquid over her shackles, where it would burn the open raw wounds.

Tara gasped, struggling to bite back the pain and jerk her hands away from the stream, but it was futile. Aiden didn't let her get away, didn't slow dousing the broken skin until her breaths came in desperate gasps of pain and the tears that she'd worked so, so hard to control streamed down her cheeks.

Then he waited for the satisfaction. For the scratching of that itch that had been clawing at him for six years. Waited for his body to say, *yes, yes, this is what we wanted. This is our moment. Our justice. And it's just starting.*

Nothing. Not one bloody ounce of satisfaction. The vengeance he'd waited for so many years was now here, and with it...with it came nothing. No prize, no scratched itch, no peace. Nothing but heartbreaking knowledge that it was Tara who'd hurt him, Tara who was trying and failing to stanch her tears of pain.

Fury spilled into his blood at the injustice of it. Spinning about, he punched the wall, putting his fist right through the plaster. Again. And again. And again. It wasn't fair. This was supposed to help and it didn't.

Looking down at his split knuckles, Aiden picked up the discarded alcohol bottle and used what remained to douse his own skin. It hurt. But at least that hurt was better than the one ripping his soul.

Aiden grabbed a chair and set it just outside the chalk line on the floor, outside their reach of each other, "Start at the beginning," he ordered Tara. "And tell me everything."

# 32

## Tara

Tara's gaze, which had been gripping a small crack right at the corner baseboard, slowly slid up to Aiden's face. His ghost-filled eyes stared at her expectantly, his face gray, his good arm dripping blood from split knuckles onto the floor. She was the one chained to the wall, yet the hell saturating the air around them belonged to him.

Tara had been little surprised by the twins chaining her up and dousing her shirt with water. And, though the alcohol had burned like lava, frankly, Aiden's outburst with antiseptic had been child's play compared to what Obsidian—what she—had done to him. Tara had expected all that and more, was ready to accept whatever the twins and Aiden wished to dole out. Deserved it. Hell, a part of her welcomed the moments of physical pain, for they drowned out the much louder hurt inside her soul.

But what Aiden was asking her, to give him a play-by-play of the interrogation, that she wasn't prepared to indulge. "An Obsidian team captured you in an ambush," she said. "We interrogated you.

You resisted. Didn't even give us your true name. We put you through hell, but you never broke."

"I asked for *everything*. From the beginning."

Tara shook her head. "No."

"Look around. You aren't in a position to negotiate. Or to risk anyone's fury."

"But I am." Tara shifted from one uncomfortable position to another. Her muscles were already cramping, but for the first time since seeing Aiden being loaded into the medevac helicopter, she tasted the possibility of doing something positive for the world. For Aiden. It made her blood run faster, her heart beat with more life and passion. "I can't stop you from hurting me, Aiden. I won't even try. I can't do much to stop you from hurting yourself either. But refusing to hurt you? That's still in my power."

He snorted without humor. "That ship sailed six years. All I want now is—"

"Is to relive every goddamn moment of torture." Energy she never thought she'd feel again seeped back into Tara's body as she felt the roots of something she'd started six years ago grip the soil. "No go, McDane. I know that look that's in your eyes. You want the details so you can savor the agony. Use it to drown out this new hurt." She almost snorted. Pot meet kettle. "Too bad. I'm not helping you shred yourself apart. Once was more than enough for my taste."

"Who died and made you God?" Aiden's upper lip curled in a snarl. "You don't get to decide what's good for me."

"You aren't doing a great job at it either just now," Tara shot back, feeling the ghostly déjà vu of the conversation. They'd already discussed this point. Six years ago. And they'd disagreed back then just as much as they did now. But some things, Tara never regretted. "There is nothing from your time in that cave that you need to relive."

Aiden's hands tightened on the back of the chair, and Tara braced herself in case he decided to strike. Her heart broke for him, for the wounds that he'd suffered, which went deeper than the scars on his flesh. If hurting her would be a balm for his frayed soul, he was welcome to it. But she feared it would not be so easy. Not for Aiden.

Drawing herself up into a kneeling position, Tara raised her chin and pulled back her shoulders, though it made the large bruise along her side ache. "Why don't we call Dani and see what she thinks?"

Aiden stared at her, his fists tightening and loosening and tightening again. "This isn't Dani's decision. And I don't want her opinion."

"But I do," Tara said evenly and jerked her head toward Aiden's fists, which were clenched once again. "I guess the question is how far are you willing to go to get me to talk whether I want to or not."

Aiden cursed, his hands rising, then dropping. "Were you always going to run?" he asked.

"No." She paused. "At first, yes. That was the plan. But once we made a deal, I had every intention of honoring it—until Cassey and Briar recognized me."

"Why didn't you tell me the truth?"

She laughed without humor. "Because I wasn't suicidal. You did tell me that one of your greatest wishes was to find and kill the people who'd hurt you."

He made that Scottish sound in the back of his throat. "Walking into the twins' lair was not a decision most compatible with a comfortable life."

"It was." Tara's face softened. "I thought I could live with everything that happened, to run and never look back, but I was wrong. Going to them was the only way forward…even if it's going to be a rather short way." Trial. Sentencing. Prison. It still frightened the hell out of her, but it no longer sounded unbearable.

Aiden turned his head, and Tara wished she could read his thoughts as he stared into nothingness.

"I didn't know you were at Crows Landing," she said, in case that mattered to him. "Katie May got hit with what was probably a stray shot. We thought we were under assault."

"You were," said Aiden.

She nodded in appreciation. "I was sending cover fire into the darkness. I saw a shape, nothing more." She wondered if he believed her, and the knowledge that he might not hurt.

Aiden didn't answer. He was staring into nothingness again. Walking in his own world. She wished she could reach out and touch him just one more time. To feel the rise and fall of his wide chest, and listen to his steady heartbeat, and bask in the warmth seeping from him. When Aiden's gaze finally refocused, it was on Tara's shirt.

"Why are you wet?" he asked.

"I presume the intention was to make me cold." She kept the answer matter-of-fact.

"Was it successful?"

"Yes."

Aiden stepped back to the first aid kit on the wall and returned with a pair of trauma shears. He hesitated only a moment before crossing the chalked line on the floor, then crouched beside her and cut the soggy fabric off completely. He tossed the rags aside, then froze, leaning forward toward the expanse of blue and black and purple that spanned Tara's entire left side and spilled slightly into her back and belly.

"Is this from the twins?" he asked.

"No. That was me tripping over a tree root that had no business existing," Tara said. "I couldn't exactly Uber from Crows Landing, and I moved by night." It was the truth. The twins had done nothing but shackle her and douse her shirt with water. A clean canvas for Aiden to do with as he pleased. From the way Aiden nodded, he'd come to the same conclusion.

The question was, what did he want to do?

Leaning forward, he brushed the tips of his fingers gently along Tara's bruised skin. The pads of his fingers were warm and callused, and the touch sent ripples of comfort along her nerves. Aiden's clean scent filled Tara's lungs.

"Does it still hurt?" His whisper tickled against her cheek.

"Not too badly. It looks worse than it feels."

Aiden's palm flattened soothingly over her ribs. "I'm glad."

Tara hung on to those words like a lifeline as Aiden rose

smoothly to his feet. Grabbing his discarded shirt, he laid it over Tara's bare shoulders. It was big and warm and dry. And it still had his scent.

Aiden nodded to something only he knew, then turned on his heel and walked away without saying goodbye.

# 33

## Aiden

Aiden sat behind the computer in his Trident Security office and tried to remember why he'd ever considered being grounded for a few days to be a punitive measure. Finishing another review that kept Trident Security running, he moved on to checking the roster for Search and Rescue. That was usually Jaz's domain, which he didn't stick his fingers into unless he wanted them snapped off, but she'd been feeling exceedingly tired the past couple of days, and Liam had asked him to pick up the reins.

It made sense. Aiden had experience running Trident Security as Liam's relief and had done so before, while Liam was away helping Jaz. Now, with his body still healing from the surgery, Aiden wasn't good for much in the field. Really, it had been only a matter of time before he got dragged back into the executive suite to help run the company.

Aiden checked the schedule. How long had he been in the office? Three days. With the phone ringing every five minutes, it felt like longer. But Jaz was still laid up and Liam neck-deep in the trial that would start tomorrow. The one where Tara—*no.* Aiden caught his thoughts gravitating toward her and redirected himself back to the rescue roster.

Keeping himself from thinking about Tara was taking up major cognitive bandwidth since everything and anything could send his mind down that rabbit hole. Knowledge that they were currently in the same building—him in the exec suite upstairs and her in the basement holding area. The scent of a flowery hand soap Liam's accountant left in the bathroom. A pop-up ad for a product that started with the letter *T*.

Aiden hoped it would get easier with time.

The phone rang.

"Front office. McDane.'

"Good morning. This is Joe from facilities. I wanted to let you know that the garage door is malfunctioning again and I've put in an order for the manufacturer to come check it. If we could keep the car traffic—"

"I'll send out an all-office notice." Aiden checked his watch for the date. "That was installed with the last upgrade and should be under warranty."

"Yes, sir. I'll remind them." Joe hung up.

Aiden reopened the timed-out browser window with the Search and Rescue schedule. They were three-people deep tomorrow. If he could—

*Ring.*

"Mr. McDane, it's Joe again. I forgot to mention—I was hoping to set up a couple of hours with you to talk about the new security upgrade proposal."

"Can that wait for Liam?" Aiden asked.

"Well, that's just it, sir, he's been so busy, and the executive assistant he's been sending me to doesn't have decision-making authority. So I was hoping to knock this out while you're here and take it off everyone's plate."

Right. It was one of those projects that wasn't urgent enough to drop everything and run to, but also had the unfortunate quality of needing to get done and refusing to go away on its own. "Aye. We can go over the plans on—"

The light for *Incoming Call* flashed on the phone. Aiden put Joe on hold and pressed it. "What?"

"McDane?" Liam's voice came over the line.

Aiden winced and rubbed his temple. "Aye. Sorry about that."

"Never mind. Jaz's water just broke." Liam's usually stone-gripped control seemed to slip for a moment as the man drew a shaking breath. They were at twenty-nine weeks. Preterm.

Aiden's chest tightened. How viable for a twenty-nine-week-old preemie? He had no idea. No idea how to make this better either.

"We're en route to the ER." Liam continued. "I need you to hold down the fort."

"Goes without saying."

"The trial. You were there for all the debriefs and … I'm sorry, I know Tara is a sore—"

"It's not a problem," Aiden said firmly. "Take care of Jaz and the twins. I'll keep the lights on here."

"Fuck electricity," Liam told him. "If you can keep Cassey and Sonia from ripping each other's throat out and eating them raw, we'll consider it a victory."

"Roger. Curtail cannibalism." Aiden's hand tightened around the receiver. "We'll make it through, Liam. Just take care of Jaz and the wee ones. Call me when you can."

AN HOUR LATER, sitting in the final trial prep with Cassey and Sonia Dancer, Aiden was worried that he'd overpromised Liam on the no-cannibalism front.

Cassey, as comfortable as Sonia seemed to not be, pressed his palm on the polished table and leaned forward. "Which part of *follow the case strategy* are you having trouble with, Counselor?"

"The part where everything our strategy is based on has changed. Tara can't testify, and our whole plan rests on her doing just that to implicate Obsidian Ops leadership in the bombing of the research facility."

"Tara can and will testify. I haven't cut out the woman's tongue."

"You chained her to a wall!"

"And she's welcome to file assault charges. But that's not the matter on fucking trial."

"The state tore up her immunity agreement. Anything she says in Denver Research vs Obsidian Ops trial can be used against her later. She would be testifying against her own self-interest." Sonia's voice rose another decibel. "Putting her on the stand like that would be unethical."

"You know what else is unethical? Murder and torture." Cassey's hand tightened into a fist. "If your horse were any higher, we could ask you the goddamn weather." Despite Cassey's military background, the man was not prone to swearing, especially around women—Sonia being the clear exception. "Couple that wonderful quality with your lack of anything resembling real-world experience, and we have the goat-rope stew we're currently wallowing in."

Sonia half rose from her seat, her pencil skirt hugging her legs. "Is there a reason you think I'm going to take legal advice from some vigilante who thinks the Geneva Convention is a suggestion? I think it would be better for all if you didn't second chair this trial."

"Wait," Aiden interrupted. "I didn't think you were barred in Colorado."

Cassey spared him a glance. "It's a universal bar state. I got my bar license paperwork over the weekend. Keep up."

Over the weekend? Of course he did… The bastard had a photographic memory. And was clearly winding up for another go at Sonia.

Aiden put out his hands and stopped both combatants in their tracks. "Let me make sure I have everything straight. Tomorrow, Trident Security, on behalf of Denver Research, is going against Obsidian Ops in court. Our strategy has been based around using Tara describing Obsidian's role in the event." Aiden channeled all his focus on the conference room drama and somehow managed to say her name without stumbling. "Except her testimony was to be in exchange for immunity, and the state no longer will give her immunity. Without Tara's testimony, we have no case. Correct so far?"

Both attorneys nodded, which was probably their first agreement since early morning.

"And Tara is still willing to testify?" Aiden asked. That question hurt because he didn't know the answer himself. Didn't know anything about what had happened to her after he walked out of the North Vault.

"Yes," Cassey said.

"And we need to advise her not to," said Sonia. "Trident Security committed to assisting with Tara's criminal defense."

"In *exchange for her testimony*." Cassey rubbed his massive hand over his face. "Attempting to flee the country and nearly killing Aiden put a kink in the fucking defense plan. Start reading the room, Counselor."

Sonia's face darkened. "Yes, let me follow your lead. Instead of treating witnesses like human beings, I too can start kidnapping them and chaining them to walls. And—*and*—I can also get into the habit of not sharing this information with the lead attorney until the day before trial."

"Maybe you should read up on the definition of kidnapping. Everyone was doing you a favor, Dancer, because you're clearly unable to—"

"Enough." Aiden raised his voice, bringing the room to tense silence. He didn't know what Liam had been thinking when he brought Cassey into the legal team or disclosing to Sonia that the twins had recreated Afghanistan in their club for a few hours, but Aiden couldn't go and ask his boss that just now. "The person testifying—or not—is Tara herself. I want to hear from her."

It was a lie. He didn't *want* to hear from her at all, not after a week of fighting off thoughts of her that kept intruding into his mind. But he did need to know Tara's intentions. They all did. Picking up the conference room phone, Aiden asked security to bring Tara up, then leaned back in his chair to feign nonchalance.

Tara was in a set of dark green scrubs when security brought her up. Scrubs, slip-on shoes without laces, and handcuffs. Security paused at the entrance to the conference room, plainly unsure how to proceed and looking to Aiden for direction. After a week of training himself to live without Tara invading his thoughts, Aiden had hoped he'd be clearheaded now. Instead, it took all his willpower to keep from getting to his feet and running his hands all over her body just to reassure himself she was all right.

"Sir?" one of the guards prompted.

"Change her cuffs from back to front, but leave them on," Aiden said briskly. He considered offering her a chair, but dismissed the thought. She wasn't part of the team any longer.

"The wrongful death trial between Denver Research and Obsidian Ops starts tomorrow," Aiden said without preamble. "Once that's done, the state of Colorado will go forward with the criminal charges against you personally. My understanding from the attorneys is that the blanket immunity you were going to receive in exchange for your testimony tomorrow is no longer on the table."

"That's my understanding as well," Tara answered as if they were having a casual conversation. Aiden didn't think he would have been as strong if their roles were reversed. He simultaneously bowed down to Tara's toughness and hated Obsidian for forcing her into that state.

"Despite the lack of blanket immunity, Colorado State and the court both may extend leniency for your situation if you testify," Cassey put in. "Trident Security's memorandum of understanding with the state also allows you to continue to be held in our custody instead of hoteling in jail."

"*Or,* you may end up saying something on the stand that gets you deeper in trouble," Sonia added immediately. "Anything that comes up in that courtroom will be on record. It can be used against you later."

Making Tara collateral damage in the fight between Trident Security and Obsidian Ops.

"What do you want to do?" Aiden asked, meeting Tara's eyes only to find himself shut out from her thoughts completely.

"The truth hasn't changed." Tara spoke over Aiden's head to the two attorneys. "I'm ready to proceed with the original plan. If there's nothing else you need from me, could I be returned to my holding cell?"

Silence reigned as security walked Tara back out of the room, then lay thickly in the air until Cassey pushed himself back on his rolling chair. "Well," he said, taking a sip of water as if it were a fine wine, "at least someone here has a level head."

# 34

## Aiden

The following morning, Aiden walked into the courtroom to find it already filled. He was wearing a suit and a freshly pressed shirt that he'd managed to iron one-handed despite the acrobatics involved with his still-healing left side. Tying his shoes had actually been worse.

Maybe it all just felt more difficult for the lack of sleep. Aiden hadn't rested peacefully since Tara left, and seeing her briefly yesterday hadn't done his subconscious any favors. He tried to remember whether sleep had been this difficult before, but wasn't sure. Either way, it was miserable now, and he needed to find a way of dealing with it.

After seeing Tara yesterday, Aiden had given up the plan of banishing her from his conscious thoughts. Not only was that unlikely to succeed, but he owed Liam better than that. Obsidian had been creating problems for years, and this was the first time they'd been able to pin them down in court. Aiden had to have his mind in the game, his whole mind. Tara included.

Now, standing at the courtroom entrance, Aiden took stock of the battlefield. A somber gravitas was built into every inch of the chamber, from the heavy polished wood paneling on the walls to the chandelier that weighed more than a man could carry. Together with the ghosts of freedoms taken and granted by the powers that exercised here, even the air had a formality to it. No matter how many times Aiden walked into a court to escort witnesses or, in rare cases, provide testimony, he felt the zinging power of the room go through him each time.

This time, however, it was different. He wasn't here to be a spectator or witness, he was here in Liam's place and needed to comport himself as such.

Aiden checked his phone one final time before turning it to mute. Jaz had delivered the twins at two in the morning by cesarean section, and the babies—twin boys—were now in NICU. Liam was a mess, and Ivy was keeping the group updated from the hospital.

Aiden was to do the same from the courtroom.

Pocketing his phone, he strode down the aisle to sit with Briar right behind the plaintiff's table. Mr. Williams, the director of Denver Research, was already there, while Cassey and Sonia were readying for the trial. At least Sonia was. While Liam's young, aggressive attorney wrote furiously in her notepad, Cassey entertained himself by balancing his chair on its hind legs.

At the defense table, two broad-shouldered men in pinstripe suits spoke quietly with each other. The shorter man with neatly trimmed goatee appeared to be Obsidian's attorney, while the man beside him— a bushy-browed bloke who might once have been in shape but had put on a paunch since—sat beside him with an unconcerned expression.

Aiden looked around for Tara, his stomach tightening when he didn't see her.

Catching his gaze, Cassey pointed to the door. Right. As a

witness, she wouldn't be called into the court until it was time for her testimony.

"Am I that easy to read?" Aiden asked, striving for a good-natured tone.

"Easier," said Cassey.

Briar snorted.

Sonia gave Cassey a look that could burn down a forest.

"All rise." The bailiff fortunately chose that moment to call the room to order, curtailing whatever sparring match the two Trident attorneys could get into before proceedings started.

As the judge walked out of her chamber and ascended her bench, the black robes waving about her, Aiden watched the men at Obsidian's table for any sign of emotion. He had no doubt at least some of the court officials were on their payroll, but no idea who or how deeply. Unfortunately, the men proved too professional to show any reaction.

"You may be seated. The matter before the court today is Denver Research Group versus Obsidian Operational Security Corporation," the judge said in the same tone one might read a shopping list. "Denver Research alleges that Obsidian Ops did knowingly run an operation targeting a facility located in Denver, Colorado, and that, as a result of this operation, three Denver Research employees perished and a computer with data valued at over five million dollars disappeared. Are both sides ready to proceed?"

"Yes, Your Honor." Sonia's clear voice rang out through the courtroom.

"The defense is ready, Your Honor," the goateed man on the other side agreed. Aiden had correctly pinned him as the attorney.

"Enter your names for the record," the judge instructed.

"Sonia Dancer, on behalf of Denver Research Group." She waited, looking at Cassey, who—as Aiden could see from his seat in the front row—was busy filling in a crossword puzzle. "I'm being second chaired by Cassey McKenzie," Sonia added quickly.

"Harry Gardener, on behalf of Obsidian Operations," said the goatee man. "Before we continue, the defense would like to submit its objection to opposing counsel."

The judge blinked. "You're objecting to names being entered into the record?"

"No, ma'am. We're objecting to the opposing counsel themselves. What Ms. Dancer failed to mention was that she collects a paycheck from Trident Security, a business competitor to Obsidian Ops. She's here attempting to litigate a competitive advantage, not represent her client's best interests."

Sonia jumped in the moment Gardener stopped for breath and quickly recited no fewer than three similar instances that had appeared before the same judge that were allowed to proceed. The ruling came down in Sonia's favor, leaving Aiden thoroughly impressed.

Cassey drew a caricature of Sonia talking and the entire courtroom snoring asleep. *Could have just asked Williams if he's satisfied with his counsel and ended this in two minutes instead of ten,* he wrote.

Sonia ignored him, reminding Aiden that discretion was the better part of valor.

"If both sides are ready, we'll proceed with opening arguments," the judge instructed, nodding to Sonia.

"Thank you, Your Honor." Sonia rose from behind her table and strode onto the main floor, her heels making a *click click click* sound against the courtroom's polished wood.

"Two months ago, an explosion at the Denver Research facility killed three employees, damaged valuable equipment, and facilitated the theft of over five million dollars of research. This explosion wasn't an accident, but part of an organized assault perpetuated by Obsidian Ops on behalf of a client. This isn't a theory. It's a fact. Today in this courtroom, you will hear directly from one of the two operatives who were there on Obsidian's orders. She will tell you about the explosive device she was ordered to build, about the Obsidian plan, and about what happened when that plan went very, very wrong." Details followed, with Sonia passionately and clearly outlining the case, but Aiden's mind snagged on the opening words.

Tara had been under orders to plant a bomb. Not new

information by any means, but now Aiden couldn't help but wonder how the hell did big-hearted Tara, who couldn't let a vicious stray cat be left behind, come to get orders from a group that tortured and killed to get their way. Either he was wrong about how that heart of hers functioned or he knew too little about the roads that had led her here. Or perhaps he did know, but just couldn't remember.

Sonia rounded off her opening by thanking the court and turned the floor over to Harry Gardener.

The man rose, took a moment to do up a suit button, then looked up into the silence. "Your Honor, thank you for granting us your time and consideration today. I only wish it was spent on more substantive matters. As you will shortly hear, the so-called facts my sister counsel refers to are nothing but the wishful fancies of a woman who had nothing to do with Obsidian Ops. A woman who likes making bombs. A woman—a murderer—desperate to do anything, even lie, to escape the punishment she justly deserves."

A second blanket of silence settled over the court, this one buzzing with questions about the defense's battle plan, which boiled down to a simple assertion that Tara was a liar, killer, and vigilante. Aiden felt a shiver run through him. Tara hadn't blown up a building of her own volition. And while she was many things, she wasn't a murderer.

*Not a murderer, only a torturer. Not a liar, only a betrayer. No splitting hairs here. Not one bit.*

Sonia called Wilson, the director of Denver Research, to the stand first. Wilson's testimony was to set the stage, which he did with compassionate efficiency. At 3:00 a.m. on the date in question, he explained, an explosion shook the entrance to the building, ending the lives of three security guards who'd been gathered there. Once the building was secure, a server with proprietary data was found missing from the fifth-floor lab, and there was evidence of forced entry through the lab window.

"Are you aware who specifically came into your facility?" Sonia asked.

"Yes," said Wilson. "One of the security cameras managed to capture the images of two people."

A large screen lit up with photographs .

"That's them," Wilson confirmed. "Tara Northpoint and Raymond Brushings, both operatives of Obsidian Operational Security Corporation."

Gardener waited for Sonia to sit down, then approached the witness stand. "I'm sorry for your loss, Mr. Wilson," he said solemnly. "Tell me, how long have you been employed by Obsidian Ops?"

"Me? What?" Wilson sat up straighter, his belly jiggling. "I'm not, and never have been, employed by those people."

"My apologies," said Gardener. "But you do have access to their HR files? Payroll? Other records?"

"No, of course not."

"I see. So then, you found some kind of identifying signage that was left behind identifying the intruders as Obsidian Ops."

"No."

"I'm confused, Mr. Wilson. How exactly do you know whether Ms. Northpoint or Mr. Brushings were employed by Obsidian?" Gardener asked.

"I…" Wilson cleared his throat. "I was told as much. By… professionals in the security field."

"You were told as much by Trident Security, who offered to represent you pro bono, isn't that right, Mr. Wilson?" Gardener demanded. "By a company in direct competition with Obsidian."

Wilson shifted in his seat. "I don't recall exactly. I'm sure we discussed it, but I don't recall when I first found out."

"Of course," Gardener agreed. "Thank you for your time, sir."

Aiden didn't need to be an attorney to know that hadn't gone well, though the only sign Sonia gave of her disappointment was a tap of a pen on the table. Cassey was still at crossword puzzles to the point that Aiden was #TeamSonia about strangling the bastard.

Sonia called a small slew of experts to the stand next. An explosives expert who established the blast radius of the ordnance, a first responder to describe the scene, a forensics expert to establish the deaths were caused by the bomb. Gardener had minimal questions for these witnesses with the exception of the forensics expert.

"How many victims were identified in total?" Gardener asked.

"Given the lack of intact bodies, we made identification based on remains. There were four individuals identified. The three Denver Research employees plus a fourth that we matched through vital records to Raymond Brushings."

"We have evidence of two people entering the facility, Ms. Northpoint and Mr. Brushings, is that right?"

The expert nodded. "It is."

"And did you find any evidence of suicidal intent by Mr. Brushings? A note, a manifesto, a video of intentions or demands? Anything at all to suggest that he intended to kill himself?"

"Mr. Gardener, we had to identify people by dental records. I don't imagine a note, if it existed, would have survived."

The attorney took a step toward the witness stand. "I'll take that as a no. In fact, you found no evidence of suicidal intent at all, did you?"

"Not as such, no."

"So let me make sure I have the facts straight. Five people were in the building. Four of them died. And no one committed suicide. That's what the evidence shows, isn't it?"

"Well—"

"Is that what the evidence shows?" Gardener pressed.

Aiden ground his jaw. Tara had said she was certain that Ray had made it out of the building alive, the evidence of his death having been planted by Obsidian's cover-up. But even in the absence of that, Gardener was warping the situation with his play on words.

"Is it?" Gardener repeated, making the expert flinch.

"I suppose."

"No further questions," said Gardener, returning to his table, where he conferred with his satisfied-looking client.

"If you have some brilliance to conjure, now would be the time to do it." Sonia said quietly to Casey. "Tara is next, and she's our final witness."

Cassey made a doodle on the side of his crossword. "Nope. You're doing just fine."

Aiden took a calming breath. "Is there any way of proving that Ray didn't die?" he asked.

"No," said Sonia. "Obsidian planted enough evidence in the debris to make it believable. Provided Tara is telling the truth."

Aiden wanted so badly to say that she was, but could not. "What about the stolen computer from the fifth floor? The millions of dollars of lost research. Where did it go if not out with Ray?"

"It was five million dollars of research in a suddenly unsecured building," said Sonia. "There are a number of ways it technically could have walked out the door."

"So this case is going to live or die by Tara's testimony," said Aiden.

Cassey snorted, finally contributing to the conversation. "Now you're getting it."

At the defense table, Gardner and Welch put their heads together. Then the defense attorney rose to request a brief recess.

"Fifteen minutes, Mr. Gardner." The judge turned to Sonia. "Who do you intend to call next?"

"Tara Northpoint, Your Honor. She is the plaintiff's final witness."

"Very well." The fall of the judge's gavel sounded as loud and final as a gunshot.

# 35

## Tara

Bending over the sink at the courthouse bathroom, Tara splashed cold water onto her face in an attempt to slow her racing pulse. She'd been about to walk into the courtroom to testify when the bailiff put an arm out to block her path.

"Fifteen-minute recess. I wouldn't stand here when the doors open in a moment and there's a stampede of people rushing out to check their phones."

Fifteen minutes? Tara wasn't sure she could survive that long without her gut exploding from anxiety. With no immunity deal, she was about to send herself to prison with her own words. Though she thought she was prepared for this, now that the moment had come, fear coursed through her veins. She closed her eyes and willed herself to breathe.

"You're wasting the little present I gave you." A Texan voice from Tara's past cut through her battle for equilibrium.

Opening her eyes, Tara saw the reflection of Gio Welch staring back at her through the chipped mirror. Though Welch was dressed in a suit for court, cowboy boots peeked out from beneath the expensive Italian trousers. For a second, Tara wondered if she'd accidently walked into the wrong bathroom, but then reality set in. This run-in wasn't an accident. And neither was the sudden recess.

Tara straightened. The last time she'd seen Gio Welch was two years ago, at a ceremony that had honored his promotion to leading Obsidian's Pacific branch. They hadn't spoken then. Just as they hadn't spoken on any other occasion their paths had crossed since Afghanistan. What the hell was he doing here now?

"I'm here on behalf of Obsidian Ops," he said, as if reading her mind. "We always have an exec sit in on these little charades." Translation: *I'm a pro at this. I'm not worried.* "You, on the other hand, would be wise to go out that corner window. Fifteen minutes is not a lot of time." He looked at his Rolex. "Thirteen now."

Tara raised her chin. "Why would I do that?"

"Because you aren't suicidal. Did that kindergartener of a lawyer not tell you that your immunity deal is gone? Gardener is going to shake off any whiff of wrongdoing, but for you… Every word out of your mouth today is going to be used against you. A ticket to—"

"Prison," Tara finished for him, making her voice sound bored.

"Prison?" Welch laughed without humor. "Oh, now, I had the pleasure of talking with the state prosecutor earlier today. You won't be facing life in prison when it's your turn on trial—they're going for the death penalty."

He was lying. Tara's gut churned. It was the kind of thing Welch would do. "There's no death penalty in Colorado."

"True. But because the bomb materials were traced to Texas, we can try the case there. And they do have the death penalty—or so my friends in the Texas State court tell me. If you don't believe me, it's your own time you're wasting." Reaching into his inside suit pocket, Welch pulled out a sheet of paper and handed it to Tara over her shoulder. She had to read it twice to understand what it meant. A memo from the prosecutor asking for exactly what Welch claimed. A venue transfer to Texas. A death penalty recommendation. "It's in draft form, so it may not have gotten to that kindergarten lawyer Trident has on the case. Or maybe it did, and Trident Security chose not to tell you."

Bile crawled up Tara's throat. She didn't think Sonia would keep something like that from her, but Cassey was on the team now too.

"It's your life, little stray," said Welch. "Or death."

"Some of us seem to be in the wrong room." The last person Tara had expected to see today strode inside and nonchalantly braced his hip against the sink, as if he made a regular habit of touring women's restrooms.

Aiden.

What the hell was Aiden doing here? They hadn't spoken since he'd walked out on her in the North Vault, not even yesterday when he'd finally come to a prep session. He hadn't so much as looked at her, leaving the lawyers to do the questioning. None of the others would tell her anything about him, giving nonresponses when she'd asked directly. As it was, Tara had no idea whether she was hated or forgiven, accepted or discarded.

And yet here he was. And despite herself, Tara couldn't help but catalog every detail of his presence. He was in a well-cut suit and fresh shaven, his strong jaw still smooth from the razor and smelling of an ocean-breeze aftershave. No sling. No sign of pain. But that didn't mean he wasn't in any.

A fresh, more urgent thought struck Tara at once. Would the men recognize each other? Would being in the same room with Tara and Welch trigger Aiden's PTSD? She drew a breath, studying both men in the reflection. Nothing. Aiden gave no sign of recognition and Welch either hadn't put it together, or else did but didn't care. Given Welch's public position for the last two years, he probably figured that if any blowback was due, it would have come by now.

Aiden shifted his weight. "If I didn't know better, I'd imagine Obsidian Ops is engaged in witness tampering. At least I can think of no other reason why I might find the defendant in the women's restroom just as our witness is there too."

Welch's smile was filled with venom. "Just the wrong door. Looks like both of us made the same mistake. I'll see you back in court in…" He glanced at his watch. "Ten."

Welch knocked Aiden with his shoulder as he passed, but since Aiden barely budged, the collision only made Welch stumble. The door closed with a crack.

"Bloody fuck." Aiden bent over gripping his side. "That hurt."

Tara was at his side in a second, her hands moving ahead of her mind as she pulled back the lapel of Aiden's suit jacket. There were a few specks of red marring the white linen. "It's all right. I think one of the stitches opened, but the bleeding's minimal."

"Still hurts," said Aiden through clenched teeth.

"I know." Tara suddenly became aware of her hands on him, of the heat that radiated from his body and caressed her face. Of the fact that he hadn't jerked away from her touch. God, she missed the feeling of falling asleep beside him at night and waking up to the safety of being in his arms. She missed offering comfort to a man who accepted none from anyone else. *And who gave him that little complex?* "What are you doing here? In court, I mean."

Aiden stepped away to straighten his suit. "Covering for Liam. Jaz… Never mind. What did Welch want?"

"What happened to Jaz?" Tara asked, a new set of fears rushing through her. "Please tell me. They were my friends for a time. It matters."

"The twins came early."

Tara's hand went to her mouth.

Aiden caught her forearm, sending a slew of sensation along Tara's skin. "They're stable, feeding, and growing in NICU with a pair of very sleep-deprived parents beside them." He plucked the memo from her hand and spoke as he read. "What did Welch want?… *Shit.*"

Clearly, he'd figured it out.

"Blackmail." He spat the word. "When the hell did this happen?"

"I think the memo's dated this morning." Not that it mattered all that much.

"Aye. It is." Aiden rubbed his hand over his face, his eyes looking vulnerable for a moment before he regained control of himself. Lowering the memo, he surveyed the restroom until his gaze settled on the top right window. The very same one that Welch had recommended she take advantage of. "You know, one thing that rubs me the wrong way about this courthouse is how lax the security is. I should make a point of it with the sergeant at arms here. I need to go back to court." He gave her one final look, then turned away and strode for the door. "They're starting up soon."

# 36

Aiden

"I'm going to file a motion about witness tampering." Sonia's face turned dark as Aiden laid the prosecutor's memo on the table in front of the attorneys. "Where is Tara? Did you escort her to the courtroom?"

"Oh, for fuck's sake." Cassey pinched the bridge of his nose. "Of course he didn't escort her back. He probably left her with enough time to decide whether she wants to make a run for it. And don't even start on the witness-tampering bullshit. Can't prove it."

Letting the lawyers argue, Aiden sank onto the back of the bench, his mind roaring. The death penalty? Tara was now facing the death penalty? It was impossible. They'd been talking about immunity just…just before she ran. Because fucking Cassey scared her off.

Aiden understood why his cousin had done it, but… "Can you two shut up a moment and tell me how we're going to unfuck this?" he demanded. "We're going to unfuck it right? This is a draft memo, not an execution warrant."

"A lot will depend on her testimony," Sonia said, giving Cassey a dirty glare.

That wasn't good enough. There had been many things on the table that Aiden had come to grips with, but this, this was never part of the deal. Especially not the one he made with himself. "What does Tara need to say? What does she need to keep her mouth shut about? Don't you want to call for another recess and hash this out?"

Cassey gave Aiden a level gaze that made Aiden's chest tighten. "She knows the answer to your questions as well as you do. And if she has any sense of self-preservation, she isn't going to walk through those doors to begin with."

"All rise," the bailiff called, driving the final nail into Aiden's helplessness.

"The court is now in session," the judge announced, settling herself in her chair. "Please be seated. Ms. Dancer, your next witness, please."

Sonia took a visible breath. "Your honor, the plaintiff calls Tara Northpoint to the stand."

The room turned toward the door, waiting for it to open. Aiden held his breath. One second. Two. Three.

It stayed closed.

"Is there a problem, Ms. Dancer?" the judge asked.

"No." Sonia cleared her throat. "If Your Honor could grant us a moment to locate—"

The door opened, cutting Sonia off midsentence as Tara strode into the aisle and set course for the witness stand.

Aiden's heart pounded in rhythm to Tara's steps. He couldn't imagine what she was thinking, what this walk must be doing to her nerves. With the black-robed judge presiding over the universe and benches filled with people all watching Tara's every move, all eager for blood.

Her short hair gleamed, and she word black slacks and white jacket that reminded Aiden of a lab professor—which had, no doubt, been the intention. Her chin was raised, but, no matter how hard Aiden tried to read her face, he found it devoid of emotion. A stone slate that gave no hint to the thoughts that had to be racing through the woman's mind.

Tara looked very much alone as she climbed the witness stand.

Because she was. The attorneys all knew it. Aiden knew it. And, clearly, so did Tara.

Yet, despite knowing that she'd been outflanked on all sides, Tara still chose to walk onto the battlefield. The warrior within Aiden couldn't help but admire that courage, even as he felt a band tighten around his chest.

"State your name for the court," the bailiff instructed.

Tara wiped her palms on the sides of her pants, then glanced over toward the defense table.

Welch's eyes slid over Tara as if overlooking a stray bit of rubbish, then he leaned over to whisper to Gardener.

Tara drew a breath, then turned back to the bailiff. "I'm sorry, what did you say?"

"I said, state your name for the court." The bailiff looked more than a little put out. Especially when a merciless little chuckle ran over the courtroom, stopping abruptly when the judge banged her gavel.

"My name is Tara Northpoint," Tara said quickly into the ensuing silence.

"Do you swear to tell the whole truth and nothing but the truth?"

"I do." Did anyone ever answer otherwise?

The bailiff seemed to accept that answer and yielded the floor to Sonia, who walked out from behind the plaintiff's table. In her proper suit and bunned hair, Sonia looked like she belonged here as much as Tara didn't.

Sonia sounded calm as she eased into the testimony, asking Tara to describe her background and standing with Obsidian Ops. They'd rehearsed this part, and after the first few couple of questions, the answers started to flow easier. Tara spoke briefly about Lucius taking her in from the streets, about being raised and educated and eventually put to work at Obsidian's compound. She described how Obsidian worked on paper, taking clients and providing security. As Tara's voice gained in confidence, Sonia pivoted to the heart of the matter.

"Tara, does Obsidian accept contracts for illegal operations?"

"Objection." Gardener was on his feet before the last word left Sonia's mouth. "Call for hearsay. Ms. Northpoint is not an Obsidian employee, much less someone involved in Obsidian's contract negotiations."

"Sustained," said the judge, instructing Tara not to answer the question.

"I'll rephrase," said Sonia. "Tara, has Obsidian Ops ever ordered you personally to do something illegal?"

"Objection." Gardener, who'd been sitting quietly earlier, was now popping up like a jack-in-the-box. "I thought we were here to discuss the matter of the Denver Research explosion, not catalog every conversation Ms. Northpoint might have had with someone since age ten."

A muscle tightened in Sonia's jaw. A large part of having Tara on the stand involved exposure of Obsidian's practices. "Your Honor, Obsidian's pattern of—"

"Ms. Dancer, I agree with the defense. Your next question better include the words 'Denver Research facility.'"

Sonia made a mark on her notepad. From where Aiden sat, he could see it was filled with fresh notes all taken in perfect handwriting. Cassey's handwriting was horrid, even on his crosswords.

"Tara, what involvement did you have with the Denver Research facility explosion?" asked Sonia.

This was it. The part where Tara would incriminate herself, setting off a chain of events that would lead to her doom. Aiden's heart stuttered.

The courtroom, already silent, somehow went quieter still. As if they all knew what was at stake. Or sensed it. And now all these people on the benches, they waited to see whether Tara would crack. Whether she would slay her own future.

She glanced at Aiden. Despite her stoic face, he could see the fear in her eyes.

Aiden shook his head at her. A tiny motion, but unmistakable. *Don't do it.*

"I was part of the two-man team that orchestrated the explosion," she said instead of accepting the wave off. "Specifically, about two months ago, I was ordered to build an explosive device to use at Denver Research. The device was to be powerful enough to create a diversion that would draw guards to the entrance. During this time, my partner—Ray Brushings—was to penetrate the facility's data storage and download proprietary information the client wanted."

Aiden stared at the witness stand, while the rest of the courtroom exploded in hushed whispers.

Sonia let the shock wave gather for a few moments before spurring the story on. "Did everything go as planned?"

"No. Ray thought I was using too little explosive, even though I was the bomb expert. We argued. Eventually he ordered me to turn the ordnance over to him and stage by the fifth-floor fire exit to help him get inside."

"Did you obey?" asked Sonia.

"Yes, Ray was the senior on the team."

"What happened next?" asked Sonia.

"Ray joined me at the staging area. He had a remote detonator. When he activated it, an explosion several times larger than it should have been enveloped the building. From the blast radius, I knew it would have killed the guards."

"So what did you do?" Sonia asked.

Tara smiled without humor. "I ran. People had just *died.* I was scared. Of the consequences. Of being associated with Obsidian Ops. I wanted out."

"Then why are you here now?" Sonia asked softly. "Why did you turn yourself in?"

Though Tara was answering Sonia's question, she looked right at Aiden as she spoke. "I couldn't live with everything I've done."

Aiden's chest tightened. Tara wasn't talking about the explosion, and everyone at the plaintiff's table knew it.

Sonia waited a beat, then tapped her pen against her notepad.

"So, to be clear..." Her voice changed to a no-nonsense rapid-fire cadence worthy of film. "Were you employed by Obsidian Ops?"

"Yes."

"And in the course of that employment, did Obsidian order you to assault the Denver Research facility?"

"Yes." Tara's clear answers matched Sonia's intensity.

"Did you follow those orders?"

"Yes."

Sonia took a step toward Tara. "One last question. Besides fulfilling your employer's orders, did you get any kind of benefit—financial or otherwise—from the assault on Denver Research?"

"Benefit?" Tara snorted. "Ms. Dancer, I'm charged with murder. I have to live with the knowledge that it was my ordnance that was altered. I have the blood of innocent people on my hands. I got no benefit, financial or otherwise. Obsidian Ops may look good on paper, but they've been committing atrocities on their clients' behalf for a decade. Denver Research is just the tip of the iceberg."

"No further questions, Your Honor," said Sonia.

# 37

Aiden

"Ms. Northpoint, you're facing a murder charge, aren't you?" Gardener asked from the defense table.

Aiden hid a wince but, up on the firing line, Tara didn't even hesitate.

"That's correct, sir," she said.

"And you're testifying today in exchange for leniency from the state, are you not? In fact, didn't you have an immunity agreement negotiated on your behalf?"

"That agreement is no longer in effect," said Tara.

"That would be a 'yes,' wouldn't it? Trident Security did negotiate an immunity agreement for you in exchange for your testimony."

"They had negotiated an agreement—"

"In exchange for your testimony?"

Tara stared at Gardener. Aiden felt his hands tighten into fists and realized he was imagining squeezing them around the attorney's neck.

"In exchange for the truth, Mr. Gardener," said Tara.

A corner of Cassey's mouth twitched toward a smile, though he continued with his damn crossword.

Gardener rose from his seat and buttoned his jacket. "You don't want to go to jail, do you?"

Sonia jumped to her feet. "Objection."

"It goes to the witness's credibility, Your Honor," Gardener said.

"I agree," the judge said, motioning Sonia to sit.

Gardener reset his sights on Tara like a sniper readjusting the crosshairs. "You don't want to go to jail, do you, Tara?" he repeated, clearly enjoying getting to say the words again.

"No, of course not."

"You'd do anything to avoid it?"

"I wouldn't lie."

"I see. Tell me, did you promise Trident Security you would testify?" Gardener asked.

Aiden saw confusion flicker over Tara's face—a mirror to his own. Where was Gardener going with this?

"I told them I'd testify, yes," Tara said.

"But then you tried to flee the country, didn't you?" Gardener said.

Tara swallowed. "I—"

"Two weeks ago, you escaped Trident Security custody in an attempt to flee the country, didn't you?" Gardener demanded.

"Yes."

"So, you lied to them?"

Tara shifted her weight. "I'm under oath now. I'm here in court to tell the truth. I paid for my mistake when my immunity was taken away. Believe me, I'm getting no benefit from this."

"You received no benefits in exchange for favorable testimony?" Gardener echoed, grabbing a sheet of paper from his table. "I have here copies of receipts from several high-end boutiques at the Denton Valley Mall. The total is over two thousand dollars. Do you recognize the items listed here?"

Tara shifted in her chair again. "Yes. These are—"

"These are clothes that a Trident Security employee purchased for you, aren't they?"

"I expected to pay for them myself, but—"

"Why did you need high-end clothes?" Gardener asked, cocking his head as if curious. "Does Trident Security dress all witnesses in their custody in Christian Dior?"

Sonia looked like she was about to stand up, but Cassey grabbed her forearm and shook his head grimly. There was no making this better.

"I was invited to Liam Rowen's wedding," Tara said on the stand.

"So Trident Security purchased you lavish clothing, wined and dined you, and took you to lavish parties—but you consider none of that to be compensation. Is that correct?"

For the first time since getting on the stand, Tara looked absolutely helpless. "It wasn't like that."

Gardener smiled. "No, of course not. Let's return to the matter at hand, though. Earlier today you claimed you were employed by Obsidian Ops. Is that right?"

"Yes," Tara said. "I've been living at the Obsidian complex since—"

"I didn't ask for your living arrangements. I asked about your employment. Were you employed by Obsidian?"

"Yes."

"The HR department does not have you on the payroll. Did you work for free?"

"Given the nature of my work, I was paid by covert means," Tara said.

Gardener picked up a stack of papers. "I have no fewer than twenty contracts that Obsidian has signed with individuals in the past five years. Is there one with your name on it?"

Tara took a breath, but leveled Gardener with an even gaze. "My name was purged from Obsidian's system when I accepted the exit package two weeks ago. You will find Raymond Brushing's records to have been purged as well."

"How convenient," said Gardener.

"Not convenient at all, sir."

A chuckle went through the room. A small score for Tara, but still one to be celebrated.

Gardener gave an oily smile. "Who at Obsidian supposedly ordered you to put explosives in the Denver Research facility?"

"I got my orders from Raymond Brushings," Tara said.

"The same Raymond Brushings who died in the explosion? The one forensics identified in dental records?"

"He didn't die in the explosion, Mr. Gardener. I saw him alive after the explosion. He's the one who stole the computer."

"So where is he?" Gardener put his hands out and looked around, as if the man might be hiding under a bench.

"I don't know." Tara's nostrils flared. "Like I told you, he got an exit package. Obsidian helped him get overseas. I imagine Obsidian's records now show that he hadn't worked with them for years."

Gardener rubbed his face as if this whole line of questioning was becoming painful. "Let me get this straight. There are no pay stubs, contracts, or executives at Obsidian Ops to substantiate your employment with them, but you'd like us to take your word for it. Contrary to forensic reports, Brushings is not really dead. He, *in*conveniently, is also the person who ordered you into Denver Research. And we should believe all this because you say so, Ms. Northpoint, and as we've established you never lie. And you received no benefit at all for your testimony."

Sonia rose to her feet, but Gardener waved her off. "No need, Counselor. I withdraw the question. Nothing further for this witness."

The judge dismissed Tara and adjourned for the day all in one breath, leaving Aiden with emptiness as the plaintiff's table gathered around for a huddle. That was a disaster. The end game. And while Trident and Obsidian could live to fight another day, it meant that Tara's sacrifice was going to be for nothing. As Tara walked slowly up to the table, Aiden searched for something to say and found nothing.

"I'm sorry," he said finally.

She wasn't listening, though. In fact, Aiden realized, as his mind spurred into action again, Tara wasn't paying attention to him at all.

"I know you took no prisoners when you were in Afghanistan," Tara said to Cassey, "but did you collect DNA samples from the cave?"

Cassey tipped his head to the side, giving Tara a long look. "We did. But we got no matches for them in the vital database."

"Of course you didn't," said Tara. "Obsidian's operatives don't have theirs listed. But you could do a one-for-one match, couldn't you? If you had a sample of someone's DNA, you could say whether it matches the Afghan sample?"

Cassey cocked his brow. "I can. Or I can simply offer eyewitness testimony to your presence there—I imagine I'd be a more convincing witness than you proved to be."

Briar clamped his hand around Aiden's wrist before he could take a swing.

Cassey put his hand into his pocket. "Unless you happen to have a contract from back then, though, it would only serve to confirm you have a history of committing atrocities—not that they were done in Obsidian's employ."

Tara's jaw tightened and she still would not look in Aiden's direction. "It's not just me you can place there. It's also Gio Welch."

"Ah." Cassey rocked back on his heels. "That would certainly change things. I'm not a crack attorney like Sonia Dancer here, but I imagine that testimony putting you in the middle of torture is unlikely to sway the prosecutor's mind about that memo, though."

"I'm going down no matter what," Tara said, straightening her spine. "I want to take the bastards down with me. I want justice."

Aiden took a step back, his gut tightening. He knew better than to fight Tara on this, but if she was going to battle for the truth, then doing that for her was the least he could do. He retreated another step. Then another until he was out of the courtroom and jogging down the courthouse steps as he pulled out his phone. "Eli," Aiden said into the receiver. "I need you tonight. Dani too. It's not going to be a pretty night."

# 38

Aiden

"If you're asking for my professional opinion—"

"I'm not asking for your professional opinion," Aiden told Dani. "I'm very clear that your professional opinion is that this is a bad idea."

"It's a horrific idea," said Dani. She'd informed Aiden and Eli of as much no less than a dozen times as they drove to the Trident Security building, but to her credit, she'd come anyway. It was night outside, and a few employees were still at work, for which Aiden was highly grateful. As they headed down into the bowels to an isolated interrogation room, Dani stepped in front of the men, evidently to give her case one more shot. "Aiden, listen to me. You can't force yourself to relive trauma for the sake of gathering information."

"That's not what you said before you knew the plan. You said I *shouldn't*. That means it's possible." Aiden opened the door to the interrogation room and unslung the bag of tools he carried.

"You want to play word games with me?" Dani snapped at him.

"Not particularly, no." Aiden ran his fingers along the walls.

"I'm just saying that given my reaction to Ivy's restraints in the ER, there is a good chance of this working."

"Let's be crystal clear, then, on what else is possible with this little PTSD role play of yours," Dani said into Aiden's back. "You know those nightmares that keep you awake? They can start coming during the day too. Phantom pain. Flashbacks that will feel so real, you'll be able to swear you taste the blood in your mouth. And if they come often enough, you won't be able to drive. Or ride that damn Harley of yours."

Aiden motioned for Eli to help him move the table against the wall. Taking out a drill and several sets of manacles, he made short work of bolting the metal to the wall. He didn't remember what the cave looked like, but Cassey and Briar didn't ask questions when Aiden had asked his cousins to draw it for him.

"There's a reason your mind blocked off those memories," Dani continued. "We peel back layers one at a time so you can process them. Conquer them. If you dive headfirst into a flame, you don't come out warmed up, you come out burned to a crisp."

There was a note of desperation in Dani's voice that made Aiden stop what he was doing and walk over to her. She was his doctor, yes, but she was first and foremost his friend. He took her shoulders gently. "Scared?"

"Very," said Dani.

"Me too," said Aiden. Hell, his heart was hammering so hard against his ribs it was a wonder Eli and Dani weren't holding their hands over their ears. "But I have to do this. If Tara is willing to die, then I'm willing to remember. Not for my curiosity or for vengeance, but because there may be something in there that can help."

Dani closed her eyes.

"I know this can end badly. But sometimes soldiers do things that aren't the best for their health, aye?"

She nodded.

"You don't have to be here," Aiden said softly. "Eli was a SERE instructor. He literally simulated torture to teach solders what interrogation might feel like and how to get through it. We've got this."

Dani's eyes snapped open. "You think for a moment I'm going to leave the pair of you to your own devices?" The indignation in her voice made Aiden lift his hands in surrender. Dani stepped toward him, poking her finger into his chest. "Just so we're clear, if you come out of this with your mind too unpredictable to do your job safely, I'm going to get your driver's license and gun permit medically suspended quicker than you can say abracadabra. Clear?"

"Abracadabra," said Aiden, kissing her on the forehead. "You should go behind the one-way mirror, though. And maybe keep the visual and audio off for a while."

"Come here, love." Eli swept his large arm around the doctor, pulling her against him. They fit together like perfect puzzle pieces, their clear affection for each other sending a small pang of envy through Aiden. Eli brushed back a lock of Dani's hair. "I've done this once or twice before, yes?"

She raised a brow. "This?"

He snorted. "No, not *this*. But Aiden is right. I do a damn good impression of a hostile interrogator—but I bring the students back too. I try to build, not break."

"Next time you go looking for your phone, I'll give you one of Ella's toy ones, and we can have a conversation about one thing being just like another," Dani snapped back at her husband, but there was no fight in it. "Fine. I'll be in the other room."

Eli waited until Dani left, the door closing behind her with a click. "She isn't wrong, you know," he said quietly.

"Aye," said Aiden. "I never said she was."

Eli did a quick check around the place, then turned the lights down slightly and took off his coat. He was dressed in his fatigues, Aiden realized, though there was no insignia to be seen. As Eli turned to him, he seemed to shift before Aiden's eyes, growing more commanding, more dominating of the room. He was slightly taller than Aiden, and now he used every bit of that height to take up Aiden's entire field of vision.

"Are you ready?" Eli's voice changed too, his natural British accent gone in favor of an American one.

Aiden felt his mouth go dry. Then he thought of Tara and nodded.

"Speak aloud," Eli ordered.

"Yes."

"On your knees. Face the wall." The rough commands sounded nothing like Eli's usual easygoing tone. Aiden obeyed. A moment later, he felt a hood he didn't know Eli had brought go around his head. The twin shocks of darkness and cloth covering his mouth and nose sent a shock along Aiden's spine. Before he could recover his equilibrium, Eli grabbed the back of Aiden's neck and forced his face down to the ground.

Aiden's side screamed. He drew a shaking breath, the fear he'd been concealing from himself now spilling into his blood.

"Here are the rules," Eli said into Aiden's ear. "I take you in, I bring you out. You argue, you're punished. You resist, you're punished. You do one damn thing to displease me, you're punished. Understand?"

"Yes."

Eli's grip didn't loosen, but his voice softened for a moment. "This will feel very real. It's meant to. But in the back of your mind, remember that this is like training. The pain is temporary."

Aiden nodded into the darkness.

Nothing happened.

Then he was shoved roughly along the floor and into the wall. "What's your unit?" a voice demanded. "Tell me your unit."

Aiden wasn't sure when it happened exactly. At first, he just gritted his teeth and bore the abuse, knowing it wasn't real. Thinking it was stupid. Idiotic. Except it *was* real. The pain. The darkness. The growing fear of what the next moment would bring. He remembered thinking that if he just got through the next hour, the next minute, the next few seconds, then maybe something would change. But then Eli would strike him or force water into his face or tighten the restraints, and that hope inside Aiden would turn to rage.

Then he was fighting, his heart pounding, his breaths so fast and desperate that he was unable to pull in enough air no matter how hard he tried. Aiden heard screaming. By the time he realized it was his own, there was no help for it. He couldn't stop. Couldn't do anything.

"Who is your commanding officer?" The man's voice, which used to be even, grew furious. That wasn't good. Fury meant punishment. Fury meant pain. Aiden shook. They'd been at this for days. Weeks. The same questions. The same demands.

Aiden felt the heat of a blazing flame. Heard the clang of metal. Smelled the stench of burned skin.

And fell into hell.

"Aiden. Aiden look at me." Eli's face came in and out of focus. It didn't match the face Aiden had been sure he shared a room with. The Brit crouched several feet away, well out of reach of what Aiden's restraints allowed. "How many fingers am I holding up?"

"Th—" Aiden licked his lips and tasted blood. He tried to speak again, but his throat was raw. Three. It was three fingers. He tried to make the sign with his own hand, but his wrist was still chained and all his muscles were cramping.

"Are you in Afghanistan?" Eli asked.

"No," Aiden forced out. "US."

Eli gave him an encouraging nod. "Good. You think you can let me close enough to unlock the cuffs?"

Even through the fog of Aiden's mind, the question seemed absurd. Aiden was restrained. Eli could do as he wished.

"I haven't touched you in two hours," Eli explained quietly. "It's been in your head. I don't want to set off another flashback by coming too close."

Two hours? Aiden blinked. It felt… Actually, he had no idea how much time had passed. He remembered arguing with Dani and seeing the change in Eli. Remembered a roller coaster of emotions. And then…then things came in flashes. Scenes from a movie. Some that repeated, some that came out of order. Enough building blocks that he knew the plot. It started with—

"Aiden. Stay with me." There was a hint of urgency in Eli's voice. "It's over. It was just training. You're in a room in Trident Security. In the US. We were simulating an interrogation, and you did well."

"No," Aiden whispered. The memories were settling now. Arranging themselves like proper puzzle pieces. "No, I didn't. Not when it was real."

Eli turned to Dani, who Aiden just realized was also in the room now. Dani shrugged. She didn't know what he was talking about, and Aiden didn't have the strength to explain it twice. Doing it in court would be hard enough.

"Can I see Tara?" Aiden asked.

"No." Dani moved forward and freed Aiden's hands. Blood burned as it rushed back into his muscles. "If you do, it can be argued that she influenced your memories. If we're doing this, we're doing this right. I'm afraid your night isn't over yet. Not by a long shot."

She motioned to Eli, and the Brit rose smoothly from his crouch and headed for the door. Once they were alone, Dani handed Aiden a blanket and bottle of water. "Tell me why you want to see Tara," she said.

And so Aiden told her. Everything.

# 39

Aiden

The courtroom looked very different from the witness stand than it had from the benches. Sitting on the witness stand while Cassey and Sonia argued about something at the plaintiff's table, Aiden got to experience the full effect. Got to feel what it was like for Tara when she sat up here, with the whole world focused on tearing her apart. He could feel the many eyes boring into him, especially those of the Tridents, who'd decided to show up in force because Eli couldn't keep his mouth shut and his worried look to himself.

Even without Eli's too-watchful gaze, Aiden knew he looked like shit. He hadn't slept, and the pain in his side was enough that he'd been forced to put his sling back on. But at least he'd managed to shave and shower and make himself into the presentable professional the court expected to see. At least on the outside. On the inside, he was barely holding on through the storm.

The one place Aiden was so very careful not to look was the middle of the front row, where he knew Tara sat. He was holding on to his composure by a shoestring, and her face would be his undoing.

The judge made an impatient sound and reminded the plaintiff that the court was awaiting their pleasure.

Cassey stood up and, ignoring Sonia's glare, identified himself to the judge. Aiden was glad it was his cousin facing him. Sonia Dancer was prepared and proper and nice, but Cassey wouldn't hesitate to push Aiden as far beyond his comfort zone as this required.

"Mr. McDane." Cassey glanced at his notepad, which Aiden knew full well contained no notes. "There's been some question as to whether Tara Northpoint is an Obsidian Ops employee. I'm hoping you can shed light on this. Can you tell us how long you've known Tara?"

*Aiden heard them before he saw them.*

*"If I were you, I'd worry more about disobeying me than anything to do with the prisoner. You're here for operational experience. So go get experienced." The male voice was familiar, but the young woman who was shoved into the cave where Aiden was chained looked utterly out of place. Her boots kicked up the rock dust as she stumbled, and, despite the fact that Aiden had been stripped naked and sported at least two cracked ribs, he'd felt an immediate protectiveness of her that he couldn't explain.*

*At first, she appeared to look anywhere but at him. When she finally did look, her face paled and she slid down along the floor to the wall.*

*"Are you all right, lass?" Aiden asked.*

*"How pitiful do I look if* you're *inquiring about my well-being?" she muttered.*

*"Fair pitiful."*

*She chuckled, the tension in her body easing slightly. Her hair was red like his, but tamer. And it cascaded down her shoulders in thick locks.*

*"What's your name?" Aiden asked.*

*"Tara." She winced. "I probably shouldn't have told you that."*

*"Probably not," he agreed.*

*"What's yours?"*

*He snorted. "Points for trying."*

Aiden blinked, dragging himself back into the present. He was on the stand. In court. And though he'd just watched a whole scene play out in his head, here in reality, a heartbeat appeared to have passed.

"I first met her six years ago," Aiden said to the courtroom. He didn't dare look around or do anything but sit tall and speak loudly enough to hear himself over the memories that threatened to become too real at a moment's notice. "She was on the Obsidian Ops team that captured me in Afghanistan."

"What was her position on this Obsidian team?" Cassey asked. "What job did she perform?"

Aiden's breath stuttered, the image of a frightened eighteen-year-old girl interposing with that of the woman he knew sat just a few paces away from him.

*Welch pressed a heated piece of metal into Tara's hand, while the other two men held Aiden still. His skin was already marked from the day's abuse, but the fear of being burned made him buck against the restraints anyway.*

*"No," Tara pleaded, recoiling from the instrument. "Please."*

*Welch backhanded her hard enough that blood spilled over the girl's mouth. As she tried to retreat, he gripped her neck and pinned her to the wall. "This ain't a pick-your-own-adventure children's book. You're either an operator or a tool." His other hand gripped the edge of Tara's shirt and ripped the fabric to expose the girl's breast. "And if you're a tool, I know exactly how to use you."*

Aiden rubbed the spot on his arm where the metal had touched and focused on Cassey's question. "Tara was one of Obsidian's interrogators six years ago in Afghanistan. They wanted details of my military unit's communication channels. One of her jobs was to get that from me."

"When you say she interrogated you, what do you mean by that precisely?" Cassey demanded with ruthless precision.

What the actual fuck? Anger flared through Aiden. "I mean that Tara Northpoint was one of the Obsidian Ops operatives assigned to torture me," he snapped. "So yes, Cassey, I can confirm her bloody employment as an Obsidian torturer."

Someone in the courtroom gasped. People shifted in their seats, making the benches creak. Aiden pressed his hand into his knee, digging his nails into the fabric to keep from giving in to the ghosts that were already gathering around him. This whole thing had seemed like a good idea last night, but now… Now Aiden wasn't sure he'd keep himself together long enough to be of help. Especially with the route Cassey wanted to go down.

Cassey turned to Gardener. "Your witness."

Aiden twisted toward his cousins. What did Cassey mean by *your witness?* They hadn't even touched on the true reason for his testimony, that Tara had been there with Gio Welch, acting on Welch's orders. Cassey had done nothing but add nails to Tara's coffin.

Cassey ignored him.

Aiden gathered himself together, lest Obsidian's lackeys found a way to capitalize on his distress. Straightening his back, he turned to the defense table and feigned patience he had none of.

The Obsidian lawyer stood and buttoned his coat. "First, you have my empathy for what took place. Reliving it in court cannot be easy, so I'll keep my questions as brief as possible. Might I ask if Ms. Northpoint wore some kind of Obsidian Ops uniform when she mistreated you?"

*They'd ripped her clothes. Aiden had been stripped naked when he was taken, but somehow, Tara's torn shirt always seemed more vulnerable to him. Maybe it was because he was a soldier and she was a frightened eighteen-year-old-girl. Maybe because for everything the men did to him, they never leered at Aiden the way they did at her.*

"Tara wore fatigues," said Aiden.

"Specialized ones, with Obsidian Ops insignia?" Gardener clarified. "Or the generic kind you can buy on Amazon?"

Aiden rubbed his face. He wasn't much of a shopper, and the material seemed irrelevant at the time. "Generic."

Gardener nodded. "But she did identify herself to you as an Obsidian operative, right?"

Ah. They were on this again. Aiden shifted in his chair. "No."

"All right, but you did see her with some kind of identification, or papers that referenced Obsidian?"

"No."

"Speak up, please."

"No," Aiden repeated, louder this time.

"Perhaps..." Gardener hesitated as if thinking. "Perhaps you overheard Obsidian Ops being referenced while she was interrogating you and verified this after you were released?"

Aiden shook his head.

Gardener sighed. "Forgive me, but how, then, did you come to the conclusion that Obsidian had anything to do with your situation?"

For the first time since Gardener squared off before him, Aiden allowed himself to stare into the man's eyes. "Because the man who pinned Tara to the wall by her neck and threatened to rape her if she didn't burn me is sitting right there with an Obsidian Ops nameplate."

Gardener froze.

At the defense table, Welch's face drained of blood.

Fucking Cassey grinned like a cat with a bowl of cream.

As the court exploded in a fury of voices, Aiden contemplated the different, but equally horrible, ways he intended to launch Cassey into the next galaxy. The bloody man could have shared the strategy instead of letting Aiden figure it out for himself midway through Gardener's cross. But to give Cassey credit, the declaration had packed a punch.

Almost as importantly, Cassey had tricked the defense into bringing up an issue they may have otherwise objected to.

Gardener, who was better trained for court than the still shell-shocked Welch, covered his setback by engrossing himself in his notes until the judge restored order.

"Mr. McDane." Gardener no longer sounded either understanding or empathetic. "The man you just pointed to has been in the public eye for years. Have you ever filed charges, called the authorities, or even just talked to him about his involvement in this alleged torture incident? I'm sorry, are you undressing on the stand?"

Aiden, who'd started to unbutton his shirt, stopped. "You said *alleged* torture, sir. I was going to show the alleged scars."

A few chuckles sounded, but Aiden wasn't laughing. And he knew that neither was Tara.

"Keep your clothes on, please," Gardener said, almost but not quite losing his controlled tone. "I fully believe your experience was real. I'm simply questioning why, before today, you never told a soul about Mr. Welch's supposed involvement. Is it possible your mind is playing tricks on you?"

Aiden paused, then shifted his attention to Welch. "I only put it together yesterday. When I saw Welch corner Tara in the restroom before her testimony."

"My question was about your mental state, Mr. McDane," Gardener snapped, losing his patience for the first time in the trial, "not other people's bathroom habits. And from what I'm hearing, after six years of amnesia, you've suddenly made a miraculous recovery within twenty-four hours. And to that end, you decided that the individual who held you was none other than a prominent Obsidian executive who is sitting ten feet away."

"I share your concern," Aiden said gravely. "Which is why I had a full psychological assessment last night. I believe Dr. Mason is in the courtroom to discuss her findings, but she appeared to agree that I'm a reliable historian."

"How…convenient." Gardener turned back to his table, where Welch whispered something in his ear. Gardener requested a few minutes from the judge, spending them engrossed in a computer file Welch had brought up. Finally, Gardener turned his sights back on Aiden. "I understand you were under the influence of some psychotropic agents when you were rescued?"

Aiden's stomach tightened. "I was."

"Those are drugs that affect perception?"

"Yes."

"Senses?" asked Gardener.

"Yes." Aiden was careful not to look at Tara, though he felt her eyes boring into him.

"These drugs also affect memory, do they not?" Gardener asked.

"Yes," Aiden said.

Gardener let the words hang in the air before turning away. "No further questions."

"I have a few more," said Cassey, striding out onto the floor. Something about the man's movements made Aiden tense, as if his body was bracing itself for whatever Cassey had in mind. "What exactly happened with Mr. Welch and Ms. Northpoint in Afghanistan that led to you having drugs in your bloodstream?"

"Objection." Gardener spun toward the judge. "This trial is about the explosion at the Denver Research facility two months ago, not allegations for something from a different continent six years past."

Cassey smiled, rocking back on his heels. "The defense spent a great deal of time discussing Afghanistan, Your Honor. In fact, it was Mr. Gardener himself who elicited testimony placing Gio Welch there. Your Honor. I have the right to clarify."

"I agree." She turned in her chair, her attention shifting between the lawyers. "You opened this door, Mr. Gardener. I'd like to know what's behind it. Mr. McDane, please cover the facts for us."

The facts. That sounded so straightforward. But as Aiden finally allowed himself to look at Tara's blanched face, he knew things were anything but.

"I was captured in an ambush," he said. "A damn good one. In the course of the next few days of interrogation, I learned that I was held by a four-person team. Gio Welch was in charge, and a young woman named Tara was at the bottom of the ladder, an apprentice of sorts, who hurt me because she was forced to and not for sport."

Tara shuddered. They both knew what came next.

*They'd fallen into a pattern. During interrogations, Aiden screamed. Tara cried. Welch moved things along at an unrelenting pace. At night, Tara would come to check on him, and even brought him water, though Welch beat her for it when he found out.*

"I started trying to convince Tara to help me escape," Aiden told the court. "I thought it was only fear that kept her under Welch's thumb, but I'd underestimated her loyalty to the one place that had given her shelter and purpose."

*The one night Tara seemed to suddenly play along, Aiden should have smelled a trap, but he was too desperate to think clearly. He poured every ounce of energy and willpower he'd had in reserve to get them out of the cave. Down a rocky path in the night's darkness. Crawling for hours along sand that abraded his broken skin.*

*And falling right into Welch's waiting shackles.*

*The betrayal had cut as deep as the punishment.*

"Eventually, a day came when it became clear that Tara and I were on different sides," Aiden said aloud. On the bench, Tara's eyes glistened with tears. He cleared his throat. "At that point, I'd exhausted all my reserves. Welch had found a way to break me."

*Aiden wished he could be angry. But he was long past anger. He was terrified. Of Welch. Of torment. Of Tara. He longed for it all to end. And if he couldn't escape with his body, he tried to do it without it. He had no tools and no freedom of movement to use them if he had, but his wounds were well open and there was plenty of filth around.*

"I purposely infected my wounds," Aiden said. Images flashed in his head, and he had to hold on to the side of the witness stand to remain upright.

*He was blazing with fever when Tara came to check on him at night. Her flashlight hurt his eyes and showed angry red streaks running along his skin.*

*"What the hell did you do?" She shook him, her eyes intense and filled with shock that only grew as she worked out what was happening. Then Tara shook her head. "You don't get to die. You hear me? You're not going to die."*

*His voice was vacant. "I already did."*

*"No." She shook her head again, locking him in a battle of wills. "This is horrid, but it will end. And you'll be alive when it does. It will become nothing but a bad memory."*

*Aiden almost laughed at that. "Not a memory I want to live with."*

*Getting up, Tara raided the medical kit they had. By the time Aiden understood what she was going to do, Tara already had the antibiotics drawn up in a syringe.*

"Tara discovered the infection—and my intentions—before the others. That's when our battle truly started. She force injected me with antibiotics and then started cooking up various concoctions to push into my veins. She said she was experimenting with a truth serum. Welch and I both believed her." Aiden felt along his forearm, recalling the phantom sting of a needle and the varying effects of whatever cocktail she'd inject. "Sometimes the drugs gave me hallucinations. Other times, they disconnected my mind from my body. Some made me lose time completely. But the one thing they all did was keep me from trying to kill myself again."

He turned away from the attorneys and spoke to Tara, who was no longer even trying to fight off the tears streaming down her cheeks. "Back then, if I'd been asked to point to the one person who I hated the most, I would have chosen Tara in a heartbeat. Now, I know that she's the one who saved my life. Who fought for me when I couldn't fight for myself."

# 40

## Tara

The judge adjourned at the end of Aiden's testimony, while Tara was still scrubbing her face free of tears. Before Aiden could clear the witness stand, he was surrounded by the Tridents, who formed an impermeable, protective wall between him and the world. Even Liam was there, though he was looking only a shade better than Aiden. A family caring for their own.

No one looked in Tara's direction as the Trident guards returned to the courtroom to escort Tara back into custody. The only exception was Sky, Cullen's wife, who stood back from the group to write furiously in her notebook. Sky's gaze touched Tara's by accident, and—after a second of awkwardness—the woman gave her a noncommittal nod of acknowledgment.

As she was led away, Tara hung on to the last words Aiden had said on the stand. Seeing herself through his eyes had shaken her to the core, but that last… It wasn't true. You couldn't drive someone to suicide and then claim credit for grabbing the knife from their hand at the last moment. Sooner or later, the Tridents would set

Aiden's head straight about it. About her. No doubt they were doing as much now.

Inside her holding cell, Tara was given the green scrubs she usually wore, her court clothes taken away. She sat on her cot and leaned her back against the wall. The holding cell at Trident Security was clean and modern, with plexiglass instead of bars, comfortable lights and fresh good-quality bedding. But it was still a cell. The kind that isolated people from a world that didn't want them.

It was good to know that Aiden was with family now. That he had people around him who loved him and would show up to support him even when he did something as harebrainedly stupid as rip away the still-healing scab from his memories. Tara still had no idea how he'd managed that little feat, but she intended to shake all involved like rag dolls if she ever got the chance.

For a moment, she couldn't help comparing Liam, who'd left the hospital to support his brother, and Lucius, Tara's surrogate father, who'd thrown some money at her through a proxy.

A knock at the door pulled her free of those thoughts. The door opened.

"Transport order," Yuli, the evening-shift Trident security guard, told her.

Tara's stomach churned. "To where?"

The woman shook her head. "Sorry, I'm not at liberty to say."

As Yuli got her ready to leave, Tara tried to ask more questions, but the woman either had no information or wasn't willing to share it. Yuli was decent people. Always respectful and polite, but a stickler for every rule and regulation. When Tara stopped to think about it, Yuli was Aiden's utter opposite.

Giving up on the pointless endeavor of getting Yuli to talk, Tara put on her shoes and held her hands out to be cuffed before following two guards to a waiting car. In self-defense classes, you were always warned about the dangers of being taken to a secondary location, but that all presumed you had some choice about the matter. Best that Tara could do was try to memorize the surroundings from the back seat of a tinted Suburban as the Trident personnel drove her out into the settling night.

The Colorado mountains pierced the orange skyline to stand sentry while the sun settled for the night. As Tara watched outside the window, the highway turned to a residential street, the grand single-family homes lining both sides a frightening reminder of the Crows Landing mansions. Tara's heart raced with possible implications of the destination when the Suburban suddenly pulled to a stop. The large house they'd arrived at looked like something from a design magazine, the sprawling front yard spoiled only by a carelessly thrown tricycle.

Where the hell were they?

Tara couldn't see what was happening behind the house thanks to a tall fence that closed off the backyard, but the smatterings of lights in the various windows said the place was occupied. Before she could get a better sense of the situation, Tara's minders took her out of the car and escorted her up the steps. Tara quickly surveyed the porch for anything she might be able to use as a weapon, but the only thing not tied down was one half of a plastic walkie-talkie.

Tara crouched to pick it up.

The door opened.

Eli filled the doorway, looking down at Tara from his massive height. He quickly took in the scene, from the guards' expressions to Tara holding the plastic toy in a vise grip. "I surrender," he said dryly.

Tara rose, the plastic toy in her hand, which she now saw had stickers of Elsa from *Frozen* on the back of the receiver hanging awkwardly between them. Might as well own it now. With a deft flip of her wrist, Tara spun the radio around and into the waistband of her scrubs the way a gangster might with a handgun.

Eli snorted.

Yuli extended a clipboard to the Trident. "If nothing has changed, you can sign for her here. This certifies that you're taking responsibility."

"I know the paperwork." Eli scribbled his signature. "I wrote half of it. If you have your key on you?" He motioned to Tara's cuffs.

As Yuli removed the restraints, Tara rubbed her wrists and gave Eli a questioning look.

Eli opened the door wider behind him and stood aside. "You've been kidnapped to dinner," he informed her. "In case no one told you." The glimmer of wry humor in his eyes left little doubt as to who exactly was behind that plan.

Eli's large foyer, the place looked a great deal more homey and lived-in than the house's pristine outside appearance suggested. A preschool-age girl who Tara recognized from Liam's wedding appeared and wrapped herself around Eli's leg.

"You're guests?" she inquired gravely.

"I believe so." She was careful to get no closer to the child. No parent would want someone like Tara to do that.

"Good," said Ella, her voice dropping territorially. "We have cake for guests. Mom said Uncle Aiden doesn't count, but maybe you do. Does she count as guests?" The last was to Eli.

"She counts as guests." Eli, who no doubt saw Tara's body stiffen at the mention of Aiden's name, disconnected Ella from his leg and set her facing the inside of the house. "Why don't you go give Mommy that good news. And Ella—no more painting Overlord's nails. Nail polish is not good for cats."

Her face scrunched up. "How did you know it was me?"

"It was between you and Uncle Aiden, but his arm is in a sling." Eli's voice dropped to a mutter. "That and he still has both eyes."

"Oh."

"Overlord is here?" Tara asked as Ella skipped away.

"Aiden is staying here for a bit. The evil cat came with the package."

"What the Brit means is that he doesn't trust me out unsupervised." Dressed in a pair of sweats and a loose T-shirt that contoured to his muscles despite the sling, Aiden walked up to them. His bare feet moved with silent deadliness over the hardwood floor, and, despite smudges of darkness under his eye, he looked better than he had earlier. "I've been declared in need of babysitting."

Tara's heart stuttered, but she stayed rooted in place, unsure of what she should do. Of why these people would invite her into a family home.

"I didn't use the word 'babysitting,'" Dani called. Dusting a bit of flour from her hands, she walked over to offer her greetings.

"I believe your exact words were that you'd leave Ella alone before you leave me," said Aiden.

Dani considered this. "Accurate. But keep in mind, Ella is very mature for her age."

Tara wrapped her arms around herself, her quickening heart now pounding in a full-on gallop. There was something off about this homey atmosphere, this greeting by the front door with kids and cooking and banter. It was the kind of thing that normal people did. Not ones who blew up buildings and tortured people. Giving up all pretense of pleasantries, she looked up at Aiden. "Why am I here?"

At Dani's subtle gesture, Eli wrapped his arm around his wife's shoulders, and the two of them disappeared deeper into the house, leaving Tara and Aiden alone. For a moment, nothing happened, as Aiden just stood there, not even attempting a smile that they both knew would be a fraud. Then, slowly, he stepped closer, his good arm tentatively extending toward Tara's face. The tips of his fingers brushed a lock of hair behind her ear, then trailed along her cheek, leaving a line of sensation in their wake.

"I wanted a chance to say thank you without two hundred people staring at me," Aiden said quietly. "This isn't exactly an unsupervised visit, but Eli and Dani will give us some privacy."

Tara shook her head. "What I did—"

"I have a fairly good notion of what you did," Aiden informed her.

She closed her eyes, shutting out the world. Aiden was so close to her, and the heat of his body caressing her skin was so damn seductive that it was difficult to fight her way back to reason. But she did. Because it was time to stop hiding and pretending she was anything but a monster.

She must have said the last thought aloud, because Aiden made one of those Scottish sounds that could mean anything in the back of his throat, then drew her closer. "You were an eighteen-year-old girl fighting a war with no allies. Welch threatening you on one side. Me hating you on the other. You had every reason in the world to collapse, Tara. Every reason to just let one of us win. But you didn't. You fought for my life, even when you were fighting against me. Even when Welch would have beaten you and worse if he suspected your defiance."

Tara shook her head against Aiden's shoulder. "You don't understand. The drugs I gave you…"

"Weren't perfect." He pulled his arm out of his sling and cupped Tara's face with both hands, lifting it up toward him. "Hell, some were damn counterproductive. Who could imagine that an eighteen-year-old amateur chemist with only her book smarts and a smattering of whatever substances she could find in a sandbox might not get every combination right?"

He looked at her intently, not moving a muscle as she took in his words, letting them settle over her mind until finally, slowly, she nodded.

Aiden nodded back. "You kept my heart beating. My lungs drawing air. You even gave my mind an occasional bit of respite from the hell around me. That was more than I could do for myself. But everything that happened, it's not over yet. Not by a long shot. For either of us."

He leaned his forehead against Tara's, and she breathed in his scent and warmth. Breathed in his sincerity. His strength. And somewhere, deep inside, found a small flame rekindling itself. Bringing her hands up to Aiden's face, she traced the pads of her fingers along his jawbone to the corner of his mouth.

"I love you." The truth flowed with Tara's breath, filling the air between them. "I've loved you for a long time, Aiden."

"Me too," he whispered, a corner of his strong mouth twitching toward a smile. "At least when I don't want to kill you. I love you at all other times."

She chuckled, though she hadn't thought she ever would again. But with Aiden, everything was different. Past, present, future.

However long or short it might be for her. Rising up on her toes, Tara brushed her mouth over his.

Aiden grabbed the kiss as if snatching a football from the air. His hand dropped to Tara's back to brace her as he took her mouth with predatory force, claiming every inch of it with powerful strokes that drove away thought and common sense. A blazing heat Tara didn't think she'd ever feel again started low in her abdomen, need and arousal spreading like wildfire. She pressed into him, taking the kiss that turned only deeper and more primal with every moment.

# 41

## Tara

Tara's mind and soul were still spinning when Yuli returned her to court the next morning. Aiden's love and forgiveness coursed through Tara's blood. While she wasn't yet ready to extend those same feelings toward herself, and—she suspected—neither were the Tridents, the winds were slowly shifting. Wherever they ended up, today was better than the day before.

Before court even started, Obsidian's attorney had already submitted a brief from an expert witness that ruthlessly dissected all the trace drugs found in Aiden's blood when he was extracted. Unsurprisingly, the hired pharmacologist came to the decisive conclusion that Aiden McDane had been too greatly under the influence for his memory to be relied on as evidence. Tara thought the conclusions went overboard into speculation and had told Sonia and Cassey as much. Cassey told her to "go sit in the back and look terrified."

She scampered back as she was told. Sonia had quickly clarified that the optics of Aiden and Tara talking, much less sitting next to each other, created too much of a collusion optic, which made Tara feel better about Aiden's sudden cold shoulder. In truth, she was grateful for the move, lest she lost all self-control and clung to him as she'd done last night during the strained dinner conversation. Dani had finally ended the ordeal early by offering "guest dessert" with the main course and excusing herself shortly after to get Ella and the baby settled, while Eli hung back pretending not to be a chaperone until her ride back to lockup arrived around ten at night.

Now, sitting alone in the back of the courtroom, Tara watched the judge open with acknowledging the Obsidian expert's memo and asking for the plaintiff's rebuttal. Another day of formal arguments was getting underway, as if Aiden's heart hadn't been torn raw for the court's pleasure just yesterday.

Sonia stood. "Your Honor—"

"The plaintiff has no objection to the brief," Cassey said from the seat beside Sonia, interrupting her midsentence.

From her seat near the aisle, Tara saw Sonia slam the heel of her stiletto shoe into Cassey's foot under the table. A sentiment that Tara shared wholeheartedly.

Instead of flinching, Cassey took his time standing up, then snatched the thick memo from Sonia's hands and flipped through it as if seeing it for the first time. Hell, for all Tara knew, it was the man's first time and he hadn't even read the thing. "The plaintiffs have no objection. We don't contest the factual conclusions of this report."

The judge stared at him incredulously. Hell, even Gardener and Welch gave Cassey a disbelieving look.

The judge cleared her throat. "You're saying that the plaintiff is fully willing to concede that, as the defense's expert asserts, the various narcotics present in Aiden McDane's bloodstream when he was rescued renders his recollection of events suspect?"

A harsh ripple of whispers rippled through the room, Tara's blood heating along with it. Cassey was throwing out everything Aiden had ripped himself apart yesterday to accomplish. Doing it without so much as a fight.

The judge leaned forward, her stern face looming from the

raised dais. "I want to be clear, Mr. McKenzie, you understand that by not contesting this report, you're waiving your right to cross-examine this expert? That, frankly, is considered an unfavorable move."

Cassey gave the judge one of his half shrugs. "Just trying to save the court's time by acknowledging the facts, Your Honor. Chemistry seems like a pretty cut-and-dried subject."

Chemistry was as far from cut-and-dried as Cassey was from the moon. Or from sanity, by all appearances.

Not that anyone was asking Tara's opinion. And despite Sonia's polite attempts at protest, Cassey's brash dominance ensured that no one was asking her opinion much either.

"All right. With the court's admonishments on the record, I'll accept the plaintiff's consent to the report," said the judge. "Do you have any more witnesses?"

"The plaintiff calls Briar Mackenzie," said Cassey.

"Objection." Gardener was on his feet. "This witness is not on the list. The defense has had no opportunity to prepare."

"I'm inclined to side with Mr. Gardener here." The judge looked at Cassey. "Is there a reason why this witness couldn't be presented to the court earlier?"

Cassey put his hands into his pockets and shrugged his massive shoulders "Well, Your Honor, given that Mr. McDane's testimony has just been unexpectedly rendered suspect by the defense expert, the plaintiff now requires a rebuttal witness."

"The plaintiff already agreed to the expert's conclusion," said Gardener. "He can't now challenge it."

"Oh, our witness won't refute McDane's chemical state at rescue," said Cassey. "He'll only substantiate the facts to which McDane testified—since the defense insisted that was required."

The judge stared at Cassey, then shook her head with a relenting sigh. "Well played, sir," she conceded. "Let's hear your rebuttal."

Tara's attention, along with the rest of the courtroom, turned to watch Cassey's double walk up to the stand. She still didn't fully understand Cassey's intent, given that Briar only saw Aiden and herself, neither of whose presence in Afghanistan was under debate.

That, together with how little Briar typically spoke, made her nervous.

"Are you familiar with Aiden McDane's capture and interrogation?" Cassey asked his mirror twin.

"Yes."

"How?"

"I led the rescue team," Briar said.

At the defense table, Welch smiled slightly. He'd gotten himself gone by the time Delta breached. If Tara hadn't been paralyzed with fear, she would have been gone along with him.

"Did you see any of McDane's captors during your rescue?" asked Cassey.

"Only one. Tara Northpoint, an eighteen-year-old girl left behind by her team when we entered." Briar's voice dripped with distaste.

"So you can only tell us that Aiden and Tara were in the cave?" Cassey clarified with such conviction that Tara hoped he hadn't forgotten what side he was representing.

"That's not entirely accurate," said Briar. "Since my orders prevented me from running down the captors, Tara was the only one I saw. However, we did collect samples of DNA from objects left behind. Toothbrushes, hair… There were some discarded Band-Aids in the trash. That sort of thing."

"Were they a match to any known individuals?" asked Cassey.

"No. But the American national registry only keeps records for convicted felons and people who voluntarily submitted a sample."

"I see." Cassey handed Briar a three-ring binder, passing a copy to the defense table and the judge. "This is a roster of all declared Obsidian Ops operatives in the last ten years. The front sheet lists those operatives registered in the DNA vital records. How many people are there?"

"There's only one name here," said Briar. "Raymond Brushings."

"Obsidian has hundreds of employees, but there is only *one* whose DNA is on file with the registry?"

"That's correct. And fortunate—without this record, the

medical examiner would unlikely have been able to identify Brushing's body in the explosion."

"Hm." Cassey paused. "But with regards to Afghanistan and those DNA samples you have that aren't a match to anyone in the registry, are we out of luck identifying who may have been there?"

"Not at all." Briar leaned forward and twisted toward Welch. "A cheek swab from Mr. Welch would definitively tell us whether he was there or not."

Cassey walked back to the plaintiff's table and picked up another sheet of paper. This one, he handed to Gardener. "Your Honor, I'm currently presenting Obsidian Ops with a subpoena for Mr. Welch's DNA. Provided he complies immediately, we can have our answer before court adjourns for the day."

Tara's hand curled around the bench, her fury at Cassey morphing into respect and then to alertness. The attorney had played his cards close to the vest with this one, but now the accusation was out in the open, there was no telling what Obsidian would do about it. One thing was certain—they would protect Welch. At any cost.

Cassey seemed to be aware of this as well, asking that Welch be considered a flight risk and placed under the court's custody until the DNA samples were collected and analyzed. Gardener made a long and valiant argument against the motion, but the judge sided with Cassey on this. Welch wouldn't be walking out the front doors of the place without the truth coming out. And he most certainly wouldn't be walking anywhere after that.

At the defense table, both men appeared to be furiously typing on their phones while waiting for the evidence tech, whom Casey must have had on standby, to come to the courtroom and collect a cheek swap from a stoic-looking Welch.

It took all of ten minutes. Ten minutes that would change Welch's life. The tech promised results by the end of the day, and the judge ordered the trial to continue meanwhile. She had to call Gardener twice before the man stood with uncharacteristic slowness and approached Briar. A snake facing a lion.

"Mr. McKenzie, we haven't had a prior chance to get to know

each other. Could you please indulge me with the details of your military service?"

Tara frowned. Who the hell cared about Briar's record?

"I joined the army. I joined Delta Force. I retired," Briar said.

Gardener smiled without humor. "Please describe all your deployments, training, and promotions. I'm just trying to understand your qualifications."

"It will take a while," Briar said.

Watching Welch still tapping on his phone, Tara suddenly got the uncomfortable feeling that this was precisely the point. Gardener didn't care about Briar's record, he cared about buying time. The lab had the DNA. There was a ticking clock above Welch's head.

The rest of the people in the courtroom had trust in procedure and the law, but Tara didn't. Something was going to happen.

Fifteen minutes later—it did. Halfway through Gardener dragging words out of Briar, the wail of a fire alarm filled the courthouse, a loudspeaker warning the occupants that this wasn't a drill. As the deafening siren coupled with flashing blue lights echoed off the walls, the judge and the others looked at each other in question as people so often did when alarms went off. Surely this wasn't really for real. Surely not in the middle of a case. Surely someone was going to come through at any moment to apologize for the malfunction. For the accidently opened fire door. For the teenager caught smoking in the bathroom.

Tara had no idea whether there was really a fire. That was irrelevant. Welch and Gardener were already on their feet, looking to get out. Unfortunately for them, Tara was seated in the back row, and her escorts—not having expected to be needed—were yet to arrive.

She sprinted out the door.

As soon as she was in the corridor, Tara ran for the women's room and pulled herself out the window Welch had pointed out to her earlier. He'd meant it for her, but she was betting he'd intended to use it as well. In a perfect world, her position would be irrelevant, with the Tridents' catching on and circling around Welch before he could escape. But one thing she knew about Obsidian was that they wouldn't hesitate to shove innocent bystanders into the men's path. Plus, the Tridents had been in the front of the courtroom. Only she was in the back.

Only she had the advantage of rushing ahead.

Though they were on the third floor, the fire escape stairs were only a foot away, and Tara raced down the steps. As she got to the bottom, she vaulted over the railing for a faster descent and managed to step into the shadows just as she heard another set of feet rush down the metal landing. She watched the two black sedans with tinted windows pull into the back alley. Welch's extraction team, no doubt activated when Cassey handed over that subpoena.

For a second, Tara wondered whether holding off the move until today was an accident or sheer brilliance on Cassey's part. Had any hint of subpoena been floated last night, Welch would have walked out of the courtroom and simply never come back. Now, however, Tara had a chance to stop it.

From the shadow beneath the stairs, Tara saw the high-end boot and pinstripe pant leg step onto the final flight of the fire escape. Welch wasn't in the kind of shape he was six years ago, and his developing belly slowed once-honed movements.

"Going somewhere?" Tara slammed her shoulder into Welch's midsection, her foot blocking his and sending him to the ground.

Welch fell backward with a satisfying thud, his goateed face twisting into a snarl. "You traitor. After everything we did for you, you haven't got a shred of decency or loyalty."

"You're a sociopath, Welch." Tara didn't know why it had taken her so long to realize as much. "You—"

A pair of strong hands gripped Tara from behind and threw her into the metal staircase. Her face hit the railing, and she tasted blood as the world swam. More figures were spilling into the back alley now, some rushing from the idling sedans, others coming the same way she had. Two. Six. Eight. An Obsidian operative in a suit was already helping Welch to his feet.

"This way, sir. We need to move. Now."

"Help!! Back alley!" Tara raised her head, screaming to whoever might hear. By the sound of it, people were stampeding toward the front door on the other side of the courthouse, the crowd's voices a dull roar that blanketed the air. "Need help in the back alley!"

Even as she yelled it, Tara knew that no one was coming. Not in time.

Pushing herself off the ground, she zeroed all her attention on the holstered weapon one of the extraction team members had on his waist. It was a small backup gun, but it would do. Tara rolled over her shoulder, coming up right as the operative took up position behind Welch to herd him to the car. Her breath stilled. Her hand tightened around the gun's grip.

The operative twisted with a snarl, throwing a fist toward Tara's head. She expected the blow and ducked, sweeping his leg out from under him. Even as he fell, Tara forgot about his existence, her hands gripping the gun. Finding the front sight. Squeezing the trigger with a precision she didn't know she was capable of.

The weapon went off with a bang, deflating the tire of the lead car. The one Welch was headed to. There was a chance the hobbled vehicle would hold off the escape. There was no chance Tara would get out of this alive. But she'd known that the moment she went for the gun. Karma had a way of rounding things out.

Two people came at Tara at once, one grabbing the gun from her hands with deadly precision while the other reached for something inside his coat. Tara saw the flash of the knife's blade and threw herself to the side to get herself away from the blade's trajectory.

She crashed into something solid and that steadied her on her feet, her body accepting the assistance before her mind could catch up.

"This here looks like a partner dance," Aiden told Tara, while the other four Tridents spilled into the melee. Liam and Eli flanked Welch's detail, while Kyan and Cullen went blow for blow with the others. Tara had underestimated how many operatives would have come to Welch's extraction, but no fewer than a dozen men now swarmed the alley. Some were dressed in tactical gear, but others wore suits, as if they had been prepared to blend into a courtroom atmosphere.

A few familiar faces flashed by Tara as she and Aiden fought their way toward Welch. Tara ducked beneath a high kick, slid behind an operative, and shoved him to Aiden—who finished the job with a solid blow to the temple. By the time they reached Welch, the bastard was already halfway through the open back door of the sedan.

Liam and Cullen had two men each on them, but somehow managed to pivot out of Tara's way as she lunged forward and grabbed Welch's shirt.

"Coward," she snarled at him.

"Ungrateful cunt." Welch kicked Tara away, trying to get the door closed.

"I'm certainly grateful," said Aiden from the driver's side window as he pointed a gun he'd somehow gotten at the driver's head. In the distance, the sounds of the approaching fire department already filled the air.

The driver pressed the gas. The car leapt into motion, uncaring about Welch's partially open door or Aiden's gun. The car backed two feet with a skidding turn that knocked Aiden and Tara away, then lurched forward, the driver taking it up onto the sidewalk to get around the hobbled vehicle.

As Tara lay on her back, she heard Aiden curse, then call out the license plate of Welch's vehicle. Cullen repeated the numbers, his voice calm. It looked like he had a phone to his ear. Probably talking to the police. With their primary mission completed, the Obsidian operatives were melting away. The ones who were still conscious. Tara rolled onto her side and was about to get up when the blinking light beneath the remaining vehicle caught her attention.

Eli already had the door open, apparently having decided that a flat tire wasn't going to stop him from pursuit.

"Eli, stop," Tara shouted at him. "Bomb! Run!"

No wonder the Obsidian operatives had fled like mice from a sinking ship. They weren't clearing the area to keep from getting caught, they were doing it to keep from getting dead. The pain clawing at Tara's mouth and back and ribs from getting knocked around in the fight suddenly receded to irrelevance, the small blinking light taking up the entirety of her world. Time slowed as she surveyed the scene. Eli had, thankfully, frozen in place. Cullen still had the phone to his ear. Liam, Kyan, and Aiden—who was climbing to his feet in slow motion—were fanned out along the field of battle.

"Get out of here," Tara shouted as she rolled herself under the car, her smaller frame giving her an advantage. "I'm going to minimize its impact." If it was the four-wire ordnance Tara thought she recognized, it had a connection that magnified the initial spark. It wouldn't stop the car from going up in flames the moment she pulled the wire, but it would contain the explosion to the vehicle. Spare the courthouse and the people there. Spare Aiden.

# 42

Tara

*Come on, come on, come on,* Tara repeated in her head as she carefully moved the top piece off the ordnance. The top popped off smoothly. Tara touched the wires with a steady hand. There was no large ticking clock like they had in movies, but the speed with which the light blinked gave a good indication of the timer. Forcing herself to hold absolutely still, she counted the timing between the blinks. Two seconds. Two minutes until boom.

Now for wiring. Red. Green. Blue. Orange. Tara breathed out a relieved breath, then cursed. And pink. What the hell was the fifth wire about?

A movement in the corner of her eye caught Tara's attention and it was all she could do to keep from banging her head on the underside of the car.

"Fuck it, Eli, which part of *bomb* was confusing to you?" she snapped. "Get the fuck away."

Eli's face appeared next to hers, his red hair falling like a mop around his face, his eyes narrowing on the blinking light. "Stop shouting. We have what, two minutes?"

Her eyes cut to him.

"I've a bit of ordnance experience," the SEAL said. "That whole demolition part of BUD/S spoke to my heart."

Tara's attention returned to the wires. "Great, then you can see there's a magnification connection here. My definition of success is to go boom without taking half a block with me. So—once again—get the hell out. And make sure Aiden does as well."

"What the bloody hell is that pink thing?" Eli muttered. "Remote override?"

That was actually a very good thought. Tara followed the wire to what, now that she knew what she was looking for, could be a remote receiver. A way for the departed operatives to set off the explosive before the timer's countdown ended. As if they didn't have enough problems.

Beside her pinky finger, the blinking light quickened. One minute.

"Fuck it, Eli. Go live to impress someone another day. Like, say, your kids."

Eli reached past Tara and pulled the pink wire free with a steady hand.

An angry *beeeeeeeep* stopped Tara's heart.

She braced herself.

The noise stopped. No boom. No boom. She let out her breath, taking a second for her heart to return to normal. One disaster averted, but the timer light was blinking still. She prayed Aiden and the others were clear of the scene by now.

Tara examined the ordnance again to assure herself that, with the pink wire out of play, it was one she was familiar with. It was. Which was how she knew there was no time to rewire it and no tools to do it with. She took hold of the blue wire. "This will reduce the explosive radius," Tara said with a voice too calm and steady to be hers. "Once I pull it, the car will ignite, but with luck, no more than that. You don't want to be here when that happens."

"So how about we not pull the blue wire," Eli suggested, unfolding his pocket knife. "I think we can reroute the green and save the boom altogether."

"Or take out half the block."

"Or that." He handed Tara the knife and held his hands at the ready. "We have about thirty seconds to do this and you know your way around the sheath better. You expose, I connect. Ready?"

Tara cut into the wire sheath.

The next thirty seconds were the longest of Tara's life. The tiny wires took up the entirety of her vision, each movement of her knife taking a century to complete. She wasn't breathing, but her heart pounded against her ribs as she peeled back the protective layers and unwound the wire cords into tiny strands that Eli's deft fingers picked up and wound together quickly.

The light switched to a constant red, only the last ten beeps announcing the countdown. Ten. Nine. Eight.

"Next," Eli said.

Tara moved over the wire.

Six. Five.

"Last one."

Three. Two.

They pulled the spark wire out together. The red light went wild and the beep became a tone. The world stopped. Shook.

Started again.

"Bloody hell," Eli dropped his head to the ground. "That was a little more fun than I had planned for the day."

An absurd chuckle escaped Tara as her body dumped the chemicals it had been storing into her bloodstream. She tried to pull herself out from under the car, but the hands that had been steady a moment earlier were now refusing to cooperate. After trying and failing two times, she let Eli pull her up.

And stood up to find the alley nothing like it was.

A perimeter had been established around the car they'd been working on, with Liam, Aiden, Cullen, and Kyan keeping everyone free of their best guess of the smaller blast radius. Lights flashed. A Denton Valley PD bomb tech was in the middle of suiting up.

She'd left chaos. She returned to a special forces op.

Aiden rushed up to them, and Eli handed Tara over to him without asking. "Primary explosive is rendered safe," he called over to Cullen and Liam. "But the perimeter should stay until secondary sweep."

"Understood," Liam called back. "Brief the PD."

There were more calls back and forth, but they started to blur together as Aiden pulled Tara against him, holding on to her with all his strength. The heat of his body seeped through her shivering chest, and she could feel the pounding of his heart though her own ribs. They stayed like that, locked together, while voices and sirens and news media anchors gathered in the background. Eventually, someone—possibly Kyan—herded them into a waiting Suburban.

Aiden pulled Tara up onto his lap as the car lurched to life and held tight all the way to the Trident Rescue office.

THREE HOURS after first getting into the conference room and recovering over lunch and coffee, Tara found her privacy with Aiden had come to a complete end. Everyone from the Tridents, to the PD, the state prosecutor and the courthouse sergeant at arms had gathered around the large conference table for a situation update.

"Denton Valley PD," Liam said, pointing to a uniformed officer. "Anything you would like to share?"

"Our bomb techs confirmed the vehicle was rendered safe by the Tridents." He gave a nod to Tara and Eli. Tara glanced at Liam, but the man didn't bother to correct the officer about Tara's particular position. The officer continued. "We did find several small secondary devices in the courtroom. Remote detonations. They appear to have been hastily set to block off key corridors, probably to secure an alternate escape route. We're going through the footage to see who entered the courthouse after Welch's DNA test was ordered. To be honest, we would never have found them if we hadn't brought the dogs in as soon as you first alerted us. As of now, all personnel are accounted for. No injuries on this one. Thank you."

Liam didn't look nearly as pleased as Tara expected.

He turned to the next person at the table. The updates came

short and fast. Welch was gone. No sign of him anywhere in the country. Gardener, the Obsidian attorney, had already filed paperwork for a mistrial. The court would return to regular business the following day.

"Ms. Northpoint." A woman in a suit who Tara had never spoken to directly before got her attention from the other side of the table. "I'm Sippy Firlander, the Colorado State prosecutor assigned to your criminal case. I would not usually speak to you directly without the public defender's office, but given the circumstances, I think it's prudent to get the ball rolling." She slid a folder across the polished desk into Tara's hands. "We're once again prepared to offer you full immunity for your testimony about Obsidian. Once you meet with the public defender and review—"

"Ms. Northpoint won't be working with a public defender." Cassey intercepted the folder before Tara could touch it. Flipping it open, he took a pen out from the inside pocket of his jacket and scanned down the page with it, stopping occasionally to cross out and rewrite several lines and make two margin notes. He slid the paperwork back. "A few tweaks before I can, in good conscience, allow my client to sign."

*His* client?

Sippy Firlander, Tara, and Sonia all stared at Cassey, then the prosecutor opened the file and put on a pair of glasses.

Tara tried to look like she wasn't about to snatch the papers from the prosecutor's hand and sign them right then and there. In blood. Frankly, the only reason she wasn't currently hopping over the tabletop to do just that was because Aiden had one of her knees in a vise grip and Cassey had just gripped the other.

"You'd like the state to provide Ms. Northpoint with new identity documents?" Firlander clarified. "And a new social security number?"

Cassey shrugged. "Her real information seems to have been purged from the system. How else do you expect her to prove that she, in fact, exists the next time she tries to sign up for a loyalty program at the liquor store?"

"Fine." She read on. "The no immunity-revocation provision is unnecessary. We have no intention of going back on the deal."

"Humor me."

Firlander rolled her eyes. "Fine." She was already on the next page, scanning the text. Stopping. Looking up sharply. "You want us to pay Ms. Northpoint fifty thousand dollars? Mr. McKenzie, she's getting off scot-free from a murder charge, never mind a human rights violation investigation."

Tara thought the prosecutor had a point. Her heart pounded. If Cassey pushed Firlander too hard, it would be her life.

"Actually, she's getting off from a death penalty charge," Cassey said, as if discussing a football game. "At least that's my understanding based on a memo that was leaked to Obsidian Ops and then used for witness tampering. I don't know whether it was a breach of human judgment or simply poor cybersecurity, but either way, the situation caused my client significant distress." He stretched like a lazy cat. "I propose we make her whole in this agreement, without us filing a misconduct suit."

Firlander took off her glasses and sighed, looking at Cassey. "I'll have to check with the state attorney general."

"Take your time," Cassey said agreeably. "I imagine he's already having wet dreams about the kind of publicity taking on Obsidian Ops is going to get him now. Incidentally, I heard Sky Hunt has been working on a story for this—and is always published above the centerfold." Cassey paused and furrowed his brow. "On second thought, time might be of the essence."

Tara couldn't believe Cassey's gall. But at least Sky writing in her notebook made more sense now.

Sonia stood from the table and left the room without saying a word, the door slamming in her wake.

Liam pinched the bridge of his nose. "If she resigns, I'll castrate you," he told Cassey.

"She won't," the man said with the kind of infuriating confidence that made Tara extremely glad he was on her side. At least for the moment.

With the legal part settled, the meeting wrapped up quickly, with everyone anxious to get back to their lives after the marathon of a day. Liam looked especially eager to be out the door, and Tara couldn't fault him one bit for leaving first. Within minutes, the place was empty except for her, Aiden, and Eli, who claimed he had some calls to make in the hall.

"Congratulations on the reprieve," Aiden said, pulling Tara in to kiss the top of her head.

"Truthfully, Cassey is the last person I expected to go to bat for me."

"He might feel a little guilty about having run you out of town the last time," said Aiden. "Or he just enjoyed needling Sonia. I can't tell with him."

Tara chuckled.

When the mirth died, though, Aiden's beautiful face became tentative. "What were you planning on doing for, um, housing?"

"I thought I was just..." Tara trailed off. She was no longer charged with murder and had already testified at trial. There was no longer a reason to have her held in custody. "I hadn't thought about it," she said honestly.

Aiden put his hands in his pockets, his shoulders hunching slightly. "I was wondering if you might stay with me for a spell. I'm afraid the only way Eli and Dani are going to let me out of their sight is if someone is there with me."

"Why?" asked Tara. Then looked into his eyes and knew. "Flashbacks?"

Aiden looked down. "Aye."

Slipping her arms around him, Tara brushed her lips over his. "It would be an honor if you trusted me to keep you company. In fact, I would like nothing better than to feel you beside me at night. And in the shower. And maybe the kitchen counter."

Aiden laughed, wrapping his arms around Tara's waist as he hoisted her up onto the conference table for a more thorough kiss. As they separated, though, Tara bit her lip. "This plan does presume that Eli and Dani consider me an acceptable sentry. This seems like a Trident inside job, and I'm not."

"I think you're well on your way," said Aiden, the words sending a wave of warmth through her. Then he cringed. "Speaking of that, did you catch Liam's face when the Denton Valley PD lieutenant mentioned Trident's work today?"

Tara nodded. "He didn't look pleased about the erroneous association."

"Oh, he was displeased, all right, but not because of that." Aiden paused as if waiting for her to catch up. He sighed and explained reluctantly. "It was more that Liam *did* associate you with Trident Security. And the whole *I'm going to run off on a suicide mission without so much as coordinating with the rest of the team,* he isn't big on that."

"So what does that mean?" asked Tara.

"It means," said Aiden, "that if you're still around and working with us when he gets back to full-time work, you're going to be in for a short chat followed by a long time of pain."

For some stupid reason, that didn't bother Tara one bit.

# 43

## FOUR MONTHS LATER... AIDEN

"Ranger, Ranger, Ranger!" Ella called to the Belgian Malinois pressed against Aiden's leg.

The dog stayed where he was, as unbothered by the child as he was by the many people swarming about Jaz and Liam's baby-transformed apartment.

"Bwoken." Bar stuck his thumb into his mouth and looked at Ella with with eyes full or toddler wisdom. He was the most curious child Aiden had ever met, which led to a lot of *bwoken*. Had to have come from Kyan's genes.

"Ranger, Ranger, Ranger!" Ella repeated, louder. "Come here, dog."

Eli swooped in before Aiden could reply. "Ella, remember how we talked about this? Ranger is a working dog."

"Uh-uh." Bar shook his head. "Bwoken. Not working."

Aiden crouched to the kid's eye level. "His job is minding me. If he senses that I'm starting to see or hear things that aren't there, he can help me stay in the present. Or make sure no one gets hurt, if I'm not acting like myself." Ranger was also being trained for police dog functions that came useful in Aiden's line of work, but the last thing he needed was to be doing bite demos with the kids around.

"That's silly, Uncle Aiden," Ella said with a giggle. "Grown-ups don't need minding. And you're a grown-up."

"Debatable." Coming up to the group, Liam weighed Aiden with a glance. "Highly debatable."

Aiden snorted and motioned for Liam to hand over the little bundle in his arms. Between their extended stay at NICU and the twins being twins, Liam and Jaz's indoctrination into parenthood had taken the trial-by-fire route that delayed the usual Welcome Home party by a couple of months. Now, their penthouse apartment was filled with people and more infant paraphernalia than tactical and rock-climbing gear combined. Given who the twins' parents were, that said quite a lot.

Aiden adjusted the baby boy in his arms. As the oldest of five brothers, he'd had his share of holding little ones—and he'd forgotten how much he enjoyed the small weight against him. "So, have you finally reached a decision, or are we still calling them Baby Alpha and Baby Bravo?"

"We're close," said Liam.

"You know, for a SEAL trained in making split-second decisions, the fact that you can't figure out a name after four month is—"

He cut off as, behind Liam, Eli shook his head in warning.

"Utterly your decision," said Aiden, quickly changing course. "So which one of the twins is this?"

Liam winced. "That's one of the reasons for the name thing," he conceded. "At first, we wanted to name them outside NICU. And then we got home, and I took off the ankle bracelets and... Let's just say Jaz is still holding that against me. Problem is, she breastfeeds and can tell by the latch. And I'm out of luck."

"I guess the question is, who does Jaz think she's holding?" Aiden speculated, looking around the room to discover Jaz sitting conveniently beside Tara. He adjusted the bundle in his arms to a more comfortable position. "Let me do some recon and circle back."

Liam looked more than a little relieved. Either he had high hopes of Aiden ferreting out the answer or else he was just glad to be baby-free for a few minutes. Both of which were valid reasons in Aiden's book.

Baby in his arms and Ranger at his side, Aiden started toward the women, but then slowed his step to savor the way Tara looked here, amid family. Her once-chopped-and-dyed black hair was growing into its natural wavy red that already reached to her shoulders and played off her rich hazel eyes. Sitting comfortably in jeans and a cropped long-sleeve shirt, Tara radiated an energy and joy that blinded him.

He imagined what she might look like with a child in her arms. They hadn't talked about kids. Actually, they hadn't talked about their future together at all. Initially, Tara had stayed at Aiden's place from necessity, because Dani insisted that until Aiden learned how his PTSD might manifest now, he needed someone around. Over the next few months, however, the flashbacks became manageable enough that with medication, exercises, and now Ranger, Aiden was fully self-sufficient. At that point, they decided that her moving out would be impractical. She had no place of her own and was needed in Colorado for the ongoing legal matters, and then there was the work she was picking up for Trident Security…

"See something you like?" Patti asked, coming up beside him. Although Patti was Liam's mother, she was making up for the estranged years with her son by actively adopting all his friends, Aiden included.

"Aye," said Aiden. Though *like* didn't begin to describe it. He loved everything about Tara. Loved her laugh. Loved giving her hell on the mat and then rubbing the knots out of her shoulders. Loved holding her as they watched reruns of *Battlestar Galactica*. Loved taking her to places that, growing up in Obsidian Ops, she'd never gotten to do as a kid. Last Saturday, they went to a trampoline park. Tomorrow, Aiden intended to use Ella as an excuse for a Build-A-Bear excursion. "Very much."

"When are you going to tell her?"

"Tell her what?"

"That you want to marry her," Patti said.

Aiden tensed, his heart speeding at the very thought as he gave

Patti a sharp look. Aiden loved Tara with all his heart—if he threw down the marriage gauntlet and she said no... He didn't want to think of the darkness that would come. "I want to give her some time," he muttered. "Don't want to push her."

"Coward."

"Aye." Stepping quickly, he started toward Tara and Jaz. Not because he was running away from Patti. He just had a mission to fulfill, that's all.

Tara smiled at Aiden's approach, but the happiness on her face flickered as her gaze slipped to the baby in Aiden's arms. He was sure Jaz hadn't noticed, but Aiden could read Tara well enough to know the meaning of that flicker. She was uncomfortable with the baby. Very uncomfortable.

*Ah.*

He braced himself for a pang of distress at the realization that the woman he wanted so badly to spend the rest of his life with had no interest in children—but it didn't come. Tara was enough for him. While it saddened Aiden to think that he would never hold his own tiny baby, he also knew that there would be plenty of nephews and nieces about. Spending a lifetime in Tara's company would be a blessing regardless.

Giving Tara an understanding nod, he joined the women's conversation. Jaz was trying to recruit Tara into rock climbing—a proposition Tara seemed to be seriously considering. With that topic running, it was a few minutes before Aiden could work in his line.

"I snatched this wee terror from Liam's hands without thinking to ask which one he was," Aiden said, holding up the baby as proof of acquisition. "Could you help me out?"

"You do realize I'm married to Liam, right?" she said. "I ask because I damn well know that no one *snatches* anything from that man's hands. Least of all a baby." Jaz squinted at Aiden. "Liam had no idea who he had, didn't he?"

The sound of something crashing came from a back bedroom, saving Aiden from having to conjure an answer. A second later, metallic rings filled the air, all accompanied by Ella's delighted squeal and Bar's disapproving *uh-oh.*

Jaz's eyes widened. "They got into my climbing gear." She was on her feet the next moment, thrusting the baby into Tara's arms. "Hold him, please."

"I—" Tara stared after Jaz, then down at the child she now held. Her face blanched. Tara wasn't uncomfortable—she was terrified.

"Easy, lass. It's a baby, not a bomb." Aiden got up and crouched in front of her, blocking her from the room's view. He shifted the baby he held to one arm and stroked Tara's shoulder with his free hand. "Talk to me."

"The baby," Tara whispered, as if that explained everything.

Aiden looked down at the child, half expecting to find the boy bleeding. The twin cooed.

"He's all right." Aiden assured her. "That's how the wee ones always look."

"No. Not him. He's perfect." She closed her eyes. "But Jaz… What am I to do once Jaz realizes who she handed her son to?"

Aiden hated seeing Tara scared, hated not understanding her fear even more. He tried to channel an inner Dani. "What do you think will happen?"

"She's going to hate herself," Tara whispered. "And she'll hate me by extension. I should never have come today. I should never have been anywhere near the children."

"Why would Jaz hate herself for leaving her son with you?" Aiden asked. Despite her words, Tara's hands wrapped round the baby protectively.

Tara stared at him as if it were Aiden who was talking crazy. "Would you want your sweet, innocent child in the hands of someone… Someone like me?"

Aiden's heart tightened, his hand stroking Tara's hair as he finally, *finally*, realized the truth. "You think that because of your past, no one would want you around their children?"

"How could they?" Tara asked, her voice breaking. "It's one thing for adults to tolerate me, but once I come near their children, even by accident—"

"Stop," Aiden commanded, waiting until Tara complied with the order and looked at him. "Tara. Listen to me. Jaz didn't accidentally thrust a child onto a stranger. She handed her baby to you. To Tara. Because she, like me, knows that you will keep that baby safe with your life."

"But—"

Aiden put a finger to Tara's lips, silencing her, then traced his thumb over her cheekbone to wipe away a stray tear. His heart broke for her. For the demons that haunted her even as they preyed on him. "You asked if I would want my child in your arms? Tara, I want more than that. I want *our* children in your arms."

She blinked. "What?"

"I want to have babies with you," Aiden repeated, raising his voice to ensure she heard every word. "I want you to be the mother of my children. I want to raise them with you. I want our son or daughter to be as proud as I am of the strong, brave, brilliant woman who is their mother."

The room hushed, and Aiden suddenly realized that it wasn't only Tara who'd heard his raised voice. It was everyone. And now, said everyone turned to stare at them.

He didn't care. He cared about nothing but what the woman in front of him might say.

Tara looked at him incredulously, cradling the baby she held closer to her skin. How had Aiden ever thought she didn't want children? "Do you mean it?" she whispered. "You want to have children with me?"

He smiled, realizing that Tara was getting blurry as his own eyes stung. "Aye. Of course I do. Children. A family. Everything."

Someone cleared her throat. Aiden glanced over his shoulder to find Patti giving him a very pointed look as if he was forgetting something. What the heck was he forgetting?

*Bollocks.* He made a noise in the back of his throat. "So, I probably should have started with *will you marry me?*"

Tara laughed through the tears trailing along her cheeks. "We did skip over that part, didn't we?"

"Aye. Just a bit."

"Right. Um. I mean, yes."

"Thank God," said Aiden. "You had me worried there."

Tara chuckled. Aiden leaned forward to brush his lips over hers. Around the room, cheers erupted, and Patti conveniently materialized at their side with an offer to take babies from their arms—but neither Aiden nor Tara were ready to let the little ones go just yet.

Their kiss deepened, two mouths combining together to share the love that flowed between them. Love and promises of the family and future they both intended to share. For all the world, Aiden didn't think he'd ever been happier than at that very moment.

You've finished Aiden's book, but there are more Tridents to get to know. Continue the adventure with the newest novel ENEMY STAND (on pre-order), that follows Casey and Sonia - or catch up with the other stories in the TRIDENT RESCUE Series.

ENEMY ZONE
*Cullen and Sky*

ENEMY CONTACT
*Eli and Dani*

ENEMY LINES
Kyan and Ivy

ENEMY HOLD
Liam and Jaz

ENEMY CHASE
Aiden and Tara

ENEMY STAND
Casey and Sonia

## OTHER BOOKS BY THIS AUTHOR:

**TRIDENT RESCUE (Writing as A.L. Lidell)**

**Contemporary Enemies-to-Lovers Romance**

ENEMY ZONE (Audiobook available)

ENEMY CONTACT (Audiobook available)

ENEMY LINES (Audiobook available)

ENEMY HOLD (Audiobook available)

ENEMY CHASE

ENEMY STAND

**IMMORTALS OF TALONSWOOD (4 books)**

**Reverse Harem Paranormal Romance**

LAST CHANCE ACADEMY (Audiobook available)

LAST CHANCE REFORM (Audiobook available)

LAST CHANCE WITCH (Audiobook available)

LAST CHANCE WORLD (Audiobook available)

**POWER OF FIVE (7 books)**

**Reverse Harem Fantasy Romance**

POWER OF FIVE (Audiobook available)

MISTAKE OF MAGIC (Audiobook available)

TRIAL OF THREE (Audiobook available)

LERA OF LUNOS (Audiobook available)

GREAT FALLS CADET (Audiobook available)

GREAT FALLS ROGUE

GREAT FALLS PROTECTOR

SIGN UP FOR NEW RELEASE NOTIFICATIONS at https://links.alexlidell.com/News

## ABOUT THE AUTHOR

Join Alex's newsletter for news, bonus content and sneak peeks: https://links.alexlidell.com/News

Find out more on Alex's website: www.alexlidell.com

SIGN UP FOR NEWS AND RELEASE NOTIFICATIONS

*Connect with Alex!*
www.alexlidell.com
alex@alexlidell.com